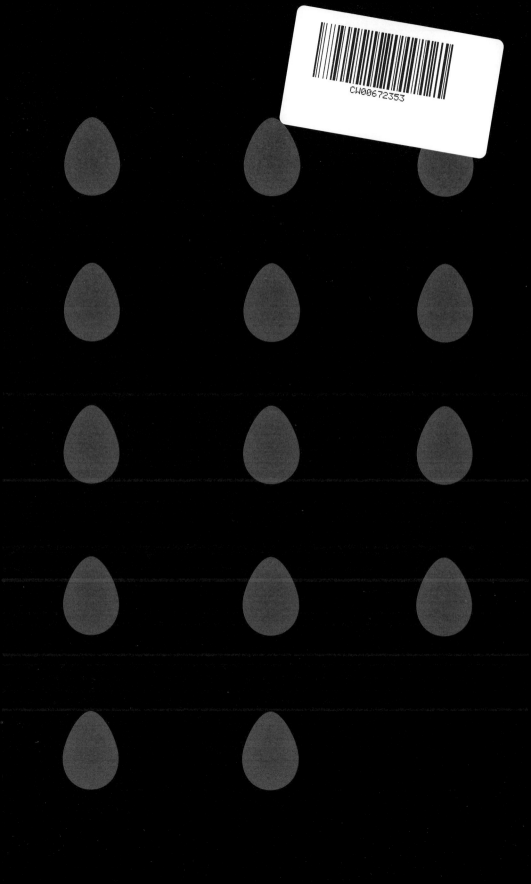

THE
IMPOSSIBLE THING

THE
IMPOSSIBLE THING

BELINDA BAUER

bantam

TRANSWORLD PUBLISHERS
Penguin Random House, One Embassy Gardens,
8 Viaduct Gardens, London SW11 7BW
www.penguin.co.uk

Transworld is part of the Penguin Random House group of companies
whose addresses can be found at global.penguinrandomhouse.com

First published in Great Britain in 2025 by Bantam
an imprint of Transworld Publishers

A CIP catalogue record for this book
is available from the British Library.

ISBNs
9781787630970 (hb)
9781787630987 (tpb)

Typeset in 12.25/15.5 pt Minion Pro by Falcon Oast Graphic Art Ltd
Printed and bound in Great Britain by Clays Ltd, Elcograf S.p.A.

The authorized representative in the EEA is Penguin Random House Ireland,
Morrison Chambers, 32 Nassau Street, Dublin D02 YH68.

Finished for Simon

Metland Farm

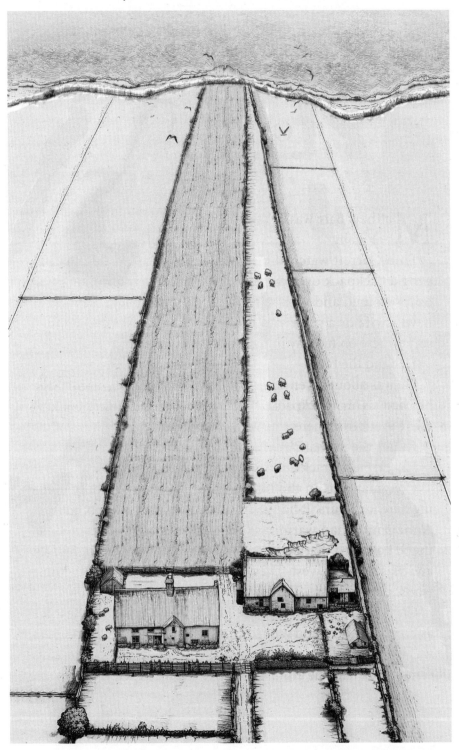

Old Habits

M atthew Barr was in the crosshairs.
Finally.

Finn Garrett watched him lock the battered old Focus and sling a backpack over one shoulder. There was a woman with him – young, and with her mousy hair tied back. Barr didn't have a wife or a girlfriend at home, so he must have stopped somewhere on his way to pick her up.

Her and the boy.

He was about seven and with hair as ginger as a biscuit. The boy had his own backpack. Something colourful. Garrett couldn't make it out from here.

'Who's the woman?'

His earpiece crackled. 'Don't know.'

Coughlan was in the trees to his left. They had been waiting here for hours. It had rained twice but they had not moved. Anticipation had warmed them. Not just now, but ever since they'd got word that Matthew Barr had left his home in Suffolk and was heading west. They hadn't had to tail him; they knew where he was going. They'd got here first and waited.

Garrett adjusted his weight on his elbows and watched the three as they left the car and walked up the hill towards the copse. Barr was whip-thin. Even without optical sights, Garrett could see his camo jacket flapping around his narrow hips. He led the way, with the woman and the boy behind, walking together, in conversation. Letting Barr take them wherever they were going to go.

'Heading our way,' Coughlan murmured.

Garrett said nothing. He practised keeping Barr in the crosshairs.

Barr's head.

The headshot.

Barr would drop to the grass like a stone. The woman and the boy would be confused at first. What had happened? No sound of a shot. Just a man who had been walking, suddenly on the ground. They'd hurry over to see what was wrong – oblivious to personal danger – and find that the top of his head had been blown clean off, as if detonated from within.

Grey jelly with white-shard wafers and a dark blood sauce, while only birdsong broke the silence . . .

Garrett put down the scope.

Old habits die hard.

The little fake family were only a couple of hundred yards from the trees now. Garrett could make out the man's pointed face. The woman's ponytail. The boy's mouth moving in time to the faint sound of childish chatter that preceded them up the hill.

It was turning into a nice day. In the sunshine, at least, although a brisk wind meant you had to keep walking. As good as it got for this time of year in the Brecon Beacons. But in the cover of the trees it was cold and dank, with the soft bed of pine needles barely soaking up the mud beneath.

Garrett slowly stretched out his ankles. Then his knees. If Barr ran, he didn't want to make any mistakes. Didn't want to stumble. Didn't want to give him even a whisper of a chance of getting away. Not this time. Not after two years of watching and waiting and hope and near misses and screw-ups and failure. While all the time he continued to kill.

Again and again and again—

Garrett felt familiar anger warming his belly against the cold ground, and breathed slowly until it dissipated.

His life was all about patience.

A hundred yards away, Barr stopped and looked up at the trees. Garrett followed his gaze into the dark woods. He knew exactly where Coughlan was, and still couldn't see him.

But Barr wasn't looking for danger – he was checking his bearings, making sure he was in the right place. Garrett already knew that he was.

The woman and boy caught up with him.

'How about here?' said the woman.

'I'm hungry, Mum,' said the boy. 'Can we eat?'

'In a minute,' Barr said. 'Let's go close to the trees to get out of this wind a bit. We can look for firewood then too. Get nice and warm, yeah?'

'Yeah,' said the boy enthusiastically. 'Can I chop it with an axe?'

'You can break it up,' said his mother.

They resumed walking to the treeline. Thirty yards from Garrett – maybe fifty from Coughlan. And stopped.

'This looks like a good spot.' Barr shrugged his backpack off his shoulders. He took out a picnic blanket – waterproof on one side, tartan on the other – which he unfolded and shook out on to the ground. The woman had brought sandwiches and a flask, and a packet of supermarket cakes. Garrett didn't need the binoculars now, but he put them to his eyes and refocused on Mr Kipling's Fondant Fancies.

He was hungry, but it would wait.

Barr put his pack on again and – while the woman continued to lay out the meagre picnic – he led the boy into the trees.

It was shocking how quickly they disappeared.

But Garrett knew where they were going.

This was what the last two years had been about – knowing where Matthew Barr was going, and what he was going to do when he got there.

Garrett stood.

Slowly.

Silently.

Draped in a cloak of needles and strips of dark bark, he only had to stand still to become one with the forest – the reddish floor, the black trunks, the mossy stumps of trees long gone.

He followed the man and the boy like a wraith. Thought he caught a flicker of movement that might have been Coughlan, moving in the same direction, but didn't look again to make sure. It didn't matter. The only thing that mattered was that Barr didn't see them. Didn't spook. Didn't stop what he was about to do.

The boy chirped – his sharp little voice blunted by the damp trees. A flash of colour from his backpack now and then. A Superman logo.

Not far now.

Garrett moved closer.

They were picking up sticks on the way. Making it look real.

Then Barr stopped and put down his sticks and turned to the boy.

'Take off your backpack.'

Garrett sank gently on to his haunches, melting back into the shadows and the needles.

'Why?'

'I've got something to show you. Put it down here.'

The boy put the backpack down. He waited. Watching. Innocent of what was to come next, Garrett was sure.

From his own pack Barr drew a small folding shovel and began to dig.

'What are you looking for?'

'Treasure.'

'Gold?'

'Better than gold.'

The boy's mouth made an O of excitement and he jiggled with anticipation.

Barr was panting a little now. He was thin but he wasn't fit. Too many hours spent in his attic, poring over his sins and the sins of the many who had gone before.

Garrett hoped Coughlan was recording this. That was the only part of this whole operation not in his direct control.

The shovel made the only sound.

Four inches. Six.

And then the *plink* of plastic.

Finn Garrett had shot men in the face, but his heart had never beaten harder than it did right now.

Matthew Barr dug more slowly, more carefully, clearing an area, unearthing . . . something. The boy knelt and peered into the ground.

'What *is* it?'

But Barr didn't speak. Instead he reached into the hole in the earth and withdrew a small plastic lunchbox. Then another. And another. And another. A fifth, a sixth, a seventh . . .

Twelve.

The boxes he had buried there nearly two years before.

Garrett remembered it had been snowing in patches; he remembered Barr's breath misting the air in visible puffs as he walked up the slope, into the trees and . . . disappeared.

The hissing panic of losing him; the agony of knowing *what* he was doing, but not exactly where. The low, angry redeployment, and then that idiot copper blundering right into Barr's path, scaring him off. Garrett had watched him hurry out of the woods and known they would have to watch him from that day forward. Where he went and what he did and who he met and what *they* did too . . . until he came again to retrieve the boxes.

And that's what they had done.

Two bloody years.

A lump in Garrett's throat told him that *this time* it had worked. *This time* it was going to be OK.

'What's *in* them?' said the boy, and Barr winked at him and beckoned him closer with a jerk of his chin, and curled back the lid of the box at his chest and said—

come and see

In a single smooth movement, Garrett rose and shrugged off his cape of needles and bark. Barr ran, but Garrett had shaken out his knees and his ankles and did not falter. Did not stumble. He was on him in yards, his heart pounding with joy that Barr had run, because it gave him the only opportunity he'd ever have to hurt him – which he did by dropping on to his kidney with the hardest of knees.

Behind them the boy was shrieking in fear, but Matthew Barr only groaned with his mouth full of needles.

Coughlan would read him his rights. That wasn't Garrett's job. All his job allowed him to do was to bend and hiss furiously against the fallen man's ear:

'I've got you now, you little *shit* . . .

'And your *fucking eggs.*'

Climmers

Bempton cliffs, Yorkshire – May 1920

Jim Chandler swept the birds off the ledge with a practised foot, and kicked their eggs after them.

The birds wheeled and squealed around him – guillemots mostly, with a few puffins and razorbills thrown in – while their eggs smashed on the rocks, spraying yolk and tiny, wet-feathered tufts into the dark blue ocean more than three hundred feet below.

Gulls and crows swooped in to pick over remains that were so plentiful they didn't even squabble.

Adjusting his grip on the rope, Chandler pushed off the sheer grey cliff-face, and swung sideways to clear another ledge.

And another.

And another.

When he had arced as widely as he could in both directions, he tugged on the handline, and was lowered carefully down another four or five feet to start on the next level.

Clearing Danes Dyke was a two-day job, and the only one Jim Chandler insisted on doing himself now. He liked to make a note of where the best eggs were to be found, and the start of arthritis meant it was easier for him to sweep eggs aside with his hands and his feet than it was to pick them up and put them in the old army satchel slung over his shoulder.

Still, he never went down without the satchel. That would be foolish.

And now – as a fluster of wings rose before his boot – he spotted an egg that justified the habit.

Normally he didn't bother. The pickings would be rich enough soon enough. Clearing the eggs early in the season meant that those birds that could, would lay again, and fresh eggs were more saleable – unspoiled as they were by the big holes required to remove chicks. But this egg was large – a double-yolker – and pale gold with only a few brown speckles near the bulbous base. Very different; very collectable. And early season too – while pockets were still full and demands unmet.

It would be nice to clamber back on to the grass with a prize. Show the lads the old man hadn't lost his touch while they were away at war.

He reached for the egg.

The guillemot did her best to stop him. She stood her ground and stabbed at his hand and spread her glossy chocolate wings and screamed for her mate.

Her best wasn't good enough.

Jim put the double-yolker in the satchel with the others and looked down between his boots at the North Sea far below. Whitecaps were scattered on the dark blue waves like blossom and, between here and there, a thousand birds – maybe ten thousand. Gulls and fulmars and guillemots and puffins and gannets and kittiwakes and razorbills. Wheeling and diving and landing and rising and swooping, and calling so loudly that the air was splintered by cries that carried for miles on a wind that never slackened, but instead drove the sea into the North Yorkshire cliffs and then whipped and whirled up three hundred sheer feet of crag and crevice and crack that hosted a million seabirds – each and every one of them drawn back every summer to the same face, the same place, the same tiny ledge, where it would lay its eggs and raise its chicks . . .

And he, Jim Chandler.

Above them all.

For a moment he just dangled there in the old leather horse collar, enjoying the sunshine.

On days like this he wondered why he left the job of collecting to his sons. Then a cloud scudded across the sun and he remembered . . . First pull was full of breakfast and expectations, and by second, a rhythm had set in. By the third they'd be working in shade, and fingerless mitts. And by fourth pull, they would be so tired that face and fingers would be numb, and they'd fear tipping backwards out of the harness.

But for now, he floated in perfect peace.

Soon, peace would be a hard thing to come by on the cliffs.

Soon there would be a broker at the top. Always. Mr Worrell or Mr Hollingberry or Mr Ambler. Often more than one, and always ready to pay top prices for the best eggs. Of course, most eggs – even scoot eggs – were dull, brown-spotted, and worth only sixpence once blown and wiped clean by Harry's lad, Kipper. Something special would fetch ten shillings, maybe even a pound. A week's wages for a precious jewel that would become the centrepiece of a grand display in some shallow, silk-lined drawer in a fancy house in London or York.

And the brokers were the least of it. By second pull there would be a carnival on the clifftop. Picnickers come up for the day in charabancs to see the birds and buy an egg to take home with them, along with the seashells, and the sticks of rock with *Scarborough* or *Bridlington* written endlessly through the sugar. Some of the men would pay to be lowered in the leather harness to pick their own egg off the cliff.

Free to go down! Two bob to come back up!

A few of the ladies were lowered too, although mostly they were content to sit and watch.

And boys.

Everywhere!

Boys running, shouting, jumping, rolling. Throwing stones off the cliffs towards the distant sea, or at the puffins and guillemots on the closer ledges. Boys rivalling the gulls with their cries and calls, being dragged back from the edge and getting their ears boxed by fathers or nurses – or by Harry if they got too close to the rope or the pulley. There was no roughhousing there. That was a serious business. Each climming gang employed a boy or two to fetch and carry, to blow eggs, to sell slop – but other boys had no place near the gang or their gear. Whether local or holiday-maker, any boy who got too close was seen off by a hard word or a hard hand, and did not approach again.

But down here . . . down here was a kind of peace – despite the noise and the stink of fish, and of guano made of fish.

Jim could tell from experience that there were already chicks in the double-yolker. That was the only shame. The hole would have to be very big to get them both out. The acid they would trickle into the shell could only dissolve so much feather and bone and beak.

Next time he'd get it sooner.

He pulled his notebook from the breast pocket of his old tweed jacket, and noted the date and where he'd found it. This was his greatest skill – recording the best eggs. His own secret code of which field, how far down, how far along. It was this that made the Chandler gang the most reliable suppliers to the great collectors of the nation and the world. Four pulls a day they made like clockwork, and forty or fifty eggs a time, competing from May to July with three other gangs working their own jealously guarded bits of cliff. Even without a jewel like this one, it was a lot more lucrative than labouring. A lot more lucrative than a lot of jobs.

Over the constant roar of the wind, the rope creaked gently beside his ear.

Jim tucked his notebook and pencil back into his pocket. Then he tugged the handline twice, and Pricky Hodgson started to pull him in.

The robbed guillemot – still furious – stabbed at his hobnailed boots as he drew away from her. He laughed – *Thank you, scoot!* – and gave her a little goodbye salute.

Now he knew this was her spot – and that in a few weeks she would almost certainly lay an identical egg.

And when she did, Jim Chandler would be waiting for it.

Celie

Everything was Celie Sheppard's fault.

Her fault they were hungry. Her fault they didn't have shoes. Her fault Molly was sick and Tom fell off the wall and the fox got the small brown hen.

Celie was to blame for every ill that befell her family, and had been from the moment of her birth, when John Sheppard's black eyes had looked down on the blue-eyed, white-browed baby seeking its first nipple.

'She takes after my mother,' Enid Sheppard had ventured desperately.

'No,' he'd spat, 'she takes after her father.' And he'd driven away from Metland Farm and never come back.

They'd found the tractor in Bridlington, but by then it already belonged to another man. There'd been early rumours that Sheppard had been seen in a hostelry in York, and then less reliable ones about bars in Doncaster and then Hertford, and finally someone said they'd heard he was heading to London, from where even rumours could not find their way this far north. But before her husband had had his first drink anywhere, Enid Sheppard had left her guilty baby swaddled in their bed, tied a towel around her breasts to soak up her milk and taken up a scythe – and the role of mother, father, smallholder, whore and outcast, all rolled into one shameful package.

Their two labouring men had left before the week was out: they'd seen the writing on the wall and, even though they couldn't read, had understood its gist. Metland Farm without its farmer was doomed to fail, its tenants doomed to eviction, and its tenants' employees doomed to go unpaid.

Only Robert had stayed, because he was a boy, and soft in the head, and so lacked the capacity to conceive of a better life in any other place, while retaining the uneasy memory of something much worse somewhere else. Robert had arrived at Metland the previous summer – in rags and without a last name – and had achieved a kind of life there. He was big for his eight years, and so could be put to most work, as long as it was properly explained to him first. He earned five shillings a week without ever realizing that the going rate was a pound, but that mattered not, because Robert never went anywhere where he might be able to spend his money. He had his food, and his blanket in the barn, where he slept with the dog, Patch. He didn't care much for people, but people were few and far between here on the clifftop farms around Flamborough and Bempton, where the lush grass bowed down before the wild wind, showing its silver.

So, Robert stayed.

Enid's brother, Giles, came to help, but his wife hated the children and the weather and the long walk to Bempton – and the shame that she fancied was an infectious disease – and they left before the baby was weaned. Enid did not try to stop them. She didn't want charity and wouldn't beg for help.

If it had been winter Celie Sheppard would surely have died for all the times she was put aside and forgotten while her sweating, lactating mother dug vegetables and cut hay. Once she was lost in the deep grass, and Enid only found her because the sheep had gathered to stare down at her like the baby Jesus in the manger, all covered in ants.

The four older, darker children wanted no part of Celie. They didn't know what she'd done wrong – only that she had come and their father had left, and they considered it a very bad exchange. Martin, Stanley and Will would not even look at her. Six-year-old Molly, who had begged for a sister since she could speak, was briefly appointed chief caretaker, but quickly relieved of her duties when Enid found the baby in the pig pen, sucking swill off her fingers.

So Celie became Robert's responsibility. He was slow, but obedient, and the other children respected his size, if nothing else, and would not dare to pinch Celie under his gaze. So Enid hoped for the best and gave Robert an extra shilling a week, which made not a smidge of difference to him, except that he now understood that this was a new duty to add to his others, and he performed it with the same silent industry as he did them all. Between feeds he carried the baby all over the farm, from job to job, enclosing her wherever he stopped to work in a small pen made of hazel that he'd devised and woven himself. It was light enough to fold up and carry with him and strong enough to keep a baby at bay against a hedge or a wall or a gate. Thus Celie survived, although she didn't grow much, or cry at all after a while, given it served no purpose in calling down aid or attention from those who heard it. She changed from an un-bonny baby to a puny child with white hair and lashes and pale blue eyes, and with skin that was so near to translucent it was hard to believe she had blood in her veins and not seawater, so blue did they show.

Once she started to walk, the wicker pen was pointless, but by then Celie had imprinted on Robert like a duckling, and followed the boy wherever he went without deviation. He gave her little quarter, barely slowed his stride: as soon as she walked, Celie had to learn to run – and to pick herself up after every fall – but that's what she did. Whether wading through grass or buffeted by wind or baulked by sheep, she was Robert's pale shadow.

Only near the slurry pit did he train her to stay well back from him, sitting against the warm wooden barn, shoulder to shoulder with Patch, pinching her nose as pig shit spattered out of the barrow and sank into the pit, whichwas surfaced with slime so green and thick that it looked dangerously like grass.

In regular letters from Scarborough, their landlord Mr Constable never stopped rumbling about his rent. Two pounds a month for their thirty-acre strip, with the house and barn at the widest inland end, and narrowing like a pennant to a point on the cliffs a mere thirty yards long. It was the smallest bit of cliff attached to any farm in Bempton or Flamborough, and squeezed from the south and the north respectively by Danes Dyke and Toon, where the climming fields yielded many fragile riches.

Although eggs were no relief to Metland. Not only was it the smallest field, it was also cursed with a cruel overhang along its entire length, so that even were a man to be strung over the edge, he'd be too far from the cliff-face to reach a single egg.

Metland Farm had never really thrived and with John Sheppard gone the family's future looked bleak. Often Mr Constable had to wait for his rent. And, although the children were always frightened that he wouldn't, for some reason he always did.

Enid and the boys and Robert, and even little Molly, had to work every minute God sent them, and every inch of the land – almost up to the drop – to keep from losing their home.

But in the end it was not work that would save them.

Neighbours

Patrick Fort thought about teaspoons all the way home.

Not unusual. He liked to stay on top of teaspoons. He'd stayed on top of them for nearly three years now in the kitchen of the Rorke's Drift, and had no other ambition.

Patrick loved to wash dishes. Loved to take chaos and make of it hot, shiny order, while Kev and Angie and Bronwyn and Rhys rushed from table to table, serving, clearing, wiping, ferrying dirty crockery and cutlery to the kitchen, where Patrick restored them to a glimmer with a system so precise that sometimes Mrs Lloyd would come downstairs just to stand and wonder at him work. Then she'd sigh and shake her head wistfully, and go upstairs again to make up the guest beds and clean the taps. She had given up trying to lure Patrick into a promotion to a more valuable role.

He was too in love with teaspoons.

The hill out of Brecon was long and steep and curled through the sheep-dotted hills like a slick black ribbon. Seven unrelenting miles that would have defeated any but the keenest cyclist, but Patrick *was* the keenest cyclist. As he hit the most brutal kick on the climb, he rose from his saddle and assaulted each pedal in turn, legs burning, lungs aching, rain dripping from his nose on to his bare knees as they rose and fell in painful rhythm:

*Tea*spoons.
*Tea*spoons.
*Tea*spoons . . .

It was almost dark when he turned on to the rutted lane that led to his neighbour's home, and then his home, and then no further. He had to pull into a gateway to let a black BMW pass too fast for comfort in the failing light.

He rode past Weird Nick's house, then got off and wheeled his bike to the back door across weed-strewn gravel and past the blackened remains of a burnt-out shed that contained the shell of a car. The cat came to say hello in the porch, then hurried back through the flap, into the warmth and light.

Patrick hung his bike on the hook, peeled off his waterproof jacket and opened the door, then stopped.

His mother called out: 'Patrick?'

He didn't answer. Didn't move.

'Patrick?'

He didn't hear his mother. His ears were present but his head was not.

'Patrick?'

Patrick closed the door again and put his jacket back on.

Walked back past the car, the shed, across the weed-strewn gravel of the old yard and along a short, well-worn track through a gap in the hedge, to the squat stone building next door.

His trainers got muddy, and Patrick suppressed a flash of panic: he should have put his boots on. Too late now.

There was a time when muddy trainers would have held him up for five, six minutes, gathering his breath until he was ready to go on. Possibly even turning back to start again in more suitable footwear. But now a casual observer would barely have noticed the break in his stride as he reminded himself that he'd been through this before and knew what to do.

It was all about being prepared for the worst.

He would take his trainers off at the door and leave them on the mat, then put them on again when he came out, and walk back home in them. There would be more mud on the return journey, and he was already bracing himself for it. When he got home he would take them off again in the back porch and clean them under the tap outside the back door, and put them on the rack over the fire. They'd be dry by morning – as good as new.

Patrick felt his breath even out as he planned the future. Felt that tight ball of panic in his stomach loosen a little. He was back on track. He was—

He stopped and frowned.

The front door was open. *That* was what he had registered as he cycled past Ty Newydd, head down.

The open door.

He stood and thought about the open door, while the rain trickled inside the neck of his jacket and made him shudder.

He'd seen the door open before, of course, but only in summer, and not at night. And never in the cold and the rain. Patrick didn't know anyone who was rich enough to waste warmth.

He understood what an open door usually meant – that some-one was at home. That was always true here. Weird Nick would be at home; he rarely went anywhere. But it was nearly dark and the lights were not on – when Weird Nick's mother was always telling her son to turn them off, and he was always forgetting, so the lights were always on.

But now the lights were not on and the front door was open.

Something was wrong.

'Hello?'

Patrick put out a hand and nudged the door aside.

'Hello?'

He would have called for his friend's mother but had never used her name. He'd known her most of his life and she had always just been Weird Nick's mother to him.

Hello, Mrs Weird.

Hello, Mrs Nick.

Safer to call her nothing at all.

'Hello?'

'Mmm.'

Someone *was* home. Or some*thing*.

Patrick took a single step inside and remembered his muddy shoes. He stopped again. His friend's mother was super-fussy about shoes in the house, so now he had to decide – take them off or keep them on.

He kept them on.

He might have to run.

He wiped his feet hard on the mat and walked into the house. He found a light switch and pressed it on. The lights didn't obey, but even in the near dark he could see that everything was out of place. Cupboards had been emptied, furniture overturned. Like a bar room after a Western brawl.

The coal had been spilled from the scuttle and across the rug like moonrocks, and there was a handbag among the lumps, with a purse sticking out, and an escaped comb.

Weird Nick's mother was lying face down on the floor by the fire, which had gone out, although as Patrick got closer he could feel its old warmth.

'Hello?' he said.

'Mmm,' she said, and when he bent a little he could see it was because her mouth had been covered by a piece of broad silver tape. The kind he'd used to fix the cracked window in the kitchen.

Patrick cleared his throat. 'Is Nick home?'

He had been asking her the same question since he was seven and had first started to walk next door by himself, so it felt good and normal to him.

'MMMM!' she said again and *looked* at him – and so he looked back at her, but was unable to hold her gaze and let his eyes drop to her shoulder, then to her elbow, her wrist – and finally to the thin strip of plastic that bound it to the other wrist in the middle of her back.

Over the past few years Patrick had learned that his concept of normal was . . . *different* . . . but even *he* thought *that* couldn't be right.

'MMMM!'

'Do you want me to . . . take that tape off?'

She nodded like crazy, and so he bent over her and peeled it off carefully and as soon as he did she burst into tears.

Patrick flinched and stepped back warily. Had he hurt her? He'd been careful. But she was crying hard, her cheek on the carpet mere inches from his muddy shoes—

'Oh sorry!' he said, and toed them off and picked them up. 'So sorry—'

But, 'Untie me!' she sobbed. 'Please, Patrick. My hands . . .'

But he couldn't untie her because the binding was made of two interlocking cable ties, so he fetched a knife from the kitchen drawer and cut through one of them, and she shouted as her arms fell apart.

She rolled on to her side. 'Where's Nick?' she sobbed. '*Nicky!*'

She tried to get up, but now he saw that her ankles were bound too. He bent down to cut the plastic ties but she jerked away and shouted in his ear.

'Leave it! Find Nicky! Hurry!'

Patrick winced at the volume. Then hurried – still clutching his trainers – through the house to Weird Nick's bedroom.

His friend was on the floor, his head nearly under the bed, and with his hands and ankles similarly bound by plastic.

Patrick cut the ties on his wrists and peeled the tape from his lips. Weird Nick rolled over awkwardly and propped himself up on his elbows.

'Is Mum OK? Mum!'

'Nicky?' On cue, his mother shouted from the darkness. 'Nicky?'

'I'm all right, Mum!'

'Oh thank God!' She started crying again.

'Is she all right?'

'I don't know,' said Patrick as he bent to free Nick's ankles.

'What do you mean, you don't know?'

'I didn't take off my shoes. I got mud on the carpet.'

'Shit, Patrick. I mean, is she hurt?'

'Hurt?'

'Yes, hurt! We were robbed and tied up by two men in ski masks!'

Patrick sat back on his heels and frowned at the window. 'But it's not snowing.'

'Jesus . . . !' Weird Nick rolled and clambered awkwardly to his feet, using the bed as an aid, and hissing as the blood returned to his limbs. He found his glasses and limped to the front room and knelt beside his mother, who hugged him and wept, while Patrick cut the ties around her ankles. Then he found the torch on his phone and swept it around the room. It was very untidy. Drawers jutted, doors awry, curtains ripped from their rings.

'They were looking for something,' Nick's mother sniffed. 'I don't know what.' She looked around wildly, as if she no longer trusted anything in the room, the house. Her life. 'They didn't even speak to me. And then they went into your room . . . and I thought they—'

She started to cry again.

'Bastards!' said Nick. 'Fucking bastards!'

'Call the police, Nicky. Call them!'

'Bastards,' he said again, less vehemently.

'Call the police!'

'There's no point, Mum. They're probably junkies looking for cash or jewellery and they didn't find any. The police won't do anything.'

'Of course they will!' she snapped. 'I don't care if they're junkies . . . or . . . or . . . *monkeys*! Someone came into our home and attacked us! *That's* the point!'

She pushed him aside and got up and hobbled to the phone. Her legs were still not fully oiled by blood and she had to hold on to the wing chair and then the table, as she lurched her way across the room to the landline and picked up the receiver.

'It's not working.'

She borrowed Patrick's phone and they waited in silence while she spoke to the police. 'They say they'll come in the morning.'

'Told you.'

'They said to leave things as they are.'

Nick was quiet for a moment, then snorted and stood up and looked at Patrick. 'Screw that. I'm going to tidy my room.'

They had been friends since they were small, but Patrick had never known Weird Nick to tidy his room. And now he was *looking* at him. Jerking his head at his own left shoulder. Patrick thought his neck must be stiff from being tied up with his arms behind him. Still glaring and twitching, Nick disappeared sideways through the door, leaving Patrick unsure of what to do next.

He was hungry so he decided to go home.

He picked up Weird Nick's mother's handbag, comb and purse. There was a twenty-pound note sticking out of the purse. He tucked it back in and zipped it shut and handed it all to her.

'Thank you, Patrick,' she said, and started to cry yet again, and hugged him. He stiffened and didn't hug her back, but he did let it happen. He was used to hugs now. Meg had told him that they would do him good, even if it didn't feel like it at the time.

Like medicine? he'd said.

Like medicine, she'd said, and Meg was nearly a doctor now, so he had to trust her.

Patrick put his trainers on at the door and left.

'Where have you been?' said Sarah Fort.

'Next door,' said Patrick. 'Is tea ready?'

'Nearly.'

He sat at the table and waited for it.

'Can you get the salt and pepper?'

He got up and got the salt and pepper.

'And the knives and forks.'

He got up again and fetched the glittering cutlery from the drawer. The drawer stuck a little and he took the time to re-arrange the utensils in the drawer below it. The potato masher was the culprit, as usual.

Patrick put the knives and forks on the table and sat down again.

His mother put a plate in front of him. Baked beans and chips. His favourite. He started with the baked beans and would finish them all before starting the chips, because of the alphabet. Then he'd drink his tea. Patrick rarely drank coffee after a meal because before C there wasn't enough alphabet to feed a mouse.

There was a knock at the back door.

Hi, Mrs Fort . . .

Weird Nick, asking if she would please go over and see his mother, as she was a bit shaken up. Then, when Sarah looked confused, he told her what had happened.

'Oh my God, Patrick! Why didn't you *tell* me?'

Patrick looked at her blankly. He knew from her tone that he'd got it wrong, but he wasn't sure how. Whatever had happened at Weird Nick's house, it was over, and there was nothing that anyone could do about it, apart from possibly the police, so he hadn't thought there was any point in revisiting it with his mother.

'Poor Jen!' Sarah pulled on her coat. 'Honestly! I can't *believe* you didn't say anything!'

Apparently there was a point.

She banged the back door, and Patrick got up and watched her and Nick hurry past the burnt-out shed and the car, and briefly fill the gap in the hedge.

Then he sat down and finished his tea before it got cold.

The Crack

1926

'Can *we* get eggs?'
Celie looked up, the wind whipping her white hair around her face.

'No.'

'Why?'

Robert frowned and Celie waited.

Patiently.

She was used to waiting for Robert to think.

They were on the cliffs. They sometimes walked here when work was done and before dark, which came late this time of year. Robert, who still had no last name, would walk ahead, with Patch behind him and Celie behind Patch – sometimes holding on to the tip of the dog's fronded tail, sometimes trailing her hands across whiskers of random wheat, or through the long grass that would soon become hay; often singing to herself – snatches of songs she hardly knew, but making up what she didn't. She never asked where they were going because she would find out when they got there.

Metland Farm ended in a bank of tall pink mallow.

Her first time at the bank, Celie had wrinkled her nose and become wary, and slowed as they approached – not seeing a way through. But Robert had not slowed; he had simply disappeared along a near-invisible track in the tall grass and flowers, leaving a lazy little whorl of seeds and bees in the air behind him.

She had followed, the purple mallow over her head in places, and her tummy tingling with something – she didn't know *what* – and then she'd emerged. And her breath had stopped.

Celie Sheppard was at the edge of the world.

A narrow strip of flattened grass and a big flat rock were all that had separated her from the sky and a sheer drop into the dark blue sea. And between this blue and that, the air was filled with birds. Beautiful birds. Celie had no number for them, having never been to school, but there were a *lot*. Many. *Manymanymany* birds. She'd recognized gulls, which often came inland to pick at innards and to shit on roofs, but there were so many others too. White, mostly, and huge, or black and big, or black and white, or brownish and smaller, and some smaller even than that – and with rainbows on their beaks!

Wherever she'd looked there were new birds and more birds and other birds, some flying, some sitting, some diving, spiralling down like leaves blown from a tree.

One huge hovering bird the size of a dog had shivered backwards away from the cliff-edge, then dipped one wing and wheeled away and down, and out of sight.

Celie had breathed again – but that breath had stuck in her throat.

Fish. The air was thick with it.

'It smells,' she'd said, but Robert was already thirty yards away along the cliff, with Patch on his heels, and Celie had had to run to catch up, along the thin line of earth that served as a path through the flat salty grass, following the ragged line of the drop for the most part, here getting closer to the edge, there detouring inland to round a slope or a tussock or a stark white scar where there'd been a recent rockfall.

Patch had glanced around as she'd joined them.

Robert rarely did.

On that first evening, they'd walked all the way to the first gang of men, and Celie and Patch had sat a little way off while Robert had given a small boy tuppence for a pail of runny egg slops scooped out of a barrel.

They'd walked home more slowly, so as not to spill it, and that night they had all eaten sizzling omelette. It had been streaked with blood and not without feathers.

But, omelette!

Celie's tummy groaned now at the memory.

This was that same kind of summer evening when, as the sun slides towards the horizon, the wind becomes a breeze and the breeze suddenly becomes a nothing – not even a whisper – and the vacuum assaults the ears.

'No rope.' Robert finally answered her question.

Celie turned away from him. She was flat on the broad over-hang that ran all the way along the Metland stretch, with her fingers and chin wedged into a long, narrow crack that split it at right angles. The crack grew slowly from its source and, at its outer edge, opened no wider than Celie's arm was long. But if she shuffled out far enough, it meant she could look through the overhang and straight down at the ocean – as distant as stars. The smell still made her wrinkle her nose but she never remarked upon it now. As with crying, she'd learned fast that when no response was forthcoming there was simply no point in repeat-ing herself. She could see two shiny brown-and-white birds on a ledge below the overhang. And she could see the eggs peeping out from underneath them – spotty and brown – and her mouth watered. She spoke into the V.

'There's rope int'barn.'

'What?'

Celie pushed herself up on skinny white arms, and turned her mouth to Robert.

'There's rope int'barn.'

He frowned at the grass.

'Us could have omelette every day,' she said. 'And not pay tuppence.'

He frowned at the grass some more.

Robert never ventured on to the overhang. He didn't say so, but Celie guessed it scared him to be on that sliver of rock with nothing beneath it but air and – finally – sea. It scared her too, but she loved to look through this crack into another world.

Now she put her head into the V again and watched a puffin return to its ledge twenty yards down with a rainbow full of quivering sand-eels. From here she could see hundreds of birds pressed against the cliff-face. And, as they shifted about, glimpses of eggs of every size and colour that she could imagine. They had chickens in the yard, of course, but they laid dull little brown eggs, and never enough to eat, only for selling. These eggs were two or three times that size, and speckled and spotted and splattered with brown and black on backgrounds that ranged from cream, through blue to green. Celie had never had a toy, but the thought of holding such eggs in her little hands made her nearly smile, with a feeling that was beyond hunger.

Carefully she crawled backwards to the grass, then stood patiently before Robert until he said: 'Who'd fetch 'em up?'

'Me,' said Celie. 'And you could hold t'rope.'

Robert looked her up and down slowly, and even that took hardly any time, for Celie at six was barely bigger than a three-year-old, with a hungry little face, and arms and legs like twigs of silver birch. Sometimes on the cliff, the wind would hit her so hard she'd stumble sideways and Robert would have to grip her arm to stop her being blown into the ocean.

Robert's dark eyes completed their detour.

Then he frowned back at the grass.

'Mebbe,' he said.

The rope was a new one. Bought in the dockyard at Hull, it was three hundred feet long, made of hemp with a steel gark for strength, and it had cost sixty pounds – a year's wages for a labouring man – and shared between the members of the Chandler gang. It was a laid twist, and prone to spin, and the much thinner handline that hung alongside the climmer was as much for stability as it was for communication – one tug, stop; two, down; three, up. It took a strong man to carry the big rope and three to pull it in. It would take the weight of a man. It would take the weight of a horse.

It would need to.

Fed out and drawn in four times a day over a wheel on a spike dug into a grassy cliff-edge, snagging on rocks all the way and with a man at the end of it, directing it up, then down, then up again, then down all the way and up again – and at each point leaning, swinging, reaching, scraping, wearing, fraying . . .

When it rained, the rope must be dried like a baby, then coiled correctly to prevent kinking, and stowed in a hole carved into the ground and secured by a door of planks and bitumen.

The rope would need no guard. Nobody who knew it was there would dare to steal something so valuable.

The rope was everything. Life itself.

In two seasons it would be worn just enough to be untrustworthy, and would be cut up and sold off to anyone who needed to tie something up or something down or to some other thing.

Some function that was not near as vital as climming for eggs.

But until that moment came, it was the king of ropes.

*

That was not the rope at Metland Farm.

Robert took *that* rope off the back wall of the barn where it had hung for ever. It was full of rat shit and slow, fat spiders that dropped to the dirt floor when he shook it.

He laid it out in long narrow loops, and they brushed it clean of most debris – the cobwebs sticking to Celie's little fingers and making her shiver.

This rope was maybe seventy-five feet long, and fraying open at both ends, so Robert tied knots to stop any further unravelling. Then he slung it over a beam and hung himself off it, testing its strength.

He fashioned a harness of sorts out of an old leather blacksmith's apron, cutting holes for the legs, and others for threading the coarse rope through. Tested that too, with Celie swinging in it, making adjustments for comfort and angles, the knot at her face, and the deep apron pocket in front – for the eggs.

After they were done, Robert coiled the rope and hung it back on its hook.

'Tomorrow?' said Celie.

'Mebbe,' said Robert, after a while.

The overhang at Metland jutted out nearly a dozen feet, and was the sole reason this narrow strip of cliff had never been plundered for eggs. Experienced eyes and sharp, greedy brains had long ago assessed the field here and concluded that it was impossible to work. The great stone ledge meant there was nowhere to dig in the pulley that kept the rope from rubbing, fraying, snapping against the sharp edge. And even if a rope were fed over without a pulley, it would leave a man dangling uselessly, yards from his quarry – and, without any purchase for his boots, would make it nigh-on impossible for him to get back without loss of eggs and probably life.

The crack was the only place on Metland where a rope could drop straight down the cliff-face, but – even at its widest point right out at the jagged lip – no climmer would have fitted through it, even without his harness and his basket. The crack was too small even for one of the young ladies from Doncaster or York who wanted to show their modern mettle by claiming their own egg.

But it was not too small for Celie Sheppard.

On a sunny, blustery evening, after the pigs had been fed and their eye-watering slurry emptied into the invisible pit, they walked to the clifftop, where Robert uncoiled their rope and helped Celie into the apron swing – she wobbling on one skinny leg at a time as the wind tried to knock her down – then he folded it around her, like enormous bloomers that reached up her back and her front. He fed the rope through the holes at the top and knotted it all in a big hairy lump at her chin.

'Reight?'

She licked her dry little lips, and nodded up at him.

Robert took up a place behind a tussock he could brace against, digging his heels into its base and leaning back, the way they'd seen the anchormen do. He wound the rope twice around his waist.

With all the winding and the knotting, the rope was now only fifty feet long.

Celie edged out on to the overhang. A dozen feet to the end of the crack – barely fifteen inches at its widest point.

She sat down with her legs dangling through the V, the hairy rope pricking at her cheeks.

Robert took up the slack.

Celie looked at the ocean a very long way down. She got a tingle of fear in her tummy and looked at Robert.

'Din' drop us!'

He tilted his narrow chin at her by way of a *yes* and said, 'Hit t'rope to come up. Three times.'

'What?'

Robert slapped the taut rope between them three times with his hand, and Celie felt the vibrations at her breastbone.

She nodded, remembering.

Then, facing Robert, and with her arms braced either side of her, Celie lowered herself slowly through the V.

There was a scary moment where her arms could no longer hold her and she dropped awkwardly and let out a small screech of panic as she fell and swung inwards – until the rope reached the narrowest part of the V, and there it stopped. And held. And Robert held too, and suddenly there she was . . .

Climming.

It really *was* like stepping off the edge of the world, because here – under the overhang – was another world entirely. The rope had twisted as she dropped, and when Celie first opened her eyes, she was facing out to sea, so that she smelled the cliff before she ever saw it. The stench was much, much stronger here than it was even at the top, where the wind played its part in protecting the nose.

She looked down but couldn't see her feet past the knot. She could see the sea though – as dark as midnight, peppered with frothy stars, and so far below that she looked once and then did not look again. Instead, she clutched the rope and kicked her legs and leaned around and slowly, slowly, she turned.

Celie had expected a cliff, but all she could see was a towering wall of birds. It was nearing dusk and most were back to roost, where a roost was any ledge that would hold an egg. Three inches would do for some of the birds, and the chalkface was dense with them, huddled wing to chocolate wing.

There were birds of every kind on Bempton cliffs, but just here almost all were guillemots. Scoots, the climmers called them. Flighted penguins with short tails and long, elegant beaks; white bibs worn over dark brown plumage.

34

Celie didn't know their real name but she could reach out and touch them and when she tried they went for her, squawking and pecking, and her heart jumped in her skinny chest and she snatched her hand away. Before she could calm, a bird brushed her ear as it swooped in to land and she cried out in fear and put up an arm to protect herself.

She hadn't known it would be like this. From the crack she'd seen hundreds of birds, but now she saw thousands – and above her as well as below. There were so many, and so close and so big. And their beaks so sharp . . .

She didn't like it. She didn't like it any more. Didn't like being under the overhang, down here with the birds where they could do whatever they liked with her and nobody could see. She wanted to be back on the clifftop, where birds were in the air and never touched her and where there was grass beneath her feet, so that she could run away—

But she wanted omelette!

Celie Sheppard was skinny and scared and white as flour, and nobody had ever loved her, but there was something inside her so *defiant* that, before her panic could render her useless, she plunged both hands under two random birds and grabbed an egg in each.

For a split second she was hot to the wrists with down and wishbones and rubbery feet, and peppered with pecks. But she *had* them! The angry scoots screamed and flapped and jabbed at her arms, but she *had* them!

Celie dropped one egg into the apron pocket so she could slap the rope frantically to go up—

But instead

she fell.

The Fall

The plummet was short but terrifying and when she opened her eyes Celie Sheppard was still alive – and covered in egg.

She breathed again, then slowly she took her fist from her chest and unclenched her fingers on a mosaic of spotted shell in sticky yolk. As she looked at it, the rope knot jerked at her chin – and then she was going back up, up, up at a rate that was almost as alarming as the drop had been.

Celie gripped the coarse rope in both hands and looked up. The overhang loomed fast, the V looked tiny, and the rope was now running through its narrow point at speed, so that she was aiming for the part of the crack that was far too small, even for her. She cried out in terror and put her hands over her head and squeezed her eyes shut and waited for her brains to be dashed out on the rock.

But she stopped inches short. Blinking.

She heard voices, and felt movement, and suddenly there was a hand at her scruff, hoisting her up and away and through the wide part of the crack, and for a moment she dangled in the air like a bad puppy, her shins scraping the rock . . . then there was grass under her bare feet and she stumbled but didn't fall, because the same hand held her up.

Celie looked around, dripping yolk and breathless with the shock of it all.

While she'd been down there, everything up here had changed.

Robert was sitting on the ground, rubbing his ear, and a big man stood over him, with Robert's rope around his waist, and she could see other men too – a small, older man and a young medium one, and whichever one still had a hold of the back of the leather apron. Satchels and baskets spilled eggs on the grass and that's when Celie knew who they were: the Chandler gang, up from Danes Dyke after fourth pull. Jim Chandler and his sons, James and Harry, who must be holding on to her, and the gang's boys, Arthur and Kipper, with their pails of slops. The big man standing over Robert was their anchor, Pricky Hodgson.

And all of them so angry!

'Is tha' gormless?' Pricky shouted at Robert as he dropped the rope around his feet. 'Is tha' soft int'head?'

Harry Chandler tugged open the knot at Celie's end of the rope. He took her skinny arm in his big brown fist and pulled the leather apron roughly down her legs, making her wobble again as she stepped awkwardly out of it. He steadied her and then let her be, and she stood just in her smock that was stiffening with egg down the front. Her mother would be angry too. Everyone was angry. Celie shivered.

Robert started to get up, but Pricky took a step at him and he fell back again, scared.

'Tha' ought t'know better. Big lad like you.'

'Leave him be,' said Jim Chandler.

'What?' said Pricky.

''Tis t'idiot,' Chandler explained.

'What idiot?'

'Idiot what lives at Metland. In't tha' reight, lad?'

Robert nodded. He was the idiot.

'Oh,' said Hodgson, 'reight.' And he stepped back a little and they all watched the idiot get to his feet.

'What was tha' at?' said Chandler.

'Nowt,' whispered Robert, still cupping his ringing ear.

'Aye,' Chandler turned. 'And ee?'

The small man's sudden focus on her made Celie feel shaky, and when she spoke her words shook too.

'We's having omelette.'

'Omelette?' He snorted. 'You'll *be* omelette if ee try owt like it agin!'

The men all laughed.

Chandler unknotted the rope from the apron and gathered it expertly into big loops on his arm – then hurled it off the cliff.

Celie gasped and watched it go, unravelling as it fell.

'Now git off home, d'ye hear?'

Celie frowned.

'But—'

'D'ye *hear*?' he repeated.

Robert started to walk away and Patch slunk after him.

Celie didn't follow them. Celie glared stubbornly at Robert's back – then turned and opened her sticky hand to Chandler.

'My egg broke,' she said.

'What of it? Better an egg than a head!'

The men laughed again.

Celie looked down at her smock and thought of all the omelette she wasn't going to be eating. When she looked back at Chandler it was with a quivering lip and eyes full of tears.

'You *made* me brek it.'

Chandler snorted, but Celie just glared up at him with her furrowed white brows.

After a bit, Jim Chandler made a sound like a horse harrumphing.

Then he shook his head.

Then finally he sighed and leaned down over his own spilled

satchel and ran his fingers over the eggs before selecting two very dull ones. He held them out to her. 'Here.'

Celie looked at them suspiciously. Two whitish eggs with brown speckles on them. Together they filled his big hand.

She hesitated. Then quickly took the eggs from him as if he might change his mind, and held them at her chest.

'What say ee?'

'Thank ee,' she muttered.

'Come *on*, Celie!' Robert called from the bank of flowers.

'You Celie Sheppard?' Chandler looked at her with new, shrewd interest.

'Aye.'

'You know me?'

'Aye,' she said. 'Mr Chandler.'

'Saved your life, reight?' he told her, and she nodded reluctantly.

Chandler picked up the leather apron and draped it over her shoulder.

'Git on now and don't try owt agin. Climmin's not for bairns.'

Obediently, Celie hurried after Robert. Walking fast, not running, so she wouldn't fall and lose another egg.

'Enjoy yer omelette!'

Behind her, they all laughed.

It was not until she was falling asleep with her belly full of omelette that Celie Sheppard remembered with a start that there was another egg, still in the deep pocket of the old leather apron.

And even though she had no way of knowing it that night – and wouldn't properly understand it for a good while yet – *that* was the egg that would change her life.

Junkies

'It wasn't junkies.'

Weird Nick paused in the back porch for dramatic effect, but Patrick didn't answer pointless statements. There had been twenty quid sticking out of Weird Nick's mother's purse. Even he knew that junkies would have taken it.

It was the morning after the night before and Patrick's mother was already next door, making sure her neighbour was all right. She'd taken her a bacon bap, in case she wasn't up to making breakfast.

Patrick didn't understand how being tied up and robbed one day meant you couldn't make breakfast the next, but rarely questioned his mother.

And she usually returned the favour.

Since what they both now called 'all that stuff' had happened down in Cardiff, Patrick and his mother had lived together in reasonable harmony in the little stone house on the Beacons. Sarah Fort worked at the pound shop and Patrick worked at the pub, and so the time they shared at home was brief, and conversation that was not meal-related generally revolved around the cat.

Patrick had always lived in harmony with himself, of course, and not much disturbed him. But whenever something *did* disturb him, it almost always started with Weird Nick.

'Let's go upstairs.' Nick bustled past him and Patrick followed him to his bedroom. They sat side by side on Patrick's single bed next to the window that looked out across the hills towards Pen y Fan.

'This is what they took.' Nick pulled his laptop out of his satchel and opened it on his knees.

Patrick leaned in to look at the screen.

It was a screenshot of an eBay listing.

OLD EGG IN WOODEN BOX. RESERVE £10.

Patrick leaned in further to look at the photo and frowned.

It was like no egg he had ever seen. For a start, it wasn't very egg-shaped, which felt like a deal-breaker. While it was rounded at one end, it was long and slim and nearly pointed at the other. More cone than egg. And it was big – three or four times the size of a hen's egg, according to the fifty-pence piece Weird Nick had included for scale.

But, most startling of all, the egg was red. A rich, bloody red around its blunt end, fading to plain pink near its point. It looked like a painting of an egg done by a child, for sticking on an Easter fridge.

'Is it real?'

'I *think* so.'

'Why is it red?'

'Search me,' said Weird Nick.

Patrick thought of the first time he'd heard another boy use those words – *search me* – and the playground scuffle that had ensued. He'd learned a lot since then.

'It was in the attic with all the rest of my dad's stuff.'

Patrick didn't remember Weird Nick's dad. He wasn't sure Weird Nick remembered him either as he had left when Nick was a baby. Patrick remembered his own dad, but never without thinking of his death, so he never lingered there.

So now they didn't have even one dad between them.

'Been selling things, see? There's all sorts up there. Got fifty quid for a crossbow alone. Raised more than two hundred quid so far.'

Weird Nick made it sound as if the money was for charity, but Patrick knew it was for a gaming chair. Nick didn't have a job and had been saving for a gaming chair for a long time now. Trouble was, he needed a really good one, because he was no lightweight, and had already broken two standard office chairs in the Call of Duty. The chair he wanted was over five hundred pounds and looked like something off *Star Trek*.

Now Weird Nick opened his photos and tapped the screen. 'The egg was in this fancy wooden box, see? That's gotta be worth something.'

There were half a dozen photos. Patrick studied them closely, enlarging each one, taking his time.

The box *was* fancy. Some kind of dark, dusty wood with carved pillars either side of a glass door, which opened with a small brass key.

Patrick enlarged them further and frowned. The carvings were elaborate. The pillars were adorned with seabirds. At least, he assumed they were seabirds, because he recognized a puffin with its distinctive beak, and the base of each pillar was splashed by wooden waves. The meticulously crafted birds wheeled and dived – and one bobbed on the grainy ocean. It had been made with great skill.

'The box alone has got to be worth that,' he murmured.

'That's what I thought,' said Weird Nick. 'All that carving. Got to be worth thirty or forty quid.'

Patrick thought more, but didn't say so. He thought about a lot of things he didn't say. Unlike Nick, who said a lot of things he didn't think about.

'It was only up five minutes and eBay took it down.'

'Why?'

'Not allowed.' Nick leaned closer to Patrick to tap the keys. Patrick leaned away from him so their shoulders wouldn't touch.

He read the message from eBay.

Your item (#78384839202) is in breach of eBay's terms and conditions. It is an item which is illegal to sell where you live. The listing for (#78384839202) has been removed and you are requested not to relist it or your account will be suspended.

Patrick frowned. 'Illegal?'

'The egg, apparently. I looked it up. You can't sell birds' eggs.'

'Why?'

'Who knows?' said Nick – another phrase that used to waste an awful lot of Patrick's time. Now he understood that it was rhetorical and could be safely ignored.

Nick lowered his voice, even though they were alone in the house, bar the cat. 'Listen, mate, I don't want Mum knowing I've been selling Dad's stuff. I mean, he's my dad, so it's pretty much mine anyway, so where's the harm, right?'

Patrick said nothing. Nick went on: 'But I googled it and eBay's right – it's illegal to even *have* a bird's egg, let alone sell it, so I don't want the bloody police knowing about any of this either. I don't want to get into shit for an egg I don't even *have* any more.'

Nick didn't bother swearing Patrick to secrecy. Patrick never told anybody anything. Unless they asked – then he told them everything. For instance, he had never told anyone that Weird Nick sometimes grew weed in the old greenhouse, but only because no one had ever asked him about it. Patrick found lies confusing, and happily unburdened himself of them at the earliest opportunity.

'You know what this means, right?' said Nick, and rolled right on without waiting for an answer. 'It means if these bastards were prepared to come here in balaclavas and tie us up to steal it, it must be worth more than a tenner. A *lot* more.'

Patrick nodded. 'But it's gone,' he said, 'so really it doesn't matter *what* it's worth, does it?'

'That's where you're wrong,' said Weird Nick, with a gleam in his eye that Patrick found unnerving. 'Because *we* are going to get it back.'

'We?' said Patrick warily. 'How?'

'Oh, don't you worry,' said Nick, tapping his nose. 'I'll think of something.'

Patrick sighed.

He knew that meant that *he* would have to think of something.

The Metland Egg

1926

George Ambler was a horse-faced young man from London. He wore a stovepipe hat, which was a most inconvenient affectation on top of a windy cliff. But it was a very good hat – and his trademark, he felt – and he liked to stand out from the hoi polloi who frequented the cliffs at Bempton and Flamborough all summer long. He wanted to make it plain, even to those who had no interest, that he was not some tourist, up to black his nose at the climmers and the birds, and that neither was he a local selling trinkets.

George Ambler was a broker.

Just as his two older brothers, Alexander and Tobias, had become City brokers of gold bars and salt, so George Ambler – after a lengthy detour through imports and a brief one through the bankruptcy court – had become a broker of eggs.

His rich brothers had rich friends, several of whom were obsessed with eggs – apportioning large sums and vast space to their collections, and communing with like-minded collectors for the purpose of comparing, contrasting and coveting.

Of course, the richer the man (and it was *always* a man), the less likely he was to procure those eggs himself. For what captain of industry or peer of the realm has the time or the inclination to shin up a tree or wade through bulrushes? Or even to travel a hundred miles in the company of the Great Unwashed, to catch his death on a northern cliff that smelled like a Shoreditch whore?

The answer, of course, was none.

So George Ambler did it for them.

He did it because he loved rich people and, despite his pecuniary improprieties, still harboured ambitions to be one himself. The opportunity to ingratiate himself with a group of wealthy men *and* to be paid for it was irresistible.

To start with, Ambler had had no interest in eggs other than in kedgeree, but he'd made it his job to find out everything about them. And what he'd found out was that the most commercial of all eggs came from the guillemot.

The guillemot, or murre, or scout – *scoot* to use the vulgar Yorkshire – was not a big bird, but it laid an uncommonly big egg. A bird that was fifteen inches from beak to tail laid a single egg that might be five inches long. And, while the guillemot was not a rare bird by any means, every egg was not only decorative – adorned as it was with whirls and squiggles, and of all kinds of colours, from white, through tan and grey and blue and green and chocolate – but was also unique. Each bird laid an egg that was unlike any other that had ever been laid by any other guillemot in all guillemot history. In the high-density fields of the North Yorkshire cliffs, where birds might roost at the rate of fifty pairs to a square yard, it was required that a bird knew exactly which egg was theirs, so that it didn't end up warming one six inches to the left, or an inch to the right.

So each bird laid an egg she knew was hers alone.

And she would lay exactly the same mark of egg the next year.

And the year after that.

And the year after that.

It was this combination of desirability, peculiarity and repeat business that had allowed George Ambler to look into the future and to see a big egg-shaped pot of gold at the end of his own personal rainbow.

He'd decided from the outset that he would be the man who bought the *best* eggs. Not for him the sixpenny shells of brown squiggles. Leave those in their thousands to Messrs Hollingberry and Worrell and other northern brokers. He resisted the lure of even *quite* interesting eggs and saved all the money he had borrowed from his reluctant brothers to buy big and sell bigger.

One day he paid Malcolm Hodgson four pounds for a big blue egg with a pale grey belt, and his position as the biggest broker on the cliffs was cemented. From then on, if a climmer found something special, his first port of call was Mr Ambler. Single-handedly he pushed up the prices of the best eggs and devalued the market for the thousands of those more ordinary.

Ambler spent every day between May and July on the cliffs with the climmers, and made it his business to know their business, so that he could sway with any favourable wind when it came to a deal.

He knew that the Chandlers and the Hodgsons were neighbours but also rivals, since Jim Chandler had pinched Malcolm's son Pricky, who was the best anchorman in Bempton. Pricky had defected because his brother Howard had stolen his lass, Maddie Slocombe, although Howard swore blind that he never knew Pricky was sweet on her, and it's quite possible that Pricky never knew either, until she was gone.

So, the Chandlers and the Hodgsons worked the cliffs alongside each other and barely made eye contact. But in the Cock of a Saturday night, when beer had been taken, anything might happen, and frequently did.

Then there were the Artleys – a staunchly religious clan who would act as peacemakers if things got too hot in the pub. They shared Mainprize Garden with the Chandlers, while the Moores worked Toon, at the edge of their own farm, together with the Hodgsons. They couldn't have worked their field alone because the old man was nearing seventy and his son only had one leg, courtesy of the Great War. But that was no handicap when that leg was only called upon to dangle over the ocean.

Each gang loosely numbered seven or eight – mostly labourers from surrounding farms – who took turns on the pulls, making up the four men in each team. The anchor, the band man, who watched the spiked pulley and stopped the rope from fouling, the climmer, and the spare, whose job was to do everything else that might possibly be needed – dry the rope, repair the swing, drill, blow and clean the eggs, negotiate with brokers, sell to tourists, and finally to help haul the climmer up at the end of each pull. For a man whose title implied that he had nothing to do, the spare's list of jobs was nigh-on endless.

Each gang always included a sharp boy or two, who were kept busy fetching, carrying, and making change for tourists. Their only compensation was the slops, but the swagger was priceless, and they were all keen to graduate to the real business of climming to earn their fortunes. The Artleys' boy was called Francis; Arthur and Kipper worked for the Chandlers, and the Hodgsons' lad was Chubby Dawkins, who was not really fat, but who had a fat face.

Ambler had learned all of this by watching and listening every day on the cliffs. Nobody had ever told him, because nobody had liked him – until he'd started to pay big money for eggs. Nobody liked him even after that, but that was all right with him, because he didn't like them either. Bandy, ignorant, weather-beaten men, who tipped their filthy caps at his face, and their fingers at his back.

He knew.

And he didn't care.

Because what fetched a pound at Bempton or Flamborough would fetch four in York and six in London. For those returns, Mr Ambler in his stovepipe hat could bear to be disliked as he waited atop Twenty Acre or Cruddy for the wealth to make its way up the cliff in old satchels and tackle baskets, and into his already-bulging pockets.

Which was exactly what he was doing one evening in June 1926 when a tiny girl no longer than his leg tugged on his coat.

'Shoo,' he said and yanked his coat from her grubby hand.

'Will ee buy an egg, sir?'

'No. Go away.'

''Sa goodun.'

Ambler looked down.

The girl was a strange one. Pale as milk and skinny as a straw. Her feet were bare and her toenails black-rimmed. The wind that had torn four hundred miles unabated across the sea from Norway had found landfall in her hair and was making the most of whipping it around her face and into her mouth and icy eyes. Ambler thought that if it weren't for her pink lips, she'd look like nothing so much as a dirty little corpse.

She obviously took his perusal as permission to continue negotiations, because before he could shoo her away again she drew an egg from the pocket of her shabby smock.

Ambler's heart—

Stopped.

Just . . .

Stopped.

And along with it, the wind and the birds and the sea below.

And in that vacuum George Ambler formed only one thought:

Impossible!

The egg was red.

Not redd*ish*. Not red-brown or pink – although any of those would have been surprising and desirable.

The egg was *red*.

He had never seen anything like it.

He didn't believe there had ever *been* anything like it.

One in a million.

A billion.

If it were real.

But it *couldn't* be real . . .

Slowly Ambler became aware that air was moving up and down his nostrils, making a slight whistling sound inside his own head, and that the child was staring up at him – and might have been for days for all he knew.

'Where did you get that?' he demanded.

'Metland.' The child turned to point as she spoke, so that the word was nearly lost on the wind.

The little liar. Nobody worked Metland. Because of the overhang.

'Let me see it.' He frowned and reached out and took the egg from her. More roughly than he normally would, because he was already angry that she was lying and trying to sell him a fake rubbed with clay or dipped in oxblood. A few years back a broker had been laughed clear out of the business after trying to sell an egg that had had the word 'GOD' inked among its scribbles by an enterprising local wag.

He licked his thumb and rubbed it hard on the red egg.

Nothing came off.

The egg's ground was a deep, tapestry red, but grew lighter as it rose from the base, fading to a pretty pink blush at the very point. There was not a mark on it. Not a spot nor a squiggle to sully the perfection.

He rubbed another place. Maybe one that was not yet dried so hard.

Nothing.

The egg was red.

And it was real.

For the first time since he was four years old and Tobias had pushed him off a pony, George Ambler felt tears spring to his eyes – so moved was he by how much money he was going to make.

The child stared at him still, and he collected himself by frowning hard.

'Five bob,' he said.

Her fine white brows met in displeasure.

'Take it or leave it,' he said, and, with every fibre of his being screaming at him to *not do it*, he handed the egg back to her and turned away and towards the gang, where they'd just pulled in young James Chandler, laden with eggs.

'Robert said a pound,' the girl said behind him.

Ambler glanced at a lad a little way down the cliff. A boy of about sixteen. Most likely a brother.

'For that?' He snorted. 'You won't get a pound for *that*.' He turned away again and examined the inside of his hat.

A long, long silence behind him.

Unbearable.

Unbearable.

But these silences were bargaining chips. He'd learned that from the grubby Yorkshiremen too. Silence spoke volumes up here. The urchin was trying to wait him out!

Slowly Ambler put his hat on.

Took another moment or two to square it just right.

And looked over his shoulder.

She'd gone.

His stomach dropped like a stone. He turned frantically – and saw her talking to the boy. He wondered what *he* was saying about the five bob. Encouraging her to take it, thinking of all it would buy? Or was he wiser than that?

Ambler itched to rush over to them, but stood his ground against the wind.

After a lifetime, the corpse-child turned and tottered back towards him.

It took *for ever*. Thirty agonizing yards. And with every step he prayed feverishly for her not to fall, to trip, to crush the jewel, or to drop it and break it. In Ambler's mind the red egg was already his, and, with her rickety legs and bare feet, the girl looked like a very poor guardian of his valuables.

'Robert says a pound.'

Ambler glared towards the stupid, cunning boy. Then looked back down at the girl. Her ugly little brows met like two chalky worms over her strange, faded eyes.

Then he tutted.

He sighed.

He pulled the kind of face that told her how *very* unreasonable she was being.

'Oh, all right then,' he grumbled. 'I'll give you a pound.'

'You bloody won't!'

Ambler turned to find Jim Chandler at his elbow. His crooked grey cigarette clamped in his lips and sending smoke curling past his slitted eyes.

'I beg your pardon?'

Rudely, Chandler did not repeat himself. Instead he held out his hand for the egg.

'Gis it.'

'Now, now, Jim, the young lady and I have—'

She'd already given Chandler the egg.

The man held it in his ghastly, grimy hand and rolled it gently from side to side. The hole in the bottom was large – must have been a late chick in it – but it was properly drilled, and the egg was clean.

Chandler shook his head in naked wonder. 'Never seen owt like it.'

'Have you not?' said Ambler. 'I hear red eggs are not un-common in Wales.'

Chandler cocked an eye at him from under his insufferable cap and Ambler made a song and dance of searching his pockets, so that he didn't have to meet it. He found his clip (because he knew exactly where it was, of course) and peeled off a pound note. The child reached for it eagerly, but before she could take it, Jim Chandler picked it clear off the end of her fingers.

So now he had the egg *and* the money.

'I trust this is t'down payment, Mr Ambler?'

'Haha,' Ambler said. 'What *do* you mean?'

'This here egg's worth more than a pound. More than two. More even than the Big Blue, I warnt be shocked.'

'I don't think that's true at all,' said Ambler. 'Even if a collector were prepared to pay, say, four pounds for it, that doesn't mean I can pay four pounds for it here on the cliff, does it? With all my overheads? My trains and my meals and my room at the Cock? For a four-pound egg I must pay no more than a pound here, you see? Come now, old man, everybody has to make a little profit along the way. It's how we all survive.'

Chandler worked his cigarette. 'T'ain't how *us* survive, Mr Ambler,' he said. '*Us* survives by not falling off a rope down t'cliff and into t'sea!'

The girl giggled up at him.

'Of course,' said Ambler hurriedly. 'I didn't—'

'And this nipper done t'same to git this egg, dint ee?'

Celie nodded her head vigorously.

'When I told tha' not to.'

The child stopped nodding and got a hint of colour in her face – possibly for the first time in her whole life.

'Hmmm,' Ambler mused with a theatrical finger on his brow. 'Well,' he said finally, 'you make a very fair point, Jim.' Then he turned to the girl and beamed as broadly as his unpractised face would allow. 'Young lady, due to Mr Chandler's most kind intervention I'd be pleased to offer you two pounds for the egg!'

Her mouth dropped open.

'Ten,' said Chandler.

Ambler wanted to throw him off the cliff. Chandler was gnomish, and old to boot, and might easily be knocked down by any taller man, even a London dandy. But George Ambler was not a fighter. Neither was he a lover. He was a money-maker, and he knew he would make money on the extraordinary egg even at ten pounds. Even at twenty. The Big Blue for which he'd so famously paid four pounds had sold to Mr Rickaby of Mansfield for thirty, making it officially the most expensive bird's egg in the known world, and Mr Rickaby the object of such envy among his fellow collectors that the man never tired of telling Ambler that it was the best thirty pounds he'd ever spent. Ambler feigned delight each time, of course, but was furious that he hadn't asked for fifty.

So *this* egg . . . this incredible, miraculous, *impossible* thing?

The sky was the limit.

But that didn't mean he was going to start throwing money at these people!

'Now, now, old man,' he smiled at Jim Chandler. 'Ten? Now really, let's not get carried away. It's not a *golden* egg, after all!'

'Not to me, Mr Ambler,' Chandler shrugged. 'And not to you. But to *her*? I reckon it might come close.'

Chandler's sons were sauntering over now, to see what their father was finding to keep him. James was rolling his sleeves down brawny arms, Harry lighting a cigarette, Arthur and Kipper hovering eagerly. Behind them, Pricky coiled the rope, with a weather eye on the action. Ambler could feel the egg about to move out of his orbit of influence . . .

'Very good,' he said with an air of finality. 'I'll give the girl five pounds. *Five pounds*. More money than she'll see in one place at one time for the rest of her life. It's an astronomical sum, Mr Chandler. You know that. The biggest bounty ever paid!'

The child looked dazed by the prospect. She turned as if to invite the boy – Robert? – over to confirm she was hearing right, but the boy just stood a way off and watched.

'Paid for what?' said Harry.

'Look ee here,' said Jim, and his sons' mouths fell open at the sight of the big red egg, and Ambler wanted to scream because it was not yet his, but could have been for a pound just minutes ago! Fifteen shillings if he was any kind of a negotiator, which he absolutely was. There were all sorts of faults he could have con-jured up and pointed out to the child to explain (once the egg was in *his* hand and not *hers*) why the pound they'd agreed was no longer on the table, and she'd never have been any the wiser. And now, here was the whole Chandler gang fawning over the egg as if it were not only gold but had been laid on the moon!

'Worth twice tha',' said Harry.

'I told ee,' nodded Jim.

'Never seen owt like it,' said James.

Ambler panicked. James and Harry were enraptured and Jim was unmoving, and if Pricky Hodgson came over, the way he looked as if he might do, then who knows? The price may go up to twenty!

'All right!' he snapped. 'Ten pounds!'

Jim Chandler pursed his lips around his vile stub and eyed Ambler while he removed a ten-pound note from his clip and handed it over to the chalk-stick child. She took it as if in a trance, then turned and ran back to the boy, shouting unintelligible stuff into the wind.

Ambler held out a trembling hand for the egg.

Jim Chandler gave it to him with a smile.

For hours after Celie Sheppard had stolen her egg, the guillemot that had laid it squawked harsh, mournful cries that were wholly unlike the regular calls of the hundreds of identical birds on the cliff under the Metland overhang.

When her mate came to roost after a long day at sea, he panicked along with her. The pair of them pecked and were pecked by neighbours settling in for the night, as they searched in confusion for their lost egg.

In the morning the bird and her mate woke on their narrow ledge and sought their egg again, squawked again, pecked again, were pecked again. Then they fed – plummeting so fast, and from so high, that in open water they might dive past the point where the ocean was blue, and pierce the black more than two hundred feet down, along with the whales – to capture eels or fish.

Then they returned to their ledge under the overhang and started their search again.

They went through this routine for days – maybe a week – while all around them dull, dark chicks started emerging from jewelled eggs like spiky disappointments.

Sometimes the guillemot and her mate would bring sand-eels back to the cliff-face and feed the chicks next door – the instinct to raise a chick so strong that they could not resist it.

But some of those chicks would be lost too. Many, in fact. Picked off by the same gulls and crows that had missed them as eggs, or by boys in boats, armed with Lee-Enfield rifles their fathers had brought home from the Great War, honing their skills by bagging the smallest targets on the cliffs.

Those guillemot chicks that did avoid early death would never become fledglings.

Fledglings fledged. They shed their fluff and feathered up and finally flew the nest.

But that wasn't how guillemots worked.

At only days old, each tiny chick would be left alone on its ledge. Suddenly without the protection or care of either parent, it would cheep and chirp and flap the puny wings that would not be able to carry it in the air for many weeks yet, while far below its parents bobbed on the ocean and called for it.

To jump.

Quick!

Before the gulls and the crows and the guns could find it making a spectacle of itself with its squeaking and hopping and flapping, and its peering anxiously off the edge of the world.

Jump! they'd cry. *Jump!*

And, if it was lucky, the fist-sized ball of fluff would live long enough to jump. A hundred feet. Two hundred, three hundred feet or more, off the towering cliff, tumbling as it dropped, tossed by gusts of wind, bouncing off ledges and jagged rocks – where the journey would end for some – until it plopped into the bitter cold of the North Sea, then bobbed there, stunned and disorientated, for its parents to find.

Not a fledgling, but a jumpling.

And the first thing a tiny guillemot jumpling would do after surviving the drop?

It would swim four hundred miles to Norway.

Across a sea frigid, rough, and thick with predators from above and below. Along the way the little chick would learn to swim and to dive and to fish and – finally – to fly.

But long before the jumplings of 1926 could start their harrowing voyage across the deep indigo ocean, the guillemots that had produced the big red egg had given up their search.

It was too late to lay a second egg – they knew that instinctively – and the only thing left to do was to set off for the winter breeding grounds.

Even without a chick to nurture along the way, they would spend weeks crossing the North Sea to that distant land where they would feed and mate.

And in the spring of 1927 they would make the long, dangerous journey back across the North Sea to England. Back to Bempton cliffs. Back to the very same three-inch-wide ledge under the supposed protection of that very same overhang . . .

To lay another egg.

Weird Nick's Attic

Weird Nick's mother was out, so they were searching his attic for more valuables when Patrick thought of something.

'Did anybody bid on the egg before the listing was removed?'

'Only one.'

'Who?'

'Hold on,' said Nick, and clambered down the ladder, leaving Patrick sitting on an old trunk with their booty at his feet: a little wooden desk calendar, a canteen of silver cake forks and a badly stuffed badger.

Nick came back up and sat alongside Patrick on the trunk with his laptop on his knees. He brought up his eBay account. 'There you go: eggman456.'

'How much did he bid?'

'You can't see that. It just shows that he made the minimum bid. Ten fifty.'

'Maybe he knew something about the box.'

'Yeah,' said Nick. 'And maybe he's the one who stole it.'

'Why would someone steal it if he was prepared to buy it?'

'He couldn't buy it, though, could he? eBay made me take it down.' Nick shook his head. 'Anyway, how would he have got my address? It's not on the listing.'

'I don't know.' Patrick was quiet for a while, then finally added,

'But somebody called eggman just seems like a big clue you should be following up.'

'You're right,' said Nick. 'Hey, you dropped this.'

'What is it?'

Nick held it up. 'Penknife.'

'It's not mine.'

'It's got your initials on it.'

Patrick shrugged. 'I don't have a penknife.'

'You got one now,' said Nick, and tossed it to him. 'Happy birthday.'

'It's not my birthday.'

'Well, when it is, remember I already gave you something.'

Patrick would. If only because Weird Nick rarely remembered his birthday, so this would be a nice change.

He shone his torch on the knife. It was small and silver and so tarnished that it was nearly black. But it did have his initials engraved on the handle – *P. F.* – in fancy letters. Patrick wondered if he'd dropped it here as a child. He thought he would remember that, but accepted that now he was in his twenties things might be starting to slip, memory-wise.

'OK then,' he shrugged, and put the knife in his pocket. 'Thanks.'

'Welcome,' said Nick. 'Happy birthday, mate!'

Patrick made a mental note to get Nick something nice in return, then he went back to thinking, while Nick cast the beam of his torch into the far corners of the attic and kept up a stream of words to which only he listened.

'Still loads to look through . . .

'Even without the egg, I reckon I'll be able to get a chair by the end of the summer . . .

'If these forks are real silver I might upgrade to the RX900. It's got—'

He sneezed violently.

'This dust effs with my hay fever . . . Jeez! Look at the size of that effing spider!'

'See if he still wants to buy it,' said Patrick.

'What?'

'See if eggman456 still wants to buy the egg.'

'What's the point when we don't *have* the egg?'

'He wanted to buy it *then*. If he doesn't *now*, then that must *mean* something. Mustn't it?'

Patrick worked hard at understanding what people *meant*. It often took him a long time to think it through, and he didn't always reach the right conclusion, but now Nick illuminated his own face in the darkness and grinned his approval.

'Genius!' he said, and sat down and tapped out a message to eggman456.

Still want this?

He hit Send and they both stared at the screen for half a minute as if an answer might pop up instantly. Even so they were both surprised when it did just that.

No thnx mate.

'Ha!' said Nick. 'One minute he's wanting to pay big bucks for it, and now he's not interested in it? You're right, it seems bloody fishy! Now what do we do?'

He waited while Patrick thought, but quickly grew restless. 'You want a sandwich?'

'OK.'

Nick was the only person other than his mother whom Patrick trusted to make him a sandwich unsupervised. He took all the rules seriously and wouldn't even use margarine instead of butter without consulting Patrick on alternative fillings – even though tuna or Marmite were the obvious solution.

Nick clambered noisily down the ladder and by the time he

got back to the attic with cheese and Marmite sandwiches and two mugs of tea, Patrick had finished thinking.

'You said you'd sold some of your dad's stuff already?'

'Yeah. Some hiking boots, fishing gear, bits and bobs, y'know.'

'Do you put your address on the label?'

'Yeah, of course.'

'Maybe that's how he got it.'

Nick frowned over his laptop, then shook his head. 'Nah. He hasn't bought anything from me.'

Patrick ate in silence for a few minutes. 'See if he's selling anything.'

'Genius!' said Nick again, and clicked on eggman's screen name. 'Hope he's not a Rolls-Royce dealer . . .'

They were in luck: eggman456 was selling off a veritable landfill of tat. Mostly it was tired-looking women's clothing – sizes 18–20 – and an array of ugly ornaments. Chipped plates, china plough-horses and haughty-looking ladies in crinolines. Scattered among the bric-a-brac were a few dirty fishing rods and reels, and several folding knives labelled *legal carry!!!*

'Just buy the cheapest thing,' said Patrick, but the cheapest thing was a Princess Di commemorative eggcup for a pound, and even Weird Nick was reluctant to sink that low.

They finally settled on a tin of two hundred and fifty .22 airgun pellets marked *almost full* for four pounds.

'Bargain!' said Nick. 'Half price, that!' He had an airgun which he claimed to be for rats, but the only time he'd shot a rat, he'd cried. Now he just peppered Patrick's mother's burnt-out shed from his bedroom window.

He was about to buy the pellets, but Patrick put a hand on his arm. 'Hold on.'

Patrick found it difficult to imagine what other people were thinking, or *had* been thinking, or might be thinking some time in the future – but instinctively he felt this was a bad idea.

'If he stole the egg, then he knows where you live . . .'

'Oh yeah, that looks suspicious. We'll use your account.'

'OK,' said Patrick. 'And have them sent to the pub. They won't mind. I get my bike bits sent there.'

None of them got much mail, but when they did, the regular postman came all the way up the lane in all weathers. However, when he was on holiday his replacements rarely showed the same enthusiasm for coming up a dirty track to two little cottages. Sometimes they got their post, sometimes they got it late, sometimes they never got it. It was wise to have an alternative.

Nick changed the account and delivery address and paid for the pellets with Patrick's money.

'Remind me to give that back to you,' he said, although Patrick knew he never would.

Nick closed the laptop and stood up, brushing crumbs off his jeans.

'Right,' he said, 'hand me down the badger.'

Need and Want

Major Howells of Anglesey, Mr Minke of Golders Green and Mr Rickaby of Mansfield were men who had everything they could possibly need.

But very far from everything they wanted.

That is why, within a week of the little scene on the Bempton cliffs, each received a stiff white envelope, sealed with wax and containing a gilded card.

An invitation to view
THE METLAND EGG
The True Eighth Wonder of the World
At the Home of Mr George Ambler, Cavendish Square, London
8 p.m., 19 June 1926
Dinner will be served
RSVP

Mr Minke immediately ordered his car to be brought around, and was driven to Cavendish Square and demanded to view the egg straight away. But Edwards, the butler, had been briefed, and fended him off with wilful misunderstanding – thanking him most ardently, as if his call were a prompt, in-person *répondez* to the invitation extended, for which Mr Ambler would be *most grateful* when he returned home *from business*, which was likely to keep him away between now until pretty much directly before soup was served at the time and date stated.

And not before was implied so strongly that even Mr Minke got the message and returned home in high dudgeon.

There was nothing for it. He would have to wait.

Before buying the Metland Egg.

Arthur Rickaby was furious.

Big Blue was the Eighth Wonder of the World!

That scoundrel Ambler had used those very words to tickle him from twenty pounds to twenty-five and thereafter to thirty. Rickaby was a little hazy as to how he'd got to twenty in the first place, when he'd never paid more than ten pounds for an egg in his life and would have scoffed at the man who'd suggested he might. But pay it he had – and he had a clear recollection of the Eighth Wonder conversation too. The Great Pyramid at Giza, the Colossus of Rhodes, and Big Blue; Ambler had whispered the words next to his ear like a lover as they'd examined the prize.

How could anyone put a price on such wonders?

Well, Ambler had, and Rickaby had paid it. And been happy to have done so – at that moment and every moment of every day subsequently.

Until now.

The *True* Eighth Wonder of the World.

The invitation was a gilt-edged dagger in Arthur Rickaby's back.

He glared at Big Blue.

It nestled in the oak case which he'd commissioned from Bartlett & Sons – the finest purveyors of taxidermy and associated paraphernalia in London and, therefore, the world. The case had cost nearly the price of the egg, but that was immaterial. Three sides glass, one side plaster-of-Paris cliff, skilfully moulded and painted by Shawcross (who knew no equal in such matters), with rugged tufts, and real murre feathers, and all dribbled white with gouache guano. And Big Blue, in situ of course, to give the impression every time Rickaby entered the drawing room that he was discovering it himself for the very first time on some blustery cliff-cum-mantelpiece.

The dreams it had evoked.

The self-satisfaction . . .

But now Big Blue meant nothing to Rickaby and he was already wondering how much he might ask for it from Bigelow or Minke.

Twenty-five pounds, he thought.

It would sting his pride to lose five pounds, but it would be twenty-five pounds he'd save on the cost of the Metland Egg, which he wanted – sight unseen – like nothing else he'd ever wanted in his life.

Major Howells responded by return. He wanted that egg. He'd been caused enough indigestion at the Oological Society dinner by Rickaby boasting about Big Blue.

Did I mention . . . ?

A lot of money, of course – thirty pounds! – but . . .

You should see it in situ. Anytime you want to come to Mansfield . . .

Mansfield?

Ha!

Howells had never been to Mansfield and neither had anyone of his civilized acquaintance. Why, he would no more go to Mansfield than Mongolia! Would not give the bumptious fool the satisfaction.

His only recourse was to beat Rickaby into silence with an egg *even more extraordinary* than his.

Major Victor Howells was not a man to be trifled with. His family had made its fortune in brewing, and beer showed no sign of falling out of favour with the masses, so his pockets were as deep as any man's in Britain.

He'd been most annoyed that Ambler had offered the big blue egg to Rickaby before him, and felt it was his absolute *right* to own this new egg. He'd been a customer of Ambler's for years – ever since the man got into the game – and had paid sixty pounds only last summer for five identical sea-green eggs with barely a squiggle. *Five* of the blighters! For five years a man had braved the cliffs at Flamborough Head and collected the same egg from the same guillemot. Then he had held on to them and sold them together. It was almost unheard of – and the pride of Howells' collection. He'd had a custom-sized mahogany case commissioned to show them off to all comers.

Who were few and far between, as Major Howells lived alone and was not a man for society, but if Mrs Pryce the housekeeper had heard once how precious those five eggs were, she'd heard it a dozen times. How lucky she was to be allowed to dust them – or to dust near them, at any rate.

But once Rickaby had started to boast about the Big Blue, the five miraculous eggs had lost a little of their sheen. The sight of them had started to give Howells a slight prick of discontent, which had made him restless.

In search of something to assuage that feeling – quickly – he had commissioned an agent to buy up the collections of half a dozen of the greatest estates of Europe – including the much-coveted Kricheldorff eggs, three hundred of which were cuckoos' – and within months had over a hundred thousand eggs in his vast rooms, awaiting curation.

Which he never quite got around to.

Each new addition to the collection lifted his hopes, but –

because his interest lay in the acquisition of the eggs rather than their organization (or even admiration) – he never quite knew what he had, or whether any of it was really worth having at all.

Any mention of the five sea-green eggs rang hollow to him now.

Everybody knew (because Ambler had told them) that Rickaby had paid thirty pounds for a single egg, and now he felt he must overtake his rival, or be diminished in the eyes of all who knew he'd been bettered.

It kept Major Howells awake at night – almost bringing tears to his eyes as he contemplated the unfairness of it all.

He *deserved* the Metland Egg.

Whatever it was.

The nineteenth of June 1926 dawned cold and grey.

But Messrs Minke, Howells and Rickaby did not notice the weather. Each woke with a feeling they'd not had since childhood Christmases, and spent their respective mornings restless, distracted and scheming – each still hoping that a strategy would occur to him, and him alone, that would stymie the ambitions of any other attendees at tonight's dinner, before it could turn into a fair fight.

From his *pied-à-terre* in Mayfair, Major Howells sent a man with an offer.

Fifty pounds.

It was unacknowledged.

As had been his first two offers.

Minke called a friend who knew a friend who had dealings with Tobias Ambler, who enquired about tonight's game to try to gauge how best to play it. The friend of a friend reported back that Tobias Ambler claimed he had no knowledge of whatever nefarious scheme his little brother might have dreamed up now, and had asked to be left out of 'the whole damned thing'.

It deterred Minke not one jot.

Arthur Rickaby – who had come down from Mansfield two days before and was now at his club – met with a buyer for the Big Blue over breakfast, and agreed the price of twenty pounds without the case. The buyer, a dubious European collector, had insisted on taking the egg there and then, and – after some prevarication, but before coffee – Rickaby had handed it over.

He finally did it because he wanted the motivation. There was no rearguard action now. No safety net. It was the Metland Egg for him, or nothing, and he had mentally committed to a purchase price of one hundred pounds. However preposterous that might sound, Rickaby was prepared to pay whatever it took to beat off any and all bidders to maintain his position as the most important collector of eggs in the known universe.

All three men skipped lunch. Partly excitement and partly anticipation of tonight's feast, to which each wanted to do justice as a preamble to victory. So that when the prize was secured, it would be on a full belly and a light head – and all three achieved at the expense of George Ambler.

Whom none of them liked.

So it was that, at around three o'clock on 19 June, each man received the news on an empty stomach that made its receipt that much more terrible, and left each of them doubly hollow.

That Mr Ambler sincerely regretted that dinner was cancelled.

And that the Metland Egg had been stolen.

eBay

The 'almost full' box of airgun pellets arrived a few days after their purchase, but there was no return address on the Jiffy bag, and so the quest to find the men who had stolen the egg was over before it had properly begun.

'Shit,' said Weird Nick. 'What do we do now?'

Patrick frowned. He saw no way forward. The police had come and gone. They'd taken no fingerprints and given no reassurances about the possibility of catching the perpetrators. Nick hadn't told them about the egg, so – given the robbers hadn't even taken cash – the best theory the police could suggest was a case of mistaken identity, which Weird Nick's mother had found the most comforting conclusion to her trauma. So effectively the two officers had come all the way from Carmarthen to deliver a leaflet about Victim Support, when a second-class stamp would have sufficed.

Patrick and Nick were playing *Call of Duty* when Patrick suddenly put down his controller and picked up the tin of airgun pellets.

'Cover me! Cover me! What the *fuck*!' shouted Nick, but blood ran down the screen as he died in a hail of machine-gun fire.

'*Nick!*' shouted his mother from somewhere. '*Language!*'

Nick hit Pause and hissed: 'What the hell are you *doing*?'

'Have you used any of these?' Patrick had unscrewed the lid and was staring into the tin.

'That dude totally turned! Don't just leave me hanging!'

'Have you used any of these?' said Patrick again.

Nick rolled his eyes. 'No.'

'This isn't almost full.'

'Whatever. Are you going to play? Or talk?'

'He said it was almost full.'

'So? He's a liar *and* a thief. So what? Come on.'

'Wait.'

Patrick got up and fetched a frying pan from the kitchen. He decanted the pellets into the pan and then counted them back into the tin.

'What are you doing?'

Patrick checked the lid. The tin had originally held two hundred and fifty pellets.

'There should be two hundred and fifty pellets but there's only a hundred and seventy-seven. That's close to thirty per cent down.'

'So?' said Nick.

'That's not *almost full*.'

'It's more full than empty,' shrugged Nick.

'But he said it was *almost full*,' Patrick explained again patiently. 'And if it's not almost full, then you can return them.'

'Can't be bothered to return them,' said Nick. 'I'll just use them.'

Patrick stared at him for a moment to see if his friend really didn't understand.

His friend really didn't understand. So he explained. 'If you return them, he'll have to give you his address.'

Weird Nick's face cleared. 'Genius!' he said. 'You think he'll take them back though?'

Patrick gave the smallest of smiles.

Slowly, Nick smiled too. Patrick was a sitting duck on *Call of Duty* but when it came to returning stuff on eBay he was absolutely ruthless. They still occasionally referred to the Great Teaspoon Incident of two summers back, when Patrick had paid thirty-five pounds for a set of six commemorative teaspoons in a shagreen box. Each had an enamelled cartouche showing a hand-painted landscape and the listing had boasted of *Six Highland Scenes.*

When they had arrived there was a heathery hillside, a bright outcrop of gorse, a fourteen-point stag at bay, a shimmering Loch Lomond . . . and two Highland cows. Not two *different* Highland cows, but the same Highland cow on two different spoons.

Patrick had contacted the seller to point out that he had received only five Highland Scenes, and had demanded not a refund – which could have been justified – but the *correct spoon.*

The seller had claimed that the set was complete and that it was common practice to have a repeated design in a box of teaspoons.

But Patrick's exhaustive online research revealed that this particular set should have been completed by a sheep at a gate, not a second Highland cow, and he had maintained that the teaspoons had been mis-sold.

It had taken months, but Patrick had worn down not only the seller (who didn't have the right spoon, but who had been so exhausted that he had finally refunded Patrick's money *and* told him to keep the set) but eBay itself, where some poor harassed minion had been commissioned to track down the sheep by a gate and have it bought and sent to Patrick in a gesture of corporate goodwill.

Patrick had placed the sheep/gate spoon in the box with all the reverence of a palace guard replacing the crown jewels after a trip to the Abbey. The whole affair had left him with a spare teaspoon, of course, which he had carried in his pocket from that day to this, as a sort of badge of eBay honour.

Weird Nick shuddered at the thought that he could still recall every detail of this insane transaction.

eggman456 wouldn't know what had hit him.

'Do your worst,' he grinned, which Patrick had learned meant his *best*.

So he logged on to his eBay account and demanded a refund due to the received item not matching the listing. Then he got a new life, but lost it again in a spray of blood when, half an hour later, eggman456 messaged back to argue the toss.

He didn't know who he was dealing with.

Patrick pointed out that 70 per cent could *never* be interpreted as 'almost' 100 per cent of anything.

After several more dogged exchanges, eggman456 ungraciously agreed to accept the return of the pellets and to refund the purchase price, but he flatly refused to pay the return postage, which was £2.65.

It was a standard back-and-forth, but it always rankled with Patrick. On principle he felt that the buyer should never be out of pocket on a mis-sold item, and that included the postage costs. Usually at this point he would have no compunction in opening a return request with eBay – confident that they would refund his money regardless and that eggman456 could whistle for his pellets.

It was only when Weird Nick reminded him of their mission objective that he grudgingly agreed to eggman456's terms.

By eight o'clock that evening, they had his address.

'Bloody hell!' said Nick. 'He's only in Cardiff. Well done, mate!'

'What are you going to do?' said Patrick.

'Go and get the egg back!'

Patrick raised his eyebrows. 'How?'

Nick waved a breezy hand at him. 'Jeez, Patrick. Don't sweat the small stuff. We just go there, tell him we know he took the egg and demand he give it back.'

Patrick frowned. He didn't quite see how this was all going to play out. For a start, his friend kept saying 'we', when Patrick was being very careful not to. He'd been stung by the word before, and never heard Nick use it without unwelcome memories tumbling back to him . . .

We should just buy it between us and share . . .

We'll take Mum's car. She won't mind . . .

I bet we won't even SEE a bull . . .

And secondly, when somebody stole something, surely the whole point was *not* to give it back? In Nick's scenario Patrick could see no reason why eggman456 would give the egg back. What would motivate him?

'Or what?' he said.

'What?'

'Demand he give it back *or what*?'

'Or we'll call the police.'

'But you won't call the police.'

'Yeah, but he doesn't know that, does he?'

'If *you* know it, won't *he* know it?' said Patrick.

'Nah,' said Nick. 'You have to remember he doesn't know we're coming. He's going to open the door to two people who cut straight to the chase and demand he return what he stole. We'll have the element of surprise.'

Patrick still felt a little uneasy, but then he often felt that way, so he couldn't be sure whether it was because of Nick's plan or because his default emotion when interacting with other people was unease. Meg had told him once that friends help each other, and Patrick had never forgotten that Weird Nick had once done just that when he had needed it most. Nick had probably saved his life, which even Patrick knew was considerably more valuable than an egg in a box.

Plus, if being alive for twenty-three years had taught Patrick Fort anything, it was that other people knew far more about human nature than he ever would.

'OK,' he said.

Weird Nick drove his mother's Ford Fiesta. He'd got better at driving over the years and no longer required Patrick to change the gears for him. But he'd not got a lot faster, and the forty mountainous miles to Cardiff took them the better part of two hours, during which time they were overtaken by several truckers leaning on their airhorns, and – on one downhill section – an entire cycling club.

It left Patrick free to navigate from directions he'd written on the back of the Jiffy envelope. He had a phone, and that phone had Google Maps, but Patrick didn't trust phones and rarely used his – although he dutifully kept it charged, as Meg had told him he must, in case of emergencies.

I don't have emergencies, he'd told her and she'd rolled her eyes and said, *Everybody has emergencies!*

But Patrick wasn't everybody.

The address they had was a side road in Splott, with terraced homes running up both sides and a dead end of a concrete wall and some brambles.

'BMW,' said Patrick. The dark-coloured car was parked across from number 22. Patrick couldn't be sure it was the same car he had seen on the rainswept lane, but it was very similar.

Weird Nick rapped on the glass front door. Footsteps from inside. A dark shadow loomed, and the door opened to reveal a tall, muscular man in his fifties, with a shiny, shaven head and in a vest. He stood squarely in the doorway and his hairy shoulders almost filled the opening.

'What?'

Patrick said, 'Hello', then looked at Nick. But when Nick said nothing, he added, 'How are you?'

The man glared at them. 'You Mormons?'

'I'm not,' Patrick said hurriedly, then glanced at Nick. He'd never asked his friend what he believed. But Nick just looked confused and Patrick thought that maybe they should have practised this in the car on the way down.

The man muttered *fucking Mormons*, then stepped backwards and started to close the door.

'You want to buy an egg?' Nick blurted out.

The man stopped closing the door, but kept it where it was, halfway. He glanced briefly over their heads, up and down the road.

'What egg?'

Nick leaned in and stage-whispered: 'The egg you bid for on eBay.'

The big man frowned again, then shook his head.

'Dunno what you mean,' he said, and shut the door.

Nick looked at Patrick wide-eyed. Then he knocked again. His hand was still mid-air when the door opened. Before Nick could speak, the big man grabbed him by the front of his jumper, yanked him forward, headbutted him, then withdrew and slammed the door. It all happened so fast that Patrick was left open-mouthed with amazement, already replaying it in his head. The door, the arm, the fist, the head, the door. It was like a very violent cuckoo clock. Now *there* was a man who'd practised . . .

'*He* had the element of surprise,' he murmured with no little admiration.

'Mate . . .' Weird Nick gripped the leg of his jeans, and Patrick helped him slowly to his feet and back to the car. Blood ran from his nose and dripped from his lips and chin.

'I think it's broken,' Nick mumbled. 'I have to go to hospital.'

'OK,' said Patrick. 'Wait a minute.'

He jogged back across the road and shoved the box of airgun pellets through eggman456's letter box, then ran back to where Nick had already started the car.

£2.65 was £2.65.

Meg

Weird Nick was no stranger to hospitals. He was a hypo-chondriac of the first order and had once called himself an ambulance because he'd found a tick in his sock.

The University Hospital A&E department was full of other hypochondriacs. At least, that's what Patrick deduced from the fact that none of them were actively screaming, bleeding or unconscious.

They waited for three hours and then – at Nick's repeated urging – Patrick called Meg.

'Patrick? What's wrong?'

'Nothing!' Patrick shouted, because he refused to hold a mobile phone anywhere near his head. Nick grabbed it from his out-stretched hand and told Meg what had happened.

'Is it actually broken?' she said.

'Well, it's bleeding.'

'Is it still straight?'

Nick got Patrick to check.

'How straight should it be?' said Patrick.

'Is it as straight as it was before?' Meg asked him.

'Kind of.'

'In that case, they won't be able to do much for it. It'll just heal by itself.'

'But I'm in *agony*,' said Nick.

Meg sighed and said she'd meet them in the coffee shop in twenty minutes and bring some paracetamol.

'Does this hurt?'

'Ow! Yes! Of course it hurts! It's broken!'

Meg winked at Patrick, who looked away and smiled.

She'd cut her hair since he'd last seen her two months ago. She had dark brown hair that had been on her shoulders; now it was just under her earlobes, in which she wore the little silver skulls he had bought her last Christmas.

Since Patrick had learned that Christmas was not all about him, he'd been all over it. Every year he started making gift lists in about May, which he narrowed down by the end of the summer, and activated by October at the very latest. By November, he would be wrapping. If he wasn't all done by the end of that month, he'd become anxious. He only bought gifts for his mother, Weird Nick, Meg and the cat, but it was still a major undertaking, and he was devoted to getting it right. Once he had decided on a suitable gift, it was nearly impossible to derail him.

Nearly.

Last Christmas his mother had derailed him.

I think you should get Meg something really special this year, she'd said.

I already have something for Meg. I need help with the cat.

I think earrings would be a good idea.

For the cat?

For Meg!

But I already bought her a book.

Which book?

Smith's Recognizable Patterns of Human Malformation.

The very same day, his mother had driven him to the jeweller's in Brecon and pointed out some diamond studs, but once Patrick had spotted the little silver skulls, the negotiation was at an end. He and Meg had met in a room full of bloated corpses, so he had known the skulls were just right for her.

Mind you, she had also really liked the book on human malformation. And no wonder – Patrick had read it before wrapping it, and it was a belter.

He'd bought the cat a fake mouse on a string.

Seeing the skull studs in Meg's soft lobes now gave Patrick a rare feeling of warm connection.

She sat down at the table with them. 'It's not broken. Just bruised. You might get a couple of black eyes, but that's standard.' Patrick pushed over the cappuccino he had already bought her and she gave him a grateful smile. 'Why would anyone want to steal an egg?'

'Why does anybody steal anything?' snuffled Nick. 'Money.'

'So what are you going to do about it?' asked Meg.

'We'll just have to steal it back,' Nick said importantly.

'Why don't you just go to the police? Call your friend, Patrick. The one who was so nice to you when you stole a man's head.'

'We can't get the police involved,' said Nick sharply. 'Not if we want the egg back. Apparently it's illegal to own a wild bird's egg, so even if they found it they would only confiscate it. And maybe even charge me for having it in the first place, even though I didn't even know I wasn't supposed to.'

'Hm.' Meg frowned. Then she clicked her fingers. 'Call the Natural History Museum! Somebody there will know all about eggs.'

'Which one?' said Patrick. 'Because the one in Tring has a quagga . . .'

*

83

It *was* the one in Tring. And somebody there *did* know all about eggs. His name was Dr Christopher Connor, but it was his assistant, Ellen, who answered his office phone.

'Dr Connor's away for a couple of days,' she told them as they huddled around Meg's phone on the table. 'He's in court for a sentencing.'

'What did he do?' asked Patrick.

'He's not the defendant!' she laughed. 'He's there as a witness in the case of an egg collector.'

Nick hissed at Meg: '*Told you!*'

'Is there anything I can help you with?'

Nick flapped his hands *NO!* at Meg, but she ignored him.

'Maybe,' she said. 'My friend found an old egg in a fancy wooden box. We were hoping to find out what it might be and if it's worth anything.'

'Do you have a photo?'

'I think so, yes . . .'

Ellen gave them her mobile number and Nick sent her a photo.

'That's a guillemot egg,' Ellen said after a moment. 'They were very collectable at the turn of the last century.'

'So they're valuable?' said Nick, leaning into the phone.

'Not generally. Most were sold for pennies. But anyway, possessing wild birds' eggs is illegal now. Your *friend's* egg should really be surrendered to a museum.'

'I— he doesn't have it any more,' said Nick. 'It was stolen.'

'Oh,' she said. 'That's a shame.' Her tone said she didn't believe it for a moment. 'Well, whoever has it should understand that the police are taking wildlife crimes increasingly seriously. In fact, we expect a prison sentence in the Barr case tomorrow.'

'What's a Barr case?' said Patrick.

'That's the defendant's name. Matthew Barr.'

'Where is he being sentenced?' asked Meg.

'Merthyr Tydfil Crown Court.'

Meg thanked Ellen and hung up and smiled at Nick and Patrick. 'How convenient!'

'What is?' said Patrick.

'Well, it's practically on your doorstep. You can go there tomorrow and watch the sentencing and then speak to Dr Connor afterwards!'

'Is that allowed?' asked Nick.

'Of course.'

Nick still looked unsure. 'You're coming too, right?'

Meg rolled her eyes. 'Not in a million years. I start three days off tonight and I'm going to sleep, eat, shower and stare at the wall on rotation until my next shift!' She glanced at her phone. 'Talking of which . . .' She got up. 'Good luck tomorrow.'

'Do I have to take ID or anything?' asked Nick.

'No, you just go in and sit in the public gallery.'

'You just walk in?'

'You might have to go through a bag check for bombs or whatever, but yes, then you just walk in.'

Nick turned to Patrick. 'You'll come, won't you, mate?'

'Rhys asked me to cover his lunchtime shift.'

'Did you say yes?'

'Not yet.'

'Then say no.'

Patrick thought about that for a moment, then said, 'OK then.'

'Good man,' said Nick.

Meg was standing now, but she lingered. 'Let me know how you get on tomorrow, OK?'

She was looking at Patrick, but it was Nick who nodded. 'Are you sure we're allowed?'

'Yep,' said Meg. 'That's why it's called a public gallery. We went to Cardiff Crown Court on a school trip once. We saw a bloke get two years for glassing someone in a pub.'

'Sounds exciting,' said Nick.

'It's not,' she said. 'It's as dull as ditchwater.'

The Letter

'Should I call the police, sir?'

Ambler looked up at the butler as if he hadn't heard him the first time, although he absolutely had.

'What?'

'The police, sir. Should I call them?'

'What for?'

'About the egg, sir.'

'No!' Ambler said sharply. And then, more cautiously, 'I know the inspector. I will take care of it.'

'Very good, sir.' Edwards dipped his head minutely, and withdrew silently.

Ambler sat at his desk, nervously fingering the note that had arrived by first post that morning.

He waited until the butler had left before unfolding it once more.

It was on plain white paper.

No return address.

No date.

No signature.

He glanced furtively around the room, as if the writer might be watching him, then reread the only words on the page.

You had best do right by that girl.

George Ambler felt a chill go through him.

The hand was not unsophisticated, and the paper was similar to his own – a simple white linen – but the words had a rough quality to them that left him in no doubt whatsoever that he was being threatened.

And that if he involved the police, they would want to know *why* . . .

And that could be . . . *difficult* . . .

The maid surprised him with a tray of tea, and Ambler jumped, then hurriedly folded the note in half, creasing it hard with his thumbnail.

Then folded it again.

And again.

Then he stuffed it in an inside pocket, straightened his tie with a trembling hand, and cleared his throat.

'Thank you, Martha.'

Ditchwater

Meg came to the court after all. She told them she'd woken early and was bored by nine o'clock, so had driven up to meet them.

She was still wearing the skull earrings. Patrick wondered if she slept in them.

Merthyr Tydfil Crown Court was a long, low barrack of a building lined with windows that seemed to shed no light at all on the interior, which was all ceiling tiles and fluorescents.

Inside, the atrium was like a regional airport of crime. Perpetrators and victims and witnesses and all their various intersections occupied long wooden benches, while barristers in yellowing wigs and black cloaks flitted between them like giant bats.

People talked in low tones, and yet the echoing space made it noisy enough to make Patrick wince.

Now and then an usher – cloaked but not be-wigged – would come outside and call a name and someone would get up from a bench and follow them through one of several wooden doors to a courtroom.

It was confusing and overwhelming. Patrick hunched his shoulders and glanced back frequently, checking his exit.

'You OK?' said Meg.

He nodded. He always felt better when she was around.

Meg asked an usher for the Matthew Barr sentencing and he pointed them towards Court Two. 'Quiet,' he said. 'It's already started.'

Patrick winced and covered his ears as a small man with very big biceps started shouting something about the unfairness of it all.

'Don't worry,' Meg murmured to Patrick. 'It'll be quieter in the courtroom.'

They crept into Court Two silently and sat in the front row of the raised gallery, almost close enough to touch the defendant. Matthew Barr was a thin, feral man wearing a big shirt with frayed cuffs, and no-name trainers. One of the laces was undone, which made Patrick itch.

Meg was right – there was only one person talking in the courtroom, but he was doing so enthusiastically. About eggs, Patrick assumed.

'. . . which makes them absolutely vital for continuing research,' the witness concluded.

'Thank you, Dr Connor,' said the judge.

Dr Connor left the stand and took a gallery seat just behind them. He was younger than Patrick had imagined a museum curator would be, and with a neat beard. He wore a tight-fitting grey suit and a thin black tie, like a hipster at a funeral.

'Calling Finn Garrett!'

A wiry man with a military jaw and a crew cut followed the usher to the witness box and was sworn in. Unlike Dr Connor, he was in jeans and a black anorak.

'The court will hear the RSPB's submission, Mr Garrett.'

'Thank you, sir. First thing I'd like to say is that Dr Connor's submission is exactly the kind of thing that makes our job at the RSPB a lot harder.' Garrett jabbed a finger on to the lip of the witness box and looked around the courtroom pugnaciously, as if challenging anyone to disagree with him. 'Egg collectors try to justify their actions by claiming that they are somehow contributing to science. Seeing their seized collections going to institutions like the Natural History Museum for so-called *research* only gives them affirmation, and they take that affirmation as permission to continue murdering thousands of birds in their nests every year. The RSPB is committed to halting this disgusting crime and we hope you will send a clear message to Matthew Barr, and others like him, that there is nothing scientific about stealing an egg, drilling a hole in it, and then killing the chick inside by pouring acid over it.'

There was a shocked silence, and Patrick winced at a chilling mental flash of a fizzing, fluttering chick.

Once more, Finn Garrett stared around the courtroom, like a man who has heard that silence before. He let the words hang over them all like a grim sword. Patrick looked at Matthew Barr, and noticed that everybody else was doing the same. Barr stared down at his feet. Patrick hoped he'd tie his shoelace, but he didn't.

Finally the judge cleared his throat. 'Thank you, Mr Garrett.'

Garrett left the witness box but didn't sit down again. Instead he stood at the door of the court with his legs braced and his arms folded, like a bouncer.

Finn Garrett made Patrick nervous.

The only sound now was the judge shuffling papers, folding some, unfolding others, until he finally held before him the one he needed.

He put on a pair of thick, black-framed spectacles.

The defendant was hustled to his feet by the stocky officer beside him, and sentenced to six weeks imprisonment with time served, and two years probation.

'Yessss!'

The judge looked over his glasses at the public gallery. 'Silence please. This is not a discotheque.'

There were a few titters, then silence again.

'Having considered both expert submissions in the petitions for forfeiture, I further order that your collection of eggs and associated paraphernalia be forfeited to the Royal Society for the Protection of Birds.'

'No!' Barr leapt to his feet. 'That's not right!'

Dr Connor stood up abruptly and left the courtroom. A smiling Garrett stepped slowly aside to let him pass but Connor didn't acknowledge the courtesy.

'Let's go after him,' hissed Meg, but the judge banged his gavel for silence.

'Mr Barr, you are free to go – unless of course you'd like to stay and spend a little time in the cells reflecting on the meaning of contempt of court?'

Barr's solicitor turned to him and whispered urgently. Barr shook his head, but said nothing further.

'I thought not.' The judge tapped his gavel on his bench and everybody stood up as he left.

Once he'd gone, the courtroom relaxed noticeably, and a low hum of chatter began.

Matthew Barr didn't look like a man who was free to go. He looked dazed and beaten. His barrister leaned over the rail of the dock and shook his hand, then Barr got up and wandered out of the dock and stood in the well of the court as half a dozen people packed stacks of papers tied with red tape into big brown file boxes. A couple of journalists wandered off the press bench, and the prosecution barrister and the defence barrister stood and chatted like old friends.

Patrick thought it all made the case seem like a play that was over.

'Let's go and find Dr Connor,' said Meg, and he and Nick trailed out behind her.

They spotted the curator across the atrium, and Meg called out his name.

As the curator stopped and turned towards them, there was a rough surge of people around them—

Fuck you, Garrett!

... And suddenly they were all caught up in a shirt-grabbing, tooth-gritting embarrassment of a scuffle, while bystanders fell back in a concentric wave. One of Barr's legal team let out a squeal and stumbled into Patrick. She dropped her box of papers, and they spilled out on to the stone floor. Patrick staggered backwards with the young woman in his arms, and only just stopped her from falling.

Two police officers appeared, and the fight was over before it had properly begun.

At its epicentre, Finn Garrett smiled grimly and waved at Matthew Barr as he was steered away by his barrister.

When the knot of people dispersed, Dr Connor had disappeared.

'Shit,' said Meg. 'Where did he go?'

'Don't know,' said Nick, who had his hand cupped protectively over his nose, just in case.

They looked around for Patrick.

He had let go of the pretty blonde clerk, and was now helping her to pick up her papers.

'Patrick?'

He didn't hear Meg.

The clerk put the lid back on the box, and dazzled him with a smile. 'Thank you so much.'

'OK,' he said.

'Can I buy you a cup of tea?'

'OK,' he said again, and followed her down a corridor.

'Patrick!' called Meg. 'Where are you going?'

He called back: 'For a cup of tea.'

The clerk's name was Ceri. She'd worked for Slee Summerville for two years and didn't like the boss, whose name was Philip, but she liked the work and had just bought her own flat in the Bay – just the one bedroom, but she didn't have a boyfriend, so it was plenty big enough – and she'd got a bargain because the owner was emigrating to Canada and so she'd knocked him down to one eighty from one ninety-five, which basically meant she had enough left over to go to Spain in September with her best friend whose name was *also* Ceri, which was quite funny, and *that* Ceri *also* worked for a legal firm, but they always had a right laugh together and were going out tonight – down to the Tiger on High Street, if he was interested . . . ?

'And *are* you interested?' frowned Meg as they all ate chips on a bench beside the standing stones an hour later.

'Interested in what?' said Patrick.

'Going to the pub with her tonight.'

'No.'

Meg groaned. 'So *whyyyyyy* are you telling us all of this?'

'Because you asked if I'd found anything out.'

'Not about *her*,' said Meg, waving a chip for emphasis. 'About the *case*.'

'I didn't ask about the case.'

'Then why did you go for a cup of tea with her?'

'Because I wanted a cup of tea.'

Meg and Nick looked at each other, then burst out laughing.

Patrick was used to being laughed at, and took no offence.

It made sense to him, and *that's what mattered*, as his mother always told him.

'What was the fight about?' he said.

'Search me,' said Nick.

'I think it was that RSPB bloke,' said Meg. 'I don't think Matthew Barr likes him.'

'I didn't like him,' said Patrick.

'Garrett?' said Meg. 'Why?'

'I don't know.'

'I don't reckon Dr Connor liked him either,' said Nick. 'He looked pretty cheesed off that the RSPB were awarded the eggs instead of the museum.'

'What difference does it make?' said Patrick.

Meg shrugged. 'I suppose it must make a difference to them, or they wouldn't have come all the way to Wales to make their cases.'

'We should have spoken to Matthew Barr,' said Nick. 'He's sure to have loads of info.'

Meg pulled a face. 'You mean loads of info about pouring acid on to living animals?'

'Just saying,' shrugged Nick. 'He's a criminal, so—'

'He's disgusting!' Meg stood up abruptly. 'I'm surprised you even *want* the egg back after hearing that.'

Nick mumbled something about his gaming chair.

'A gaming chair!' Meg's eyes blazed. 'You'd pour acid on to a bird for *that*?'

Nick couldn't look at her. Patrick couldn't look anywhere else.

'Somebody stole that egg from the bird that laid it. Now somebody has stolen it from you. Sounds fair to me.' She got up, scrunched her chips into a paper ball and slam-dunked them into the bin.

'Are you angry?' said Patrick curiously.

'Yes, I am!' she said.

'With me?'

'No! With—' Meg stopped, suddenly looking on the verge of tears, then cleared her throat and started again. 'With *people*.'

'Why?'

Meg gave a hopeless shrug. 'Because life should be lived, not destroyed for our stupid pleasure. Makes me angry *and* sad.'

Angry and sad. Patrick didn't feel either of those things. And yet, there was something in *Meg's* anger and sadness that made him want to . . .

What?

He didn't know. Feelings were difficult things to understand. But he did know that Meg was right about most things, so he was sure she was right about this.

'OK,' he nodded.

Meg sighed and wiped the back of her forearm across her eyes. 'I'm going home.'

'OK.' Patrick frowned. Something had changed, but he wasn't sure how. All he knew was that Meg had been *with* them and now she was leaving. He was sorry about that, but he didn't know how to stop her, or even if he should want to. Or if she *wanted* him to.

So he did nothing.

Meg hugged him goodbye, but so briefly that he barely minded, and said, 'Bye,' to Nick.

Then Patrick watched her walk towards the station until she turned a corner and disappeared.

'Pass us her chips, mate,' said Nick. 'Waste not want not.'

The Deal

Celie Sheppard was helping Robert to pick wild oats out of the far field when the box arrived. So she was not there to see the faces of her mother and her siblings as they carefully opened the huge wooden crate and released the straw, as if unpacking a bear.

'Keep that wood!' fussed Enid – as if she had to. The crate was made of good lengths and they all knew it was not to be wasted.

Then they removed the twelve wooden pegs that secured the lid on the inner box . . . all the time chattering about what might be in it, and who might have sent it – with Father being the favoured suspect, and great excitement emanating therefrom – but with Mother minutely checking and rechecking the bill of lading to ensure that the crate really was addressed to *Miss Sheppard of Metland Farm*, and not to some more lofty local address, which would be so disappointing, and yet so much more likely.

When they finally managed to open the inner box – which had stencilling on the side that meant nothing to them – there was a basket inside it, made of thick brown wicker and with leather straps, and big enough to hold Molly with barely a cramp.

But when they undid the straps and opened the creaky lid of the basket they were further stymied by what they found there.

Two dozen packages, each wrapped in muslin or waxed paper,

and all tied with pretty bows or string, or sealed with black wax blobs that bore the initials *F&M*.

'Toys!' said Molly, and they all reached, but Enid slapped their hands away before they could touch. She picked up the first package, which was a box carefully wrapped in white paper, secured by a blue velvet ribbon, which held fast a thick card on which was written (in a beautiful hand): *Scottish Shortbread*.

Enid knew of shortbread, of course, but had never eaten it, or dreamed of having the sugar to waste on making it, let alone of receiving a box of it without any immediately apparent accompanying sacrifice.

She frowned suspiciously.

'What does it say, Mam?' said Will, but Enid remained silent as she carefully removed and examined – but did not unwrap – every parcel in the hamper, her lips moving slowly as she read every label.

There were quails' eggs and bon-bons and Italian ham and German sausage and relish, and cheeses from France, and chocolate from Switzerland, and Irish soda bread. There were numerous tiny tins of something called *pâté* and something else called *olives*, both of which were mysteries to the Sheppards, and would remain so for ever, as they did not possess a tin opener.

There were also bottles. Enid read the labels aloud. They were port, sherry and a very large bottle which she took a moment to work out was champagne, because the 'g' threw her off.

Attached by a slim golden tassel to the magnum was an envelope of such quality that Enid had to ask Will to fetch the knife in order to open it, and then did so with the care of a surgeon so as not to leave a ragged scar.

Inside was a sheet of quality linen paper, folded precisely in half.

Enid unfolded it and read it.

Then she read it again.

And a third time . . . before she barked a single big laugh – as if she could not believe what was written therein.

'What is it, Mam?' said Will.

But Enid could only shake her head and laugh and wipe her nose and eyes on her hands as she put the letter in her apron pocket and packed everything quickly back into the wicker hamper, and the hamper back into the box, and the box back into the packing case.

The children sat silently, unnerved by her display, and watching the food disappear again with big, anxious eyes.

As she was about to close the lid on the packing case, Enid hesitated. Then she leaned in and opened the box again, and undid the leather straps on the basket.

The Sheppard children held their breath.

It was the aroma of boiled ham that sucked Celie and Robert in from the far field fully an hour before sundown.

They found the kitchen in chaos – the table set as if for company, her siblings hysterical with anticipation, and Celie's mother singing over the stove.

'What happened?' Celie said. 'Why is it all happy?'

'Ham!' danced Stanley. 'Ham!'

'Ham!' shouted Molly.

'Ham!' laughed Will and Martin together, and banged on the table and Enid didn't even stop them, but only laughed.

Celie and Robert stood, uncertain, only watching and waiting until things became clear.

And finally they did, in the shape of a shiny pink boulder rising from the steam, then rocking the big tin platter. Enid sliced it thinly on top of their bread and cabbage, but nothing could halt their joy at the feast before them.

Robert always ate in the barn, so took his dish to the door, and waited there for grace to be said. But they were all too excited to think about God, let alone thank Him, so he slid quietly from the kitchen and closed the door behind him. Then he stood on the top step and shovelled the food into his mouth so fast that he choked and spat and cried through the entire thirty seconds it took him to finish the lot, and stood panting in amazement at what had just happened.

When his breathing evened out he was suddenly crestfallen. He'd eaten so fast that his little knot of a stomach ached with the rude stretch of being filled. How he wished he could start again and do it all more slowly.

Too late now.

Instead he walked to the barn, licking his tin plate all the way and with Patch drooling at his heels. Inside the door he put the plate on the floor to be cleaned again by the dog.

Then, as he straightened up, his sharp eye was caught by something in the near dark. Something . . . *different*.

Robert stood and looked at it for a long minute before he approached. There, on the same hook where he had hung the old blacksmith's apron, was a new rope.

Not a *new* new rope, but a new rope to Metland, for sure.

This rope was not covered in cobwebs and was not frayed; this rope had been cut down and then neatly spliced at both ends.

This rope was made of hemp, with a steel gark for strength.

This rope was *safe*.

Celie was used to the smallest portion, but the wisp of ham on top of her cabbage looked mean, even to her – especially given the size of the joint, which had barely been shaved by the meal.

She nibbled the sliver, trying to make it last all through her mountain of greens. Barely a third of the way down, she ran out of ham, but her tongue had been electrified by the salty succulence and buzzed for more.

There were flakes of meat on the table and she reached for one.

Enid slapped her hand hard.

'Not for you,' she said. 'You'll get fat.'

Celie blinked at her in confusion. *Fat* was not a word she'd ever heard applied to a human being – only to the pigs and sheep as market time approached.

A slow dread crept up from Celie's toes to the top of her tingling head. A dawning realization that children too might be sold at market if ever they were fat enough. The steaming ham sat before her as evidence of what might happen after that.

'Eat your food.'

Celie ate her cabbage and watched the others eat the ham – happy mouths filled with pink mush, and brine dribbling down their chins in snaily trails.

And although everybody was happy, Celie couldn't shake an uneasy feeling that something had started that none of them would be able to stop.

As she readied for bed that night, Enid Sheppard took the stiff white letter from the pocket of her apron and read it one more time. Then she laid it carefully between the pages of the family Bible.

It seemed fitting, given the salvation it represented.

For the letter was not really a letter at all, but a contract.

A contract from George Ambler that promised to pay the staggering sum of twenty pounds for next year's red egg.

And the same price for each one after that.

Until, it stated, *the bird lays no more.*

The bird that had laid what quickly became known as the Metland Egg knew nothing of the deal struck between George Ambler and the Sheppard family.

The next year she arrived in early May, a few days ahead of her mate, and laid her impossible egg before the month was out.

She did her best with pecks and squawks and a great flapping to stop Celie Sheppard from taking it. But taken it was and, when it was, she and her mate were just as confused as they had been that first time. They spent nearly a week crying and fretting and trying to foster another egg or another chick without success.

But nature is a wonderful thing.

And because this egg was stolen in May and not in June, the hen laid another egg three weeks later, every bit as big and as red and as beautiful as the first two had been.

When Celie Sheppard took that as well, the pair went through the same process all over again – as if this had never happened to them before. Just as confused. Just as fretful. Squawking just as loudly – as all around them hatchlings hatched and jumplings jumped and the crags of Bempton and Flamborough slowly emptied of guillemots.

Until

somehow

nature told the pair that even if they did find their egg, it would be too late now for any chick to survive the long, cold journey north.

The bereaved bird and her mate seemed to come to this

understanding at the same time as each other. They sat for one whole day, neither flying nor feeding – just huddled together on the narrow ledge under the overhang where they had made their doomed home.

If birds mourn, they mourned.

The next day they left for Norway, without a chick for the second year running.

Next year, they would be back to try again.

Scarborough

Celie stood in a basin in the yard while her mother scrubbed all the colour off her, then brushed her hair until she cried.

Then she was dressed in an old dress of Molly's that still had some prettiness about it. Although Molly had grown out of the dress at four, it swamped six-year-old Celie, and Enid made her take it off again and stand shivering in her knickers while she made rough alterations.

When she was dressed, her mother tried to curl her lank hair into ringlets but gave up when the irons started to smell of burning. She glared and tutted, and then she took the blue velvet ribbon off the shortbread and tied the hair in a bow instead.

Then she stood Celie in a corner under threat of mayhem should she move a muscle towards anything grimy, and put on her best clothes and hat.

Celie had never seen her mother dress with such care – not even for church. Her good dress had a tear to the sleeve, where she'd caught it on a splinter coming through a gate. Enid had sewn it, but the repair was obvious, so she put her wool jacket over it, and checked that the snag was covered.

'Where's us gannin?'

'You'll see,' said her mother, but the little frown never left her face, and it did not reassure Celie. She recalled wondering whether children could be fattened for market like pigs and sheep, and watched her mother with a growing sense of unease.

Suddenly Mr Bonnington's cart arrived in the yard, and before she knew what was happening, Celie was lifted into the back and made to sit on a bit of sacking her mother provided for the purpose.

She started to cry.

'What's with you?' said Enid.

'Is I off to market?'

'To market?'

'Like t'pigs.'

Mr Bonnington laughed and Enid rolled her eyes and said *daft as a brush* but Celie only bawled harder, imagining she had only been dressed up to fetch a good price.

Under Enid's direction, Robert loaded the hamper into the cart, and then was directed to get in too, along with the sack trolley. Celie was reassured that Robert was coming, as she knew he was far too valuable to Metland to be sold off.

Enid sat up with Mr Bonnington, but after he'd touched his cap and said *Morning* on arrival, he had said not a word to anyone but his horse, whose name was Bucket – a great big animal with shaggy white feathers all the way to his knees, and a little bell tied into his mane that jingled when he trotted or shook the flies off his gigantic head.

Celie was wide-eyed all the way to Bridlington. She had never ridden in a cart and it was a mix of excitement and terror. The ground was so far down and the ride so fast and bumpy that she feared falling out at every turn of the wheels, and yet the experience was also exhilarating. She clung to the rail and her hair trailed out behind her, shortbread ribbon and all.

The air was already the kind of warm that promised hot, and whenever they slowed for a corner or a crossing, pollen and midges floated around them, along with the white dust that rose from the wheels.

By the time they got to Bridlington, all she could smell was Bucket.

Then came another new thing – an even more extraordinary thing! A train! Celie was terrified of the houses on wheels that emerged screaming from a plume of grey smoke, and at first refused to get on the train because she thought it was on fire. Robert hung back too, until Enid snapped at him to take the hamper to the guard's van and wait with it there until Scarborough. Even with his orders, he waited until the last possible moment to get aboard, and would not have done so if the conductor hadn't shouted at him even more harshly than Mrs Sheppard had.

Against the odds, they all alighted safely at Scarborough on what was now a very hot day.

Enid had been to Scarborough only rarely since her honeymoon, which had been three days in a guest house with a view of a glum courtyard and a high grey wall. But she remembered the grand hotels along the Esplanade, and headed for those, with Celie holding her hand and Robert zigzagging about behind them with the trolley, so gormless was he at every single thing that was new to his eyes – which was all but the sky and the gulls.

They sold the hamper to the cook at the very first hotel they came to – the Royal – for five pounds, which was only a pound less than Enid had dreamed of, and she was so giddy with it that she gave Robert half a crown.

For the first time in his fourteen years, Robert was in possession of money while also in a place where money might be spent, and his lingering at every shop window finally made Enid dismiss him – telling him to meet them at the railway station at two o'clock. When he looked concerned about that task, she pointed the station out to him, for they had walked nearly a straight road from there, and told him to ask any gentleman for the time.

'How will I ask?'

'Politely,' she said sternly.

'But . . . what will I say?'

'You'll say, "Please, sir, can you tell me the time?" And when he's told you the time you say, "Thank you kindly."'

'Thank ee kindly,' he nodded, still full of worry, and yet not so worried that he could overcome his desire to spend the half-crown. Even as he spoke, his eyes were darting here and there, and over Enid's shoulder, to see what he could spot in this window or that.

So they left him there on the Esplanade, and Enid led Celie away from the hotels and down streets where the sand-coloured stone houses were almost as big but had no signs outside showing *Vacancies* – just brass numbers on their glossy doors.

Enid had to ask the way three times, and Celie started to worry that they were lost and might never find their way back to the station and home, but finally they mounted six broad yellow steps to a door with the number 17 on it, and her mother rang the huge bell, then spat on Celie's fringe and straightened her dress and looked at her very seriously.

'Best behaviour now, Celie.'

Celie nodded.

She held her mother's hand as they waited. She noticed that it shook slightly.

After a few moments there was the sound of coughing from inside, then a little silence, then the door was opened by a frail-looking woman.

'Can I help you?' she said.

'I'm Mrs Sheppard of Metland Farm come to see Mr Constable.'

Celie glanced up at her mother, who was suddenly using her church voice.

The woman nodded politely. 'How do you do, Mrs Sheppard? I'm afraid my husband is not at home today. May I be of assistance?'

Celie winced as her mother's grip tightened, but she didn't pull away or complain because she'd promised to behave.

'I'm . . . not . . . No, I'm . . .'

Celie glanced up and saw that Enid suddenly looked more lost than when they had been lost.

'I . . . I have come to pay the rent.'

Celie was surprised. And she was also confused, because there was a collector for the rent. His name was Mr Bastard – first name, *That* – and he came every month and was always very rude when he did. None of them liked him, and her mother didn't like him so much that lately she'd hidden in the barn when he came, and the rent collector had had to leave empty of hand and foul of mouth. Yet, here her mother was, come all the way to Scarborough to pay the rent in person, as if she'd had it all along.

'That's most kind of you, Mrs Sheppard, but I'm sorry you've troubled to come here yourself. I hope there is no issue with Mr Crouch?'

Again Enid looked slightly flustered and said, *Oh no*. Then she opened her little cloth purse and took out a roll of notes, bound with string.

'Twelve pounds,' she said. 'For three months.'

'Thank you, Mrs Sheppard. Please do come in and have some refreshment, if you've come all that way.'

She opened the door more widely and smiled down at Celie, who smiled back, despite her crushed fingers.

Enid hesitated, and then said, 'Thank you.'

They stepped into a grand hallway with a tiled floor and wooden walls so polished that Celie could see her own grainy face in them. The panelling went on for ever and she almost tipped over backwards trying to see the ceiling, which – when she found it – was domed and the colour of the sea, with fishes painted in red and gold.

'May I take your coat?'

'Oh no, thank you,' said Enid, then explained hurriedly: 'I'm a little chilly.'

'Of course. It is a little chilly in here.' Then the woman bent slightly and put her hands on her knees. 'And what's your name?'

Celie whispered it.

'What a pretty name,' Mrs Constable said. 'And how old are you, Celie?'

Celie glanced up and Enid mouthed *six* and then she whispered that too.

'Well, well.' Mrs Constable smiled. 'Six years old. What a wonderful age. Now you wait here, Celie, and I'll get us all a nice cup of tea.'

'Please don't go to any trouble,' said Enid, but Mrs Constable said *No trouble at all* and patted Celie on the head as she went, which gave her a start.

She disappeared through a door.

'I'm hot,' whispered Celie, but her mother did not respond. She stood like a statue, pale as marble. Celie turned and flinched as another child appeared beside her. Then giggled as she realized it was her own reflection. They had a mirror at home but it was small and hung over the basin, and they could only see their black-spotted faces in it. This mirror was the size of a sow and showed her right down to her feet. Celie was fascinated to see all of herself. She looked much smaller than she felt, and Molly's dress was still too big on her, although not quite long enough to hide her knees, which were like knots tied in string. Her mother, who had looked fit to be Queen when they'd climbed into Mr Bonnington's cart this morning, was made strangely tired by the mirror. It made her look worried too – despite the money she had in her purse.

Just then Mrs Constable came back and ushered them into a vast pale yellow room with a window at one end as big as a wall. It was so bright and beautiful that it felt like a palace to Celie, who had barely recovered from the hallway.

There was a small table with four chairs, and they all sat there, although Mrs Constable had to lift Celie on to her chair.

'I'm sorry the rent is a little late.'

'Please say no more about it. Ah, here's tea.'

A maid came in with a large silver tray with a silver teapot and silver milk jug and silver sugar bowl, and three white cups on white saucers, all covered with pink roses and with gilt rims. There was a rose-covered plate too, with a selection of biscuits. If the maid had brought gifts of gold, frankincense and myrrh, Celie could not have been more impressed.

'Thank you, Sally. Now, shall I be mother?'

Mrs Constable poured the tea in a delicate golden stream that made a satisfying tinkling sound.

She handed a cup to Enid, who smiled a thank-you.

Celie noticed that Mrs Constable smelled of flowers, and of something she couldn't place but which made her think of Dr Wardlow, who came once when the ram broke Will's wrist.

Now that they were away from the farm, Celie could tell that, for all her efforts, her mother smelled *of* the farm. She wondered if she did too, and sniffed her own arm until she caught her mother's eye.

She didn't dare drink her tea. The cup was so thin that she could see the sun shining through it. It reminded her of that first egg that had smashed in her hand, leaving behind pale blue shards, and she knotted her little hands together to avoid the temptation of touching it.

'Don't you like tea, Celie?' Mrs Constable was smiling at her.

Celie squirmed slightly and nodded at the cup. 'Mayhap he'll brek.'

Mrs Constable nodded as if she'd been thinking just the same thing. 'My niece hated these silly old cups. We'll get you something much nicer. Sally?'

The maid, who had been about to leave with the tray, stopped. 'Ma'am?'

'Would you fetch this young lady the doll cup? The one Lisette liked so much when she was small?'

'Yes, ma'am.'

Mrs Constable winked at Celie, and Celie liked her, whatever the doll cup was.

'You're very kind, ma'am,' said Enid.

'Not at all,' said Mrs Constable. 'We were never blessed with children and our nieces and nephews are all grown, so it's a treat to have a little girl at our table again.'

The maid came back with a dear little cup with two handles and dolls in blue dresses dancing around the bottom. Celie couldn't help giggling when she saw it.

Mrs Constable poured tea and milk into the cup and asked if she took sugar. Celie looked at Enid to see if she did or she didn't, and when Enid nodded, she said that she did. Mrs Constable held out the bowl to her and showed her how the tongs worked and allowed her shakily to plop two lumps of sugar into her own tea and stir it carefully with a silver spoon. Then Celie raised the doll cup to her lips and drank the best drink she'd ever drunk in her whole life.

No more was said after that about the rent or the farm – only about the weather and the general strike, and the ever-present threat of seagulls.

As they took their leave, Mrs Constable told Celie she could keep the doll cup. Enid protested, which gave Celie an anxious moment, but in the end the lady of the house prevailed, and they waited in the hallway while she had the cup washed and dried and wrapped in tissue, and then placed in a small plywood orange box for the journey home.

Celie considered the whole day a raging success and was bursting to talk about the cup and the fishes on the ceiling and the giant mirror and the sugar lumps, but something in her mother's face and pace kept her quiet.

They met Robert at the station and caught the train.

It turned out that, unaccustomed as he was to spending, Robert had had great difficulty in ridding himself of his half-crown. Finally he had only managed to spend a little over a shilling and had neglected to buy anything at all for himself. For Celie and each of her siblings he had bought a whole stick of Scarborough rock, and for Enid, a tiny bottle of toilet water.

She thanked him kindly for it, and then burst into tears.

Celie and Robert sat in befuddled silence, while Enid Sheppard sobbed all the way back to Bridlington, as if her world had ended.

The Guardians

At the top of the tallest pine for miles around, a golden eagle sat on two eggs.

From down here in the hide, Lynne Sweet could only see the hen's head, bobbing out of sight now and then as she tore up the meal her mate had brought to her.

'Red squirrel,' she said with a sad note in her voice.

Alan Sweet adjusted his own glasses and squinted up at the nest, then nodded and murmured, 'Red in tooth and claw,' as if it were something he'd just made up and not something they'd said to each other at least once a day during nesting season for the past eleven years.

'Supper?' sighed Lynne.

'Hm.' Alan put the binoculars down.

With at least one of their charges fed, they both sat down in their camping chairs and busied themselves with tin plates and foil before the light completely left the sky. They had a gas lamp, but they enjoyed the idea of being as unobtrusive as possible, and rarely used it. It meant they had to eat supper a bit earlier than they'd have liked, but it was a small sacrifice to make, and they could always eat biscuits in the dark.

The Sweets had been RSPB Nest Guardians for this particular pair of golden eagles for the past eleven years, and had the lanyards to prove it. The couple looked upon the birds as they would members of their own family. They had married late in life – she at fifty and he at fifty-eight – and never had children of their own, but had bonded so successfully over their interest in birds that their lives now revolved around the one hundred days they spent each year here in Scotland's Glenmore Forest, making sure that nothing disturbed the eagles they had nicknamed Fred and Ginger.

Early every March – even before the feathered couple began to line their huge, messy nest – Lynne and Alan would pack their supplies into their Volvo and leave their home in New Deer. They'd got it down to such a fine art that for the last three years they hadn't even had to go to the shops once during their vigil.

The RSPB officer who had trained them had called Nest Guardians the 'first and last line of defence' and Lynne and Alan had never forgotten it. Other Guardians would only do week-ends, or withdrew to their camper vans when it rained too hard, but the Sweets prided themselves on being hyper-vigilant and in the little wooden hide twenty-four-seven.

The fact that they had never once been called upon to actually physically defend the eagles in their care made no difference to their zeal.

'Just us being there is enough,' they told anyone who ever asked, although both liked to imagine – but never voiced aloud, even to each other – that one day they would have to actually confront an intruder intent on harm, and make a citizen's arrest. In Alan's fantasy there was a brief struggle and he had to punch a man in the face, then stand over him with his fists clenched like Burt Lancaster. Lynne's fantasy was exactly the same, except with Alan as Russell Crowe, so it's a pity they never shared.

Supper was always baked potatoes with something. Tonight it was tuna and sweetcorn. The foil-wrapped potatoes had been smouldering for much of the day in the fire pit, and were perfect.

For pudding they always had chocolate chip cookies, dunked in tea.

The days were still short and by the time they finished eating, it was entirely dark. The silence of the forest was only broken by their occasional whispers and rustling as they packed away their meal and wrapped up warm for a long evening of whispered word games and silence.

Once they were settled, the Guardians' ears were alert to the slightest noise.

The darkness stopped them watching.

But it didn't stop them being watched.

From the blackest shadows, a man had been watching the Sweets for five days and four nights. And because they were creatures of routine, he could anticipate every one of their moves.

He had seen Alan put the potatoes in foil and then into the pit this morning. He knew they would eat at dusk. Potatoes with tuna or beans. He knew their dessert of choice was chocolate chip cookies, with tea made on a camping stove and in a small kettle with no whistle.

He had watched them through night-vision goggles – and listened too, through a small parabolic microphone. Listened to the crackle of the foil, and to their low, boring chat and to the kettle bubbling, and then the rustle of the biscuit packet. Alan always had two, Lynne never had fewer than three.

Crunch crunch crunch.

He had watched them, and he had listened to them . . .

And he had timed them.

The whole affair of supper took twenty minutes. Sometimes more, but never less. Twenty minutes of movement, of foil unwrapping, of eating, of kettle boiling, of crunching, and then of more movement while they both bustled about, tidying up. Twenty guaranteed minutes of noise and distraction when Lynne and Alan Sweet were focused on their own needs, rather than those of two birds at the top of a very tall tree.

The man had watched the birds too, of course. He guessed there were two eggs. There often were – although whichever chick hatched first would almost always be the sole survivor.

If it was allowed to hatch . . .

It was late March now, so he knew he had to act soon while the eggs could still be easily blown – both chicks breaking up and dribbling out through the smallest possible hole. No collector wanted a hole that was any bigger than it ought to be. Especially for such premium eggs.

Two golden eagle eggs would fetch thousands on the black market, or give bragging rights for life. Whether sold or kept, they were a prize to tempt any collector who had the knowledge and the guts to evade the Guardians, climb a tree in darkness and brave two angry birds – each as big as a man, and with talons like knives.

The hide was fifty yards from the tree. After the disaster of 1987, where two Guardians were killed by a falling Scots pine, hides were always a safe distance away.

It would make the man's job just that little bit easier.

In his mind, he had already climbed the tree a dozen times. Examining every branch, every possible foothold, planning his route up, and his route back down.

Speed was of the essence, so he had decided that when the time came, he would use spikes, but no ropes.

The branches of the pine grew conveniently horizontally, thickly at the bottom but more sparsely near the top, nearly seventy feet above the ground. There he would have to identify the branches that would lead most obviously to the nest.

So he had twenty minutes. If all went well, he thought he could do it in fifteen. He liked a cushion but never planned to use it.

It was starting to get dark when the mic picked up Lynne Sweet saying, *Supper?*

The man in black covered his face and moved instantly, smoothly – almost soundlessly.

The climb would have been much easier to conceal under the cover of darkness, of course, but he had decided that the distraction of the impending meal would be more valuable to him than night and silence.

By the time Alan Sweet was bending to uncover the potatoes, the man was a mere shadow at the foot of the tree, hidden already by the low, dark needles. He wore a thornproof jacket, thick leather gauntlets, and a hard hat with a sturdy face shield. Golden eagles were not to be taken lightly. If he had done the job by day, he could have made his move while only the hen was on the nest. But by night, both would be there, and he was taking no chances.

He started to climb. He made good time. Handholds and footholds were many, and at first he didn't need to use his spikes.

He proceeded carefully, not wanting to risk rushing and snapping a branch and alerting the Guardians.

Forty-five feet up, the branches started to thin, and to thin out.

Now he dug his spikes into the trunk – not trusting every foothold.

At fifty feet he stopped. The lowest point of the vast, messy funnel of a nest was just above him now.

His next choice would be critical.

He had examined this section from afar countless times, so that now he was right there it seemed not unfamiliar to him. He knew that from here on, there were only a limited number of branches that could be relied upon to take the weight of a man.

He inched upwards, hugging the trunk, until he reached a point where there were only a couple of possible handholds above him. He dug in his spikes and gripped the trunk in the crook of his elbow.

The black ground was a dizzying drop away. If he fell now, he would definitely die.

Careful never to lose his elbow's grip on the trunk, the man unfolded an expensive tungsten tree saw from his belt.

Then he reached up and started to saw through the first of the handholds.

The eagles stirred and grumbled, and he stopped. Waited a full minute until they settled again, mentally thanking the cushion he'd built into the operation.

Then he continued, unhurried, sawing almost all the way through that sturdy branch. He brushed away the sawdust and raw splinters, then started on the branch beside it. And then the two branches below them . . .

Five minutes later he squinted up at his handiwork.

The cuts to the branches were almost imperceptible.

He hooked the saw back on to his belt and descended slowly and so silently that he could hear the kettle boiling.

His boots pressed softly into the bed of old needles at the foot of the tree.

By the time Lynne Sweet was on her third chocolate chip cookie, the man in black was halfway to his car.

Freebies

Patrick was carefully feeding an old wooden aeroplane propellor out of the small attic hatchway when Nick's phone rang and he abandoned his end of the equation, leaving the prop teetering on one narrow rung of the loft ladder.

'Nick?'

But Nick had walked away and Patrick could hear him talking animatedly on the phone, so did his best to steady the prop on the rung until Nick reappeared, which he did about two minutes later.

'Guess who that was!'

Patrick thought about it. 'Mrs Capstick.'

'Who the hell is Mrs Capstick?'

'Our English teacher at the primary.'

'Jeez, Patrick. No! Not Mrs Capstick from a hundred years ago! Why would our old English teacher suddenly call me? She's probably *dead* by now!'

'OK.'

'Anyway, it was Dr Connor.'

'From the Natural History Museum?'

'Yes, him. He's invited us to the museum as his guests!'

'Why?'

'He said his assistant showed him my picture of the egg. And he thinks we'd be interested.'

'In what?' said Patrick. 'Can you take the other end of this?'

'Eggs, of course!' Nick took the other end and they lowered the propellor to the floor.

'But you're *not* interested in eggs.'

'I'm interested in getting *my* egg back, though.'

'So how's this going to help?'

'Well, he knows all about eggs, see?'

'OK,' said Patrick, who didn't see.

They each took an end of the propellor and carried it to Nick's bedroom and put it in a corner. Nick brushed his hands on his jeans, then shrugged and said, 'Free day out, innit?'

It wouldn't be a free day out, Patrick knew. Nick's free days out never were. His friend had once won two tickets in a raffle to a West End show he didn't want to see. *We Will Rock You*. Patrick didn't want to see it either, but he had spent well over three hundred pounds doing just that.

Nick loved a freebie and would take anything for nothing, regardless of how much it cost him. His mother's garden shed was packed to the roof with broken vacuum cleaners, rusty gardening equipment, tools, pressure washers, five old bicycles and three lawnmowers, even though he didn't have a lawn and wouldn't have mown it if he had. He just couldn't say no.

Nick slid the ladder back into the loft. 'Guess how many eggs they've got there.'

'A million,' said Patrick, closing the hatch.

Nick looked deflated. 'How did you know?'

'Why? Is it a million?'

'Yeah. Anyway, he's going to take us all round and show us everything.'

'Why?'

'Oh my God.' Weird Nick rolled his eyes and flapped his arms. 'Why why why! You're like a bloody toddler!' Then he stomped off and slammed his bedroom door and Patrick went home.

This happened sometimes and meant nothing.

As he walked through the gap in the hedge, Patrick thought about toddlers. He hadn't met a toddler since he'd stopped being one, but if they were always asking *why* then he thought he might like to.

Tring

Patrick couldn't drive and so was in no position to critique his friend's driving, but that didn't stop him being nervous.

Even on the motorway Nick barely reached 50mph and the little Fiesta was constantly tailgated by trucks that filled all their mirrors with grilles and headlights and angry airhorns.

But Nick seemed oblivious to his own faults behind the wheel. *What's his problem?* was his regular refrain, interspersed with tuts and sighs and, *Look at this idiot.*

By the time they finally reached Tring, Patrick was drained from the stress of the trip.

Tring cheered him up.

For a start, it sounded fictional, but wasn't. It was a thriving town, and its core was made of pretty old houses with fancy little shops selling candles and wooden toys from what used to be their front rooms. The museum was discreetly signposted up a narrow side road that looked to be leading nowhere, but which ended in a small car park.

Weird Nick pulled in beside a shiny black Mercedes with a personal number plate that read B1RDY. He cut the engine and for a moment he and Patrick sat and looked at the place.

In scale the museum was a mansion, but in style it was a mish-mash. A sprawling house at the foot of a wooded hill and with neat lawns and shrubbery, it was full of nooks and angles – red brick in places, pan-tiled in others and mock Tudor at its multiple gable ends. Its windows were leaded or sashed or Crittall, bay or flat, with crowns or cornices or crenellations. Even its steep red roofs had suffered aberrant stylings: here an afterthought of a clock tower, there a curled touch of old Dutch.

Patrick thought it looked like a building that couldn't make its mind up.

They walked up the front steps and waited for Dr Connor in reception, from where they could glimpse the vast galleries of animals awaiting them. Dead ahead was a huge polar bear.

Dr Connor appeared, now wearing jeans and a polo shirt. He looked a lot more cheerful than he had in the courtroom, and shook Nick's hand warmly, so Patrick stepped away from him just in case.

'Don't mind Patrick,' said Nick. 'He's not big on touching.'

'Don't blame you,' said the curator. 'You don't know where I've been.'

'Exactly,' said Patrick.

'That your Merc in the car park?' said Nick.

Connor nodded. 'It is.'

'Thought so,' grinned Nick.

'What gave it away?' laughed Connor.

'What are you a doctor of?' said Patrick bluntly.

Connor winked. 'Not much! I have a PhD in applied oology, so if you cut your finger, you're on your own.'

Patrick asked, 'Why?' and under his breath Nick muttered, *Don't start, mate,* but Dr Connor took the question in his stride.

'I just mean, I'm not a medical doctor, so I'm basically useless in a crisis unless it involves eggs.'

Patrick frowned. 'What sort of crisis involves eggs?'

'God knows!' He laughed. 'Never had one! And, having established that the title is meaningless, you can call me Chris.'

So they did. Well, Nick did anyway. Patrick found names too familiar at the best of times, and preferred to call him nothing.

The curator led them briskly past tall glass cases filled with dead animals. It all flashed by too fast for Patrick's liking. Far too soon, they were ushered through a dark oak door marked *Staff Only*, past a bathroom and along an echoing corridor to a small office that looked out on to a black drainpipe and a laurel hedge.

There was a desk covered with piles of paperwork, and a framed photograph of Dr Connor in an evening suit, holding an ugly award – both washed out by the flash.

The curator gave them endless forms to fill in which required their names, addresses, ages and the Fiesta's registration number. They had to submit their passports for copying and have their photos taken, before finally being issued with visitor passes on lanyards.

'Blimey!' said Nick. 'It's like *Mission Impossible* getting in here!'

'Yes, I'm afraid it is,' Connor said ruefully. 'We used to let any old Tom, Dick or Harry come to do research, but then some bastard made off with some of our rarest feathers. Now to gain entry you have to sacrifice your firstborn son!'

'I'm the *only* son,' said Patrick. 'We both are.'

'In that case,' said Connor, 'you're both in!'

The egg collection was nothing like Patrick had expected.

It was not on public display. Unlike the animals behind polished glass, the nation's egg collection was housed in a series of vast, high-ceilinged halls, made dim by sturdy mesh at the windows, and filled with row after row of towering metal cabinets that grew out of one wall of each room like giant breakwaters, leaving only a narrow passageway along the opposite wall. Sturdy wheeled ladders ran down the aisles between rows to access even the top drawers, which were eight feet high. Everything was a deep cream colour; but the effect was still of some dystopian filing system.

Every now and then the curator stopped and unlocked a column of drawers using a small silver key – one of hundreds attached to a huge ring that absolutely bristled with them.

Patrick was mesmerized by the keyring. There were smaller rings clipped to the big ring and even smaller rings clipped to those. All of the keys looked identical to him, so he imagined there was a system, and tried to work it out as Dr Connor opened drawer after drawer to reveal the wonders inside, from humming-bird eggs the size of a pea, to the spectacular golden eagle eggs, and ostrich eggs as big as his head.

As they moved from one room to the next through noisy swing-doors, Dr Connor fired an enthusiastic stream of infor-mation at them. Weird Nick looked a little dazed, but Patrick was engrossed. He had never learned so much so fast.

He learned that until a day or two before it's laid, an egg has no shell; that one is constructed as it travels out of the uterus, like a car on a production line – with thousands of blobs of calcium fired at it to form a shell that's both breathable and waterproof, which is then painted in a pattern unique to each species and – in some cases – to individual birds.

He learned that hens' eggs – having travelled all that way pointy end first – somehow flip over to be laid facing the oppo-site direction. This last miracle discovered by a man armed with a pencil, an uninhibited hen, and a very tolerant wife.

He couldn't wait to tell Meg.

Dr Connor even showed them the egg of a great auk – giant flightless birds a yard high that were predator torpedoes in water and yet so slow and clumsy on land that men killed them for food or feathers faster than they could breed. As they gazed down at the big black-and-white egg, Dr Connor mused, 'The last known pair were strangled by Icelandic fishermen in 1844.'

Patrick flinched. 'Why?'

'Because a collector wanted their skins undamaged,' the curator said sombrely. 'The egg they were hatching was smashed, and that was the end of the great auk.'

Nick shook his head. Speechless for once.

Connor continued. 'We're losing bird species every day. That's why monitoring changes in shell composition is so critical to protecting future generations. For instance, without eggshell research we'd never have known that acid rain or DDT were so dangerous.'

'The science,' murmured Patrick.

'Indeed.' Connor nodded. 'It's not even in dispute. That's why we're allowed to collect a small number of eggs under government licence, but it's never enough to do adequate research. Which is why we always apply for possession of any eggs seized in criminal cases.'

'But what about what that RSPB officer said?' asked Nick.

'Garrett?' snorted Connor. 'The man's a philistine.'

Then he sighed and went on more gently, 'Look, it's a thorny debate. I can see his point. Unfortunately he can't see mine. But the truth is that without continuing access to modern eggs to compare to the older ones, we simply may not know how birds are being affected by current environmental changes until it's too late to save them.'

'But surely,' said Nick, 'their value to science does encourage people to collect eggs?'

Connor snorted. 'Of course it doesn't. Trust me, if all the museums in the world disappeared overnight, eggers would get up the next morning and collect eggs. They don't care about the research or the birds, they're simply hoarders. It's just unfortunate that for some reason Finn Garrett has made it his personal crusade to make sure we don't get the eggs – and he usually wins.'

'Because of that thing about the acid?' said Nick.

'Exactly.' Connor nodded ruefully. 'He knows it gets people right in the guts. After that, trying to explain the importance of cataloguing, or the subtleties of shell thinning and sand-eel decline . . . well, it's not a fair fight.'

'How do you catalogue an egg?' said Patrick.

'Ah, good question!' The curator brightened. 'To be able to properly authenticate and catalogue eggs, you need data.'

'You mean like a spreadsheet?' said Nick.

'Well, a very old-fashioned one. But not dissimilar. The thing is, unlike with trees or rocks, it's impossible to tell how old an egg is, so data is absolutely vital. It's like the signature on a painting – without it you can only really make an educated guess about whether it's a Rembrandt or one of his students, or even a modern fake. Here, I'll show you.'

He stopped randomly and rifled through his keys, then unlocked a drawer and slid it open. Inside were a dozen bird's nests, each one filled with little blue eggs.

Patrick's stomach gave a lurch. He had expected eggs, of course. But for some reason, he hadn't expected nests.

His father had once shown him a nest. He'd parted the hedge and allowed him to peer in for a brief moment at the three baby sparrows, each barely as big as his four-year-old thumb. The little cup of twigs had been spiky on the outside but smooth and beautiful on the inner, and so carefully lined with wool and moss that no chick would be snagged or harmed, even at its most naked and vulnerable. Patrick had never forgotten how cosy the nest had looked, or how after that he'd often imagined growing smaller, not bigger, until he also might curl into a ball inside that safe, fluffy cradle.

But no chicks were ever cradled in this robin's nest. No chicks had tapped themselves free of these eggs, and been fed and fledged and flown away. These chicks had been pulled out in pieces through the neat hole drilled in each shell.

Patrick felt slightly queasy.

Connor removed a small strip of paper from one nest. It was barely three inches long, and looked to have been torn from a lined page. In faded pencil was scribbled *Robin. South Downs. June 1922.*

'This is data.'

'That little scrap?' Nick was plainly disappointed.

Connor smiled and nodded. 'It's the egg's only provenance, you see? A contemporaneous note of what the egg or the nest is, and where and when it was collected.' He picked a similar bit of paper from the next nest. *Robin. South Downs. June 1923.*

'June 1924, June 1925, and so on,' he said. 'When you work with these things all the time you come to recognize the handwriting of the biggest collectors. This is the Reverend Jack Andrews. The hobby seemed to attract a disproportionate number of vicars!'

He turned to Nick. 'Did your egg have the data with it?'

'I *think* so,' said Nick.

'Think so?'

'Yeah. I think it was in the box.'

'Not any more?'

'Well . . . no. Not now. I mean, I didn't know what it was. I didn't know it was *data*. I just thought it was a bit of old paper.'

'So what did you do with it?'

Nick looked abashed. 'I just . . . threw it away.'

The curator said nothing, just raised his brows, then carefully replaced the paper among the little blue eggs.

Patrick was still staring into the drawer. 'Why take the whole nest?'

'Makes for a better display.'

Patrick looked around at the walls of cream drawers. 'But they're not *on* display.'

'They used to be,' Connor shrugged. 'And anyway, collectors are completists. No egg left behind!'

'And what about the birds?'

'The birds?'

'That made these nests?'

'I suppose they built other nests.' The curator closed and locked the drawer and led them out of the hall.

Nick fell into step beside him, while Patrick followed them. 'So what would an egg like mine be worth?'

'Without the data, not much.'

'Shit,' said Nick. 'Really?'

'Really,' said Connor. Then he added, 'Well, it really depends on the individual egg. You might use the word *priceless* in its most literal sense, because illegal eggs cannot be legally bought or sold, whatever the price. But of course, on the black market, some eggs can sell for hundreds of pounds. Even thousands.'

'Thousands?' Nick gave a low whistle. 'Is there a big black market?'

'Sadly, yes. There are still collectors all over the world willing to pay big prices for the best eggs.'

'Like Matthew Barr?'

'God, no. He's small fry. But he's indicative of a sizeable minority who continue to collect illegally, or who are still holding on to historic collections.'

'So who would steal my egg?'

'I imagine it was stolen to order for a particular customer.'

'But it was only on eBay for five minutes,' said Nick.

'That's long enough. Collectors monitor sites like eBay and Marketplace and egg forums. It's all so much easier now with the technology available. They're really looking for people like you, who don't know what they've got. You would be amazed at what they will do to find these things. And as you've found out, they won't stop at much to own them. Violence or blackmail. There have even been cases where thieves have posed as police or RSPB officers to seize entire collections. Old eggs are particularly sought after because, if you have data showing that the egg was collected before the 1954 ban, then it can be legally owned. You know, the way they do with ivory now? If it's old enough, it's lawful to keep it.'

'My egg *looked* old,' said Nick.

'It can *look* as old as it likes,' shrugged Connor. 'But without the data, you're screwed.'

Nick nodded mournfully, then cheered up. 'You mean whoever nicked it is screwed!'

'Indeed they are,' said Connor. 'Got anything else of interest in your attic?'

'You mean eggs?' said Nick.

'Eggs? The Holy Grail . . . ?'

'Got all sorts up there,' laughed Nick. 'Want to buy a badger?'

Connor smiled. 'I believe we have one of those somewhere around here . . .'

Nick got serious again. 'But if somebody stole my egg, surely it *must* be valuable!'

Connor raised his eyebrows and said, 'Follow me,' and led them through another swing-door to the fifth and final hall. 'Pick a drawer, any drawer!' he said with a theatrical sweep of his arm.

'OK.' Nick led them down the rows of cabinets and turned into an aisle about halfway along. He stopped a few paces in and pointed to a slim, wide drawer near the top of a column. 'That one!'

'OK!' Connor slid the ladder into place with a soft squeal. Patrick noticed that it had left faint trails on the parquet floor from years of being pushed back and forth.

Again the curator picked through his keys. Then he climbed the ladder and opened the drawer Nick had pointed out. He removed a large display case, then turned and sat down on a low, broad rung of the ladder, resting the case on his knees, and opened it towards them like a spiv selling watches.

Inside were dozens of eggs of assorted colours – blues, yellows, browns, greens – each covered with Pollock-esque scribbles and drips in various darker shades. It was a dazzling display.

'Sorry to disappoint you, Nick,' he said. 'Guillemot eggs are beautiful but they're not exactly rare. At the height of the egg-collecting craze they were without doubt the most popular eggs because they're so brightly coloured and each one is unique to a particular bird. We call this the guillemot room. It holds over fifty thousand guillemot eggs – all the work of a single collector.'

Nick looked crushed. Patrick stared around at the cabinets, thinking of the drawers filled with thousands of eggs just like these. 'Everything in this room belonged to *one* collector?'

Connor nodded. 'That's right. George Ambler was obsessed with guillemot eggs. When the museum bought his collection the sheer number of eggs was overwhelming, and either his curation left a lot to be desired, or things were jumbled about in transit, so it was a right old mess. There simply wasn't the time or the staff to inventory the collection – or to match all the eggs with the scattered data. Here's Ambler's data, you see? So at one time he must have kept it up.' He pointed to the little scraps under each egg, each with a pencilled note of the date and location of the egg, and the scratchy initials, *GFA*.

'But by the time it arrived here, much of the collection was missing data, or it was mixed up, which meant it couldn't be displayed properly – back when we *did* display eggs – and it wasn't even useful for research because of course—'

'There's no way to date an egg without the data,' finished Patrick.

'Exactly.' Connor nodded. 'So for twenty years everything just sat around in boxes in the basement. Finally the museum recouped their costs by selling half of Ambler's collection to the American millionaire John du Pont—'

'The Foxcatcher guy?' asked Nick.

'The Foxcatcher guy,' nodded Connor. 'You know, he once paid a million dollars for the most valuable stamp in the world and slept with it under his pillow!'

'Why?' said Patrick, and Nick muttered, *Don't start.*

'Rich but crazy, I imagine,' shrugged Connor. 'Anyway, du Pont was buying up collections all over the world back then for the museum he was founding in Delaware. So I suppose he wanted to buy in bulk, and it was advantageous for the museum to sell that way too. I understand they covered the initial cost of the entire collection by selling only half of it.'

'That's not bad business!' said Nick.

'It was very good business,' agreed Connor. 'The story goes that du Pont arrived in a Rolls-Royce with two lackeys, to choose his half of the Ambler collection.'

Patrick was surprised. 'He came in person?'

'He did,' nodded the curator. 'I imagine he wanted to make sure he was getting all the best eggs, but everything was in such a mess that it was impossible to evaluate what was good and what was junk. Apparently he was one ticked-off millionaire! Eventually he flipped a coin, and then pointed to one half of the room and stormed off. Everything in that half of the room was packaged up and sent to Delaware. And years later, here we are. But even with only half of Ambler's collection remaining, the cataloguing is far from done and – to be frank – may never be completed. We just don't have the money or the manpower.'

He stared at the eggs on his lap for a moment, then sighed and put them carefully back in the drawer. As he came down the ladder, he opened other drawers in the same column, showing that each was full of eggs – some in glass cases, others just jumbled on top of a layer of cotton wool laid down to protect them. 'See what I mean?'

'So my egg was just one of thousands,' said Nick despondently.

Connor nodded as he relocked the column of drawers. 'I'm afraid so. But still collectable, of course – *if* it had the data with it that showed its proper age.'

'I'll remember that,' said Nick. 'If I ever get it back.'

'If you do, let me know. Although we're no longer allowed to pay for eggs, I'm sure the purchasing committee could stretch what it's prepared to pay for *the box*.' He made air quotes around the last two words. 'Even the data would be worth *something*.'

'The data I threw away, you mean?'

'Yes,' said Connor, '*that* data.'

Patrick followed them back through the vast halls, back past Dr Connor's office, a storeroom and a bathroom.

Connor held open the *Staff Only* door back into the main exhibition rooms. 'Were the police any help with your egg?'

'They said it was junkies.'

Connor pulled a face. 'What would junkies want with an egg?'

'He didn't tell them what was stolen,' explained Patrick.

'Oh,' said Connor.

Nick blushed. 'I didn't know it was illegal to have an egg, see? I was hoping I could get it back myself.'

The curator nodded. 'You had any luck with that?'

'Well, we tracked down the only bidder, but—'

'He broke Nick's nose,' Patrick chipped in again.

Nick glared at him. 'Thanks, mate.'

'Oh dear,' said Connor. 'These people don't fool around.'

'Too right,' Nick nodded. 'I only wanted to raise a bit of cash for a good cause.'

'Good for you,' said Connor. 'What are you raising money for?'

'A gaming chair.'

'Oh!' He laughed. 'That *is* a good cause! What do you play?'

'*Call of Duty.*'

Connor gave a little salute. 'Lance Corporal Jack Hammond at your service.'

Nick returned the salute. 'Sergeant Mick Savage reporting for duty!'

'Stand down, soldier!'

They both laughed.

'What Rank are you?' said Connor.

'Thirty-one,' said Nick.

Connor gave a low whistle. 'Nice. I'm still at twenty-five.'

Patrick was ranked six, and stopped listening as they walked back towards the main entrance past more long-dead animals looking at each other with sad glass eyes. They were almost back at the polar bear when he said, 'Where's the quagga?'

'Sorry?'

'Where's the quagga?'

'The quagga? Oh. It's upstairs.'

Patrick stopped and looked back the way they had come, but Dr Connor didn't break his stride – just carried on talking to Nick.

'I'm really more of a *Resident Evil* man. You play?'

'No. Patrick's still into *GTA*. And he usually gets us both killed in *Call of Duty*, so . . .' He ended with a helpless shrug that indicated that the calibre of his comrade made *Resident Evil* a cyber-risk too far.

Patrick trailed behind them and caught up at reception.

'I've seen it on YouTube!' Nick was saying. 'Jill Valentine or Ada Wong?'

'Wong.'

'Is the *right* answer!' They laughed and bumped fists, and Nick said that Ada Wong was welcome round his house anytime.

Patrick didn't know either woman, but that wasn't unusual. Apart from his mother and Weird Nick's mother, Meg was the only woman he knew. The girls at the pub were always chattering to him and around him, but he didn't *know* them. He was surprised to hear that Nick knew two girls. It would be two more than Patrick had ever seen him with.

They gave in their lanyards and Dr Connor walked them to the doorstep and shook Nick's hand. 'Give me a call if you find anything else in that attic of yours – eggs, data, anything, OK?'

'Thanks, Chris. Will do,' said Nick. Then he saluted. 'See you in Las Almas!'

Connor laughed and saluted Nick as he headed across the car park. Then he turned to Patrick and stuck out his hand.

Patrick quickly tucked his hands into his armpits, and the curator withdrew with a smile.

'Sorry,' he said. 'Force of habit!'

'Come on, mate!' shouted Nick, but Patrick stayed where he was and frowned at Dr Connor. 'You said Ambler was obsessed with guillemot eggs.'

'Well, yes. Collecting on that scale is always liable to tip over into obsession.'

'Then why would he sell his collection?'

'He didn't,' said Connor. 'I believe the museum bought it from Ambler's estate after he died.'

'Oh,' said Patrick. 'OK.'

Nick tooted the horn on the Fiesta, and Patrick went down the steps and broke into a jog across the car park.

'Bye,' Connor called after him.

Patrick stopped and turned. 'How did he die?'

'What's that?'

'How did George Ambler die?'

Connor frowned.

'He was murdered.'

Mud

At the British Oological Society annual dinner at the Grand Hotel in York, George Ambler's name was mud.

The primary business of the night was for fifty rich men to smoke cigars, get drunk, and to show off their eggs. But all the after-dinner talk concerned an egg that was not even there.

'I don't believe it ever existed,' said Mr Minke. 'Did anybody see it?'

'Not I,' said Major Howells as he sliced the end off a cigar the size of a banana.

He had his five sea-greens laid out in silk nests beside him on a purpose-built stand.

Minke had brought along the same large sickly yellow egg with white markings that had caused quite the stir last year.

But this year, nobody cared about any of them. This year all the talk was of the Metland Egg.

'I went round there, you know,' said Minke. 'And got the brush-off!'

'From Ambler?' said Howells.

'From his man,' said Minke. 'Didn't even *see* Ambler.'

'Should have pushed the damned fellow aside,' said Howells, pouring himself another glass of port. 'Bloody cheek.'

'Quite right!' Sir Oliver Bigelow raised his glass to *that*.

Minke reddened as he realized far too late that now everybody

would know he had been fobbed off by a servant. Worse –
they would imagine that he must have been treated so ill because
he was a Jew. He hadn't considered it himself at the time, but now
that he did consider it, he prickled with shame.

There was a long silence in which Howells pinched his yellowing moustache with his nicotine fingers.

'How did you come to hear of it, Minke?'

'Hear of what?'

'Ambler's egg.'

'Why, I had an invitation to view. That's why I went around.'

'An invitation to view?'

'Well, an invitation to dinner to view, yes. Eighth Wonder of
the World, it said.'

Howells gave a non-committal grunt. Until that very moment he
had assumed Ambler's invitation had been to him, and him alone.

This was sobering news.

Howells was Ambler's oldest and wealthiest client, and yet two
years before, Ambler had sold Rickaby the Big Blue. Howells
had let him know that it had been a grave error. That in future
he should be given first refusal on *any* egg. Certainly on any egg
that was worth showing off at the annual dinner. Not that he'd
have paid whatever Rickaby paid, of course, but even so! Now
it turned out that he had been just one of several invited guests.
Possibly one of many.

Ambler had even invited the Jew!

He had let the Big Blue go, but this was too much. He didn't
trust Ambler any further than he could throw him – and with
his gammy knee that was no distance at all. A gammy knee, he
always hastened to add (even in his own mind), that had been
earned in the Great War. Ypres, to be exact. Which was absolutely true. Ypres was the *where* – although if anybody enquired
exactly as to the *how*, Howells always waved the question away,

gruffly insisting that other men had done more. Which was also true – unless any man had done less than fallen down the stairs into the wine cellar of an abandoned chateau.

Regardless, Major Howells considered himself a war hero, and was sorely aggrieved that Ambler had deceived a man such as he.

'Didn't bother going round myself,' he said. 'Sounded fishy from the off.'

The other men all grunted and nodded, because allowing a chap to lie his way out of an embarrassing situation was what a fellow gentleman did.

'Good for you, Major,' said Bigelow. 'Ten to one on, Ambler bought an egg thinking it real and then found it was made up by some crafty bumpkin. We must rib him about it.'

'Indeed!' Minke looked around the room, keen that the baton of scorn should pass from him. 'Where is he?'

'London, I imagine,' said Howells. 'No brokers allowed, you know. Only gentlemen.'

Minke hadn't known. To cover this latest *faux pas* he said quickly, 'Cotton did tell me that one of the Chandler gang said something about a red egg at Metland.'

Cotton was a less-fashionable broker whom Minke patronized only because they'd both gone to Westminster.

'Nonsense!' Howells ejected smoke from his nostrils like a cartoon bull. 'Show me a red egg and I'll show you a child with a paintbox.'

Bigelow threw his head back and laughed and took another glass of whisky from a passing silver tray.

'Nobody works Metland,' Howells added, 'because of the overhang.'

They all knew that was true, although none of them had ever been there to see it. For all they knew, there might not even be a cliff at Bempton.

'Mark my word,' Howells went on, 'Ambler's been duped. And it'll be a cold day in hell before I buy from him again.'

'Absolutely!' said Bigelow. And then he frowned. 'Although he did find the Big Blue.'

Howells snorted. 'Blue is not red.' Then, before anybody could remark that sea-green was also not red, he leaned back in his chair and looked around the room. 'Where *is* Rickaby anyway? I haven't received this year's invitation to bloody Mansfield!'

They all laughed – even Minke – and followed Bigelow's finger to where Rickaby stood by the fireplace, swaying slightly, with an empty glass in his hand.

Minke raised an eyebrow. 'Didn't know he was a drinker.'

'Probably how Ambler got him to pay thirty pounds for an egg!' said Howells.

'Have you seen it?' asked Bigelow.

'Seen what?' said Howells.

'Rickaby's egg.'

'That's not the question,' snorted Howells. 'The question is, is there a man alive who has NOT seen Rickaby's blasted egg?'

'He doesn't seem to have it with him,' said Bigelow.

They all turned again to look at Rickaby, who had braced one hand against the mantel to keep himself still, and was glaring into the fire.

'He tried to sell it to me, you know,' said Minke.

'Really?'

'Yes, just after Ambler's invitation came, I had a note from him offering to sell Big Blue for twenty-five pounds.'

'Well, well!' Howells sat up in his wing chair.

'You weren't interested, Minke?' said Bigelow.

Minke shook his head. 'Not when Ambler had something even better. Why spend money on second best?'

They all nodded in agreement, and Minke felt he'd recovered a little ground.

'Call him over,' commanded Howells, stubbing out his banana.

Bigelow did. Rickaby looked up but didn't move.

'Go and fetch him, Minke.'

Minke was stung by the tone, but got up and headed for the fireplace, feeling like a waiter.

'Rickaby, old man. Join us.'

Rickaby stared at him and Minke cleared his throat. 'We were just talking about the Big Blue.'

Rickaby swayed.

'Is it here? Sir Oliver was asking.'

Rickaby turned his gaze slowly towards Bigelow, and then back to the fire, missing out Minke completely.

'Or did you sell it after all?' Minke grew more and more uncomfortable the longer Rickaby stayed silent. He wondered if Rickaby was angry he hadn't bought the egg. 'Sorry I couldn't oblige you myself. I was keeping my powder dry until I'd seen this egg of Ambler's. But then of course that all went pear-shaped and, well . . . Did *you* see it?'

Rickaby regarded Minke with a bloodshot eye. 'Did anyone?'

'No!' Minke raised his brows. 'Not that I know of anyway. Actually we were only just saying that we doubt the thing ever existed. Maybe Ambler—'

'Maybe Ambler should watch his fucking back.'

Minke blinked. He had never heard a man openly make a threat to another man, let alone when the men concerned were gentlemen. He stood for a moment, wondering if there was anything he might say to Rickaby that could possibly improve things, but if there was any such thing to be said, it did not leap in a timely fashion to Mr Minke's mind, and so instead he merely raised his glass at Rickaby and then drifted away from his angry orbit until he found himself once more in the snug.

'So! Did he sell it?' demanded Howells.

'He didn't say,' said Minke. 'But he's frightfully angry with Ambler.'

Howells laughed bitterly.

'Aren't we all?'

The Collector

Weird Nick swung the Fiesta out of the museum car park and peered this way and that, trying to find a sign to the ring road. There was a one-way system, and roadworks, which didn't help.

Patrick called Meg. On speaker so he didn't have to put the phone anywhere close to his ear.

'Hi!' she said cheerily. 'How's it going?'

'We're just leaving the museum,' said Patrick.

'Did you see the quagga?'

'No!' said Patrick vehemently. 'It was up—'

The brakes squealed as Nick almost mowed down an old lady on a zebra crossing.

'Patrick! Are you OK?'

Patrick unpeeled his fingers from the dash. 'Yes.'

He glared at Nick, who shrugged: 'She came out of nowhere!'

'Was the curator any help?'

'Not really.'

Nick called out, 'Chris is a top bloke, but I thought he was going to help me to find my egg. Instead he just showed off all of *his* eggs!'

'Oh well,' said Meg breezily. 'It sounds to me as if you've done all you can.'

'I don't think so,' said Nick. 'Maybe we should speak to that bloke from the RSPCA.'

'The RSPB,' said Patrick.

'Right,' said Nick. 'We should ask them about it. They bring these cases to court, so they must know all the criminals. Probably got a register or something.'

Patrick said nothing.

Nick glanced at him. 'What?'

'What?' said Patrick.

'What's wrong with going to the RSPB?'

'I don't like Finn Garrett.'

'I don't like him either,' said Meg. 'Seriously, Nick, I think you should stop this now.'

'Stop what?' said Nick.

'Trying to get the egg back.'

'Why?' said Nick crossly. 'It's mine and I want it back!'

'But it's *not* yours. That's like saying a shrunken head is yours. Or a horse-hoof ashtray. It's—'

'*Oh for fu*—' said Nick as they drove past the museum again, and had to start over.

'OK,' said Meg brusquely. 'Keep me in the loop.'

'OK,' said Patrick. 'Bye.'

He hung up. 'What's the loop?'

'It means, keep her informed,' scowled Nick. 'If you want to.'

Patrick nodded. 'OK.'

For a moment they drove in silence. Then Nick said: 'I wish we'd spoken to Matthew Barr when we had the chance.'

'The egg thief? Why?'

'Because Chris and Garrett have their own agenda when it comes to stolen eggs. They're both trying to do what they think is right for the birds by fighting their little court battles, but basically they're the establishment working against the egg thieves. If we're going to get my egg back, then we need to speak to thieves.'

'Your nose already tried that.'

Patrick rarely made jokes and didn't know he'd made one now until Nick guffawed.

'Good one!' he said. 'But we shouldn't give up so easily.'

Patrick didn't answer. He thought that *easily* sounded like the best way to give up.

'Hey! You think that woman would give you Matthew Barr's number?'

'What woman?'

'That lawyer you had a cup of tea with.'

'Ceri? No.'

'Why not?'

'Because I think she'd get fired.'

''Spose so,' sighed Nick. 'Shit, we're going to pass the bloody museum *again*. How the hell does anyone get out of this place? Where's the sign to the motorway? Help me look for it, will you?'

Patrick paid closer attention until he finally said *Ring road* and pointed at a sign that was almost completely obscured by a banner strung across the street that read *TRING FESTIVAL OF FIRE*.

'Thank God for that,' said Nick and swung out of the one-way system.

'I know where he lives,' said Patrick.

'Where who lives?'

'Matthew Barr.'

'You know where he *lives*?'

'Yes.'

Nick turned to look at him. '*Where?*'

'Eleven Eddery Road, Newmarket.'

'You're shitting me!'

'No, I'm not.'

149

'*How* do you know?'

'It was on one of the documents Ceri dropped outside the courtroom.'

'Bloody hell, Patrick! And you didn't think to mention this before?'

'No.'

Nick shook his head and muttered something Patrick couldn't make out.

He could tell that Nick was annoyed with him, but he couldn't think what he'd done wrong. Nick hadn't wanted to know how to contact Matthew Barr until now, so why would he have mentioned it before? What would have been the point of giving Nick information he wasn't ready to use?

Patrick remembered a time when he tried to tell people what they needed to know. He had gradually learned that nobody ever thanked him for it. And then they always forgot it anyway and had to ask again later when they realized they *did* need to know it after all. That meant he had to access it twice. This way he only had to access it once, when it was needed.

'Can you get Barr's address on Google Maps?'

'Yes,' said Patrick.

'Go on, then.'

'Why?'

'Because we're going to see him!'

'Now?'

'Yes, now. We're already halfway across the country. It's logical.'

'It's already nearly three o'clock and your mum needs the car for work tonight.'

'Bloody hell, mate! Where's your sense of adventure?'

Patrick didn't answer. He'd already accidentally had one adventure in his life and it had been very stressful. He didn't really fancy another.

But Nick was buzzing. 'Stop wasting time! Fire up Google Maps and let's go!'

Patrick sighed. He knew that the longer he tried to talk Nick out of this plan, the later they would get home.

So he took out his phone again and fired up Google Maps.

The Egg Thief

In a long terrace of small but neat houses, Matthew Barr's was the carbuncle. Weeds sprung eternal in the little front garden behind the broken gate, paint peeled off the front door, and the windows were blinded by what looked like old blankets – although it was hard to tell, because the glass was so dirty.

'You sure this is it?' said Weird Nick nervously.

Patrick didn't answer pointless statements.

'Careful,' he said. 'He's got a dog. A big one.' There was a fresh turd on the crumbling concrete path.

Nick dithered for a moment, but finally took a deep breath and knocked on the door.

Matthew Barr opened it almost instantly, smoking a rollie and wearing only a pair of drooping Y-fronts. He looked at them suspiciously.

'What's up?' he said.

'I . . .' said Nick. Then he stopped and started again. 'I'm Nick,' he said.

'Yeah?'

'And this is Patrick . . .'

'And?'

Nick went red and Patrick sighed. Once again, they should have practised.

Nick tried again. 'We were . . . we were just . . .'

'You were just what?' said Barr. 'Hurry up, mate. I'm letting all the heat out.'

Patrick intervened. 'We were in court when you were sentenced.'

'So?'

'So,' said Nick, 'I've got an egg.'

'Bully for you.'

'Well, I *had* an egg. It was stolen and we were wondering . . . y'know . . . if you . . .'

Matthew Barr's eyes hardened. 'If I stole it?'

'No, we didn't—'

'Just because I'm up in court you think I must have nicked your egg.'

'No, we were only—'

Barr sucked the last ember out of the cigarette and crushed it against the door frame.

'I collect my own eggs. I don't steal other people's eggs. Or other people's *anything*.'

'I didn't mean that,' said Nick.

'Then what the fuck *do* you mean?' Barr flicked the stub past their heads, and Patrick flinched and took a step backwards.

'Mind the—' said Nick.

Patrick lifted up his foot and grimaced at his trainer.

Barr snorted.

'Shit!' said Nick. 'You're not getting in my car like that.'

'OK,' said Patrick.

'Take them off, then!'

'OK.' Patrick toed his trainers off and stood holding them away from his body. 'Now what?'

'Oh hell,' muttered Nick, and looked around him. Nothing was to hand. Finally he appealed to Barr. 'You got a plastic bag, mate?'

Barr sighed and withdrew silently, but he left the door open, so they waited. He reappeared a few moments later with a flimsy Spar bag and held it out to Patrick, who dropped his shoes into it and tied it firmly at the top.

'Bloody nightmare,' said Nick crossly. 'I *knew* this would be a waste of time. Come on! We'll ask someone who gives a shit.'

Patrick carefully avoided the squashed turd, and followed Nick to the gate.

From behind them, Barr said, 'What kind of egg?'

They turned.

'What?' said Nick.

'What kind of egg?' he said again. 'Got stolen?'

'Guillemot. I found it in my attic.'

'Just one?' said Barr.

'One attic?'

'One egg.'

'Oh. Yeah. It was in a fancy box.'

Matthew Barr pursed his lips, then peeled himself off the door frame.

'Come in, then,' he said. 'But leave the shoes outside.'

Warily, they followed him into the house.

Indoors there wasn't even flooring – just bare concrete and a big, flattened cardboard box doing double duty as a rug under a breeze-block coffee table. From the state of Barr's Y-fronts, Patrick would have bet good money that he didn't own the washing machine that had come in the box.

The blankets at the windows meant the room was dim and grey. The only decoration was an empty frame on the window-sill; a small photo of a red-headed boy had been tucked into one dusty corner.

Barr turned on the overhead bulb and waved a wiry arm at a

sofa that looked as if it had been recovered from a skip. Neither of them sat down.

'I'll make some tea.'

It wasn't a question.

Patrick and Nick stood in silence and stared at the sofa, which sagged under the weight of its own filth.

Patrick's feet grew cold through his socks. He moved on to the cardboard rug.

Barr came in holding two chipped mugs, then went back to the kitchen for his own while Patrick stared aghast at his KitKat mug. 'It's dirty,' he whispered.

'Just drink it,' hissed Nick.

Patrick didn't. He could barely hold it.

Matthew Barr came back in with his tea.

'Have a seat.' He nodded at the sofa, so there was nothing to do but sit on it. Nick went first and Patrick took a deep breath and followed, trying not to think about the velour's greasy embrace.

Barr sat on a wobbly wooden stool and rolled another cigarette. He seemed even thinner than he had been a month ago in Merthyr. Patrick guessed he was thirty but his face looked forty-five. His skin was tanned, but also strangely grey and taut, and his hair was short and yet somehow lank. He crossed one sharp knee over the other and, between sips of tea, he chain-smoked roll-ups that had left a permanent yellow stripe on his lower lip.

'We wanted to speak to you in Merthyr,' Nick started. 'But then there was all that . . . fuss . . . outside court.'

Barr picked a bit of baccy off his tongue. 'Oh yeah. Garrett.'

'He seemed like a bit of a dick.'

Barr snorted. 'You don't know the half of it. The man's a bloody maniac. I mean – total psycho. I'd like to meet him down a dark alleyway one night with a crowbar.'

'Why?' said Patrick.

Nick dug his elbow into Patrick's side.

'You know – to rearrange his smug bastard face for him!'

'Why?'

'Why'd you think?' Matthew Barr got angry fast. 'It's not bad enough he took my eggs? He's got to laugh about it right to my face? Did you hear what he said to me? *Say goodbye to your eggs.* That bloody *wanker.* I spent twenty years of my *life* collecting those eggs. Out all hours in all weathers, cold, wet, hungry – driving thousands of miles, using all my money and all my skills to find those birds. Up to my nuts in freezing water, or hanging forty foot up a tree with a fucking hawk trying to kill me. Was sleeping in a field once and a cow shat on my head! All for eggs. And then this . . . this . . . Royal Society *arsehole* just comes along and takes them all away. You got any idea what that's like?'

He glared at them, so Nick nodded vigorously.

'And it's not just my eggs he took, it was my cabinets too, and that's just not right! That's where I draw the line. The eggs . . . well, the law has spoken on the eggs and there's nothing I can do about that. But I got those cabinets made special by an old bloke in London – he's like a zillion years old and makes cabinets for royalty. You know the royals all got eggs, right?'

They didn't know that.

'Well, of course they fucking do! Every rich bastard's got eggs, but who does Garrett pick on?' He swept an arm around his dingy room.

'You?' guessed Patrick.

'Exactly,' nodded Barr. 'I mean, those cabinets cost me a thousand pounds apiece. And I had fourteen of 'em.'

'Fourteen!' Patrick's eyes widened. Fourteen custom-made cabinets at a thousand pounds apiece, and they were balancing their dirty mugs on breeze blocks . . .

'That's right,' said Barr. 'And Finn bloody Garrett just come in here and took 'em. Fuck knows where. Wouldn't be surprised if he keeps 'em himself. Too bloody lazy to get his own eggs so nicks them off the *real* collectors. Wouldn't surprise me one little bit! Twenty years of sweat and tears and hard bloody work. Gone. Now I'm sitting here with fuck-all. No eggs. No cabinets—'

'No carpet,' Patrick pointed out helpfully.

'Fuck *carpet*!' Barr said forcefully. 'Fuck carpet and tables and chairs. Stuff like that – those are sacrifices you have to make, see? Job. Family, even. Whatever. Doesn't matter. And I don't mind that. Don't miss 'em. Because eggs is all you need, see? Works of art. Every day I looked at them. Every single day. When you're doing this kind of work, it's not a hobby, it's your *life*.'

He stubbed out one cigarette and lit another, sparking flecks of tobacco that made him blink.

'And it's about the environment too, see? What with climate change and everything. It's proper science. Like that museum bloke told the court – without us collectors all the birds would be dead from DDT! We wouldn't even *have* birds! That's what people don't understand—'

Barr stopped suddenly and rubbed his face and suddenly Patrick thought he recognized the expression. 'Are you sad?'

'Too right I'm sad. Sad and . . . fucking . . . *furious*.' Barr looked around the room as though exhausted. 'Those eggs were all I had. They were museum quality. Everybody who saw them said so. Look here . . .'

He picked up his phone from the floor, where it was charging, and started to scroll through his photos.

'Got pictures going back years here. I mean, look at that . . .'

He flashed the phone at them. 'Bullfinch eggs. Six of 'em. Rare, that.' He carried on scrolling and talking. 'Went back for that clutch four years running. Fella up in Newcastle offered me two hundred quid for 'em. I told him to fuck off! Four years' work and he thinks he can buy me off for two hundred quid!'

'Did you sell a lot of your eggs, then?' ventured Nick.

'You don't *sell* 'em,' Barr snorted without looking up from his scrolling. 'I'd sell my granny before my eggs! Every egg's got a memory attached, see?'

'I see,' said Nick.

'So what do you do with them?' said Patrick.

Barr did look up this time. 'You . . . *collect* 'em!' he said, as if Patrick were stupid. 'And then you *look* at them! And you show them to other people. You *have* them. That's the whole point.'

Barr then went back to the phone – flashing it at them briefly now and then, as if they knew what they were looking at.

'Skylark. *Impossible* to find. They try to trick you by running away from the nest before they take off, so you run to that spot and it's wrong, see? Cunning little bastards! But I'm wise to that . . .'

Nick made another attempt to steer Barr back to his own missing egg. 'Got any guillemot eggs?'

But Barr only shook his head. 'Not my bag, guillemots. Cliffs. I'm a field and tree man, me. Old school. We all got our skills. Mine is trees. I can get up a fifty-foot fir in sixty seconds flat. Sight unseen. I love a good tree, me. Just spike up and go.'

'What's spike up?' asked Patrick.

'Tree spikes, y'know? Spikes you strap on your legs and you dig in as you climb. You get really good you can *walk* up a tree, and I'm the fucking best. Here you go. My cabinets.'

Barr headed across the room to show them the photos, and Patrick leaned away in horror, sandwiched as he was between the ghastly sofa and Matthew Barr's approaching underpants.

'I've got a photo of my egg . . .' Nick held up his own phone.

Barr stopped like a vampire before garlic.

'What's that?' he said sharply.

'It's a photo,' said Nick, uncertainly. 'Of my egg.'

Barr snatched the phone from him and then glared at him. 'Is this for real?'

'What do you mean?'

'Did you make this, or is it for real?'

'It's for real. I *think*. I mean, I didn't *make* it, I found it. How would you *make* an egg?'

'People make 'em,' said Barr, but without any tone of real accusation. 'Paint 'em. Fake 'em, you know?' He held the phone close to his face, enlarging the pictures with his ochre fingers, the better to study them. He was so fixated that he almost seemed to forget Nick and Patrick were there.

For two full minutes, there was complete silence.

'What do you think?' said Nick finally.

Barr took a moment to raise his head, and when he did he seemed disorientated, as if his world had stopped and now he'd have to catch up again. He took the cigarette out of his mouth and dropped it in his tea, then stood up and started pacing about the room. Every few paces, he looked at the phone again.

'Where'd you get it?'

'It was my dad's.'

'This is the egg that was stolen?'

'Yep. Two men broke in and took it. Balaclavas, cable ties, the whole nine yards.'

Barr nodded. 'Makes sense.'

'Does it?' said Nick doubtfully.

'Does to me. Does if this is . . .'

'Is what?'

Barr looked at Nick, his eyes shining. 'I know it sounds crazy, but . . . d'you think it could be the Metland Egg?'

'What's that?'

'You don't know what the Metland Egg is?'

'We don't know *any* eggs.'

'Shit . . .' Matthew Barr laughed, then stopped pacing and looked again at the phone in his hand and then around the room, as though searching for someone who'd actually appreciate it.

'Bloody hell!' he said. 'Bloody *hell*!'

'So what is it?' said Nick urgently.

'The Metland Egg is . . . famous. More than famous – it's . . . *mythical*.'

And he looked at them with such excitement that Patrick felt a little thrill pass through him, even though he had no idea what the man was talking about.

Barr struggled to put words together – barely able to tear his eyes from Nick's phone as he spoke: 'It is the greatest mystery in the history of eggs.'

'Seriously?'

'Seriously. It was this pure-red egg collected back between the wars. Worth a fortune . . .'

'A fortune? Dr Connor at the museum said guillemot eggs aren't valuable.'

'But this one was,' said Barr. 'It's *red*!'

'But they come in all colours.'

'Not red like *this* is red. I mean, look at it! It's a *red fucking egg*!'

'Go on about the Metric Egg.'

'Metland. Metland Egg. It was found on the cliffs at Metland Farm up near Bempton under this overhang – this big fucking rock where nobody could go except – I don't know who, but *some* crazy bastard – and it was bought every year by the same broker—'

'George Ambler?' said Patrick.

'That's right.' Barr nodded. 'They say every year it was sold to Ambler and then . . .'

He stopped and shook his head, lost again in the photograph.

'Then *what*?' said Nick impatiently.

'Then every year the egg just . . . *disappeared*.'

'What do you mean, disappeared?'

'I mean it wasn't bought, it wasn't sold, it wasn't shown at Oological Society dinners . . . I mean – nobody's seen a Metland Egg for a hundred years!'

There was a sharp knock and they all looked at the door.

Barr hurried to the window and moved the dirty blanket a mere inch to one side.

Then he let out a strangled shout and tore it from the rail in a great cloud of dust that billowed in the sudden light of the dipping sun.

'My eggs!' he yelled. 'They've brought them back!'

They *had* brought them back.

Two men in RSPB anoraks were unloading the cabinets from the back of a large white van. Matthew Barr flung open the front door and rushed to the nearest one.

Patrick and Nick followed him out into the cool early-evening air, where commuters walked past briskly and schoolchildren stopped to stare at the scrawny man in Y-fronts cooing over a chest of drawers.

It *was* beautiful though. Patrick didn't know what kind of wood it was, but it was a gorgeous grain, and was highly polished. He joined Barr, and watched as he smoothly slid open a wide, flat drawer to reveal dozens of jewel-like blue eggs, clustered into clutches in cream silk nests, and with data written in a careful hand – each piece of paper pinned to its silken nest by an identical pearl-headed pin.

Barr closed that drawer and opened another, then another.

'They're all here!' he shouted, and broke into a little dance of wild joy. 'They're all here! Oh my God, thank you! Thank you!' Barr was beside himself. Pumping the hands of the taciturn RSPB men, stroking the cabinets, peeking into drawers.

'They're all here! They brought them back!' He turned to Nick and Patrick with shining eyes. 'Can you help me get them in? Hold on, I'll get my shoes.' As if shoes and Y-fronts were all he needed. He hurdled the turd and ran past them into the house.

Nick and Patrick waited on the doorstep.

The men finished unloading and were now just hanging around. Patrick hoped they'd stay to help too. The cabinets filled the little garden and looked like an awkward size, given the narrow doorway.

He peered indoors to see where Barr was.

'Shit,' said Nick, and when Patrick turned to see what was wrong his stomach clenched.

Finn Garrett.

He walked through the gate and Patrick made an effort to remain motionless. His feelings were nebulous things, but there was something about Garrett that made him want to run and hide.

'He's getting his shoes on,' one of the RSPB men told Garrett quietly.

Garrett gave a short laugh, then glanced at Nick and Patrick. 'Who are they?'

'Don't know.'

'Who are you?' said Garrett.

'What's it to you?' said Nick.

Garrett paused, then said, '*Nothing*,' and Patrick shuddered.

Matthew Barr returned in his pants and no-name trainers, and stopped dead between them at the sight of Garrett.

'Hello, Matthew.'

Barr was silent, but Patrick saw goosebumps pop up all over his shoulders and chest, and felt an odd kinship.

Garrett walked slowly out of the garden and to the van, and was momentarily hidden by the open back doors.

When he emerged, it was with a sledgehammer.

'Shit,' murmured Nick again.

'What are you doing?' said Barr.

Garrett walked back into the garden casually, as if he wasn't carrying a fifty-pound hammer.

'*What are you doing? Get out of my garden!*'

But Garrett strode towards the nearest cabinet, the sledge-hammer swinging in a long slow arc that started at his side, passed high over his head, and ended in a detonation of polished wood.

Matthew Barr screamed.

Panic jolted through Patrick like lightning. He ran. Jumped the low wall into the next garden, out of that front gate and into the road. He sprinted fifty yards then ducked between two parked cars and crouched there, shaking and with his hands over his ears, so that the sound of Finn Garrett destroying Matthew Barr's egg collection was just a series of distant thuds. But he couldn't block out the sound of Barr's hysterical cries of protest.

Finally, the hammering stopped and Patrick could hear only Matthew Barr's wailing and his own squealing, desperate breathing.

He crawled to the kerb and peered around the bumper of the car in front of him.

Nothing.

Two little girls in gingham dresses and long white socks stared at him. 'What are you doing?' said one.

'Hiding,' panted Patrick.

'Who from?'

Patrick ducked as Finn Garrett walked out of the garden. Easily, the man swung the sledgehammer into the back of the van, where it landed with a deep clang, and slammed the doors.

Then he turned, looked up and down the street – and headed straight for Patrick.

Patrick shuffled backwards between the parked cars on his hands and knees, his throat solid with fear. He looked up at the girls standing watching him.

'Go away!' he croaked, but the words barely found their way to his lips.

Garrett's tread was gritty on the pavement and Patrick reversed into the road. A car swerved around him and hooted angrily, and Patrick pressed himself against the back wheel of the car, then bent low to watch Garrett pass.

But Garrett didn't pass.

He stopped.

The girls had blown his cover!

And Patrick knew that any second now, Finn Garrett would step off the pavement and come round the back of the car and find him and—

What?

Patrick didn't know *what*. He just knew it would be bad. He couldn't run away in his socks. Garrett would catch him easily.

He reached up and tried the door handle next to his ear.

Miraculously, the door opened.

In a fluid movement, Patrick slid into the rear footwell behind the driver's seat and let the door click gently behind him.

There was a tartan rug on the back seat and he pulled it over himself in a desperate attempt at camouflage.

He knew it wouldn't work. Not if Garrett peered through the windows . . .

But Finn Garrett didn't peer through the windows.

Instead, he opened the driver's door.

Then he got behind the wheel, and drove them both away.

Confrontations

1930

The Society dinner had gone to the dogs.

Major Howells glared around sourly through the haze of cigar smoke that blurred the edges of the room.

Four years on, and the best egg in the place was still Rickaby's Big Blue – although of course it was not Rickaby's any more. Rickaby himself had never again attended the dinner, although he continued to blacken George Ambler's name from afar. The interloper who had bought Big Blue wasn't even English, so nobody in Howells' circle had anything to do with him. Not that the younger members seemed to care as they clustered around, oohing and aahing . . .

Of the founding members, only Minke and the Reverend Jourdain continued to bring eggs to show off every year – as though anyone was interested in that grim yellow thing that Minke insisted on introducing as the Golden Egg, as if just repeating it could make it true.

As for Bigelow . . . each year he sunk lower and lower in his leather chair until now he sat opposite Howells – slumped, half asleep, and with port staining his shirtfront like a man who'd been downed with an elephant gun.

No, the Oological Society dinner was not what it used to be.

Time was when it had been the highlight of Major Howells'

year. When all he'd had to do was sit with a snifter of brandy and bask in the reflected glory of his sea-green eggs.

Now he didn't even bring them.

The Big Blue incident had been bad enough, but Howells was not about to see his five sea-greens even further relegated by the Metland Egg. The new owner had not yet attended the dinner, but now everybody knew that two spectacular red eggs were being bought by George Ambler every year on the cliffs at Bempton, so it was only a matter of time before he made his appearance.

For four long years Major Howells had been on tenterhooks about the inevitable day. The projection played out in his mind on a near-daily basis: the way the red egg and its mysterious owner would be hidden by the dinner-suited mob clamouring to see it, flushed with whisky and wonder, raising their glasses to the miracle. Then the throng would part to allow him through to view the *Eighth Wonder of the World*.

As he passed, every face would turn towards him.

And in every eye he would see the reflection of his own humiliation . . .

No, the Metland Egg had ruined everything.

They all knew now that it must never have been stolen. That Ambler had lied to them and made fools of them all. That he must be accommodating a mystery client who had taken precedence over even the oldest and the richest of them.

Who was that man?

Nobody knew, but Major Howells still attended the dinner every year for the sole reason of finding out. Each year he anticipated the appearance of the Metland Egg like a spot on his lung, but he could not help it: he *needed* to know the worst. Once he had seen the egg then he could find fault with it, pour scorn upon it; be openly and loudly glad that he had not been overcharged for it.

But until it had been seen, the Metland Egg was unimpeachable.

'Penny for your thoughts?'

Howells glared at Bigelow. What *was* the man talking about? Didn't they all share the same thoughts? Bigelow must know his thoughts – or at least he would if he were ever sober. He only grunted in response.

Unabashed, Bigelow waved his glass in the air, and a waiter brought a decanter and refilled it, and Bigelow tapped the side table to let the man know to leave it there.

'Royalty,' he slurred after another minute or two. 'Mark my words. King himself, I wouldn't wonder.'

Howells pursed his lips. He hadn't thought of it, but Ambler having sold the egg to royalty *would* explain it. The lies. The secrecy. He didn't hate the idea. Royalty would at least be a respectable way out. Losing to royalty was nothing to be ashamed of.

He would have engaged with Bigelow but the man was snoring again, his drink listing precariously on his knee.

Minke flopped down into the wing-back between them. 'Have you seen Corbin's six?'

Howells frowned. 'Who the hell is Corbin?'

'Tall fellow in the corner. Six small brown murre eggs. Unmarked. Like hens' eggs!' He laughed. 'Damnedest thing!'

Howells made a face that left Minke in no doubt that he had no interest in Corbin or his eggs.

Bigelow snorted awake. 'Penny for your thoughts!'

'Oh, do shut up, Bigelow!' said Howells, and reached for the decanter. 'Nothing worse than a whimsical drunk!'

There was a long, difficult silence, during which Howells took a long gulp of port and surveyed the room.

Minke looked uneasy. He changed the subject. 'It's been a while since we've seen your nice sea-greens, Major.'

It was a blatant attempt to lighten the mood, but Howells only glared at him.

This was what it had come to – pity from a Jew.

Under that glare, Minke flushed and shifted awkwardly. He cleared his throat and tried again. 'The Golden Egg is causing quite a stir.'

'Your egg is the colour of vomit,' said Howells. 'Everybody is laughing at you.'

'I say, Howells!' said Bigelow.

But the Major merely downed his port while the air between the three of them thickened and seemed almost to settle upon them like a dirty fog in a hollow.

The silence dripped.

'Nobody is laughing at *me*, sir,' Minke said finally in a low voice. 'And nobody is laughing at Rickaby. Indeed, everybody feels very bad for him because he sold the Big Blue and then could not buy the Metland Egg.' He gave a bitter little smile. 'Nobody feels bad for me, of course, because I am a Jew.'

Howells tutted, and Bigelow said, 'Now, now, old man.'

But Minke waved away the protest. 'I understand this. Nobody really expected a Jew to be allowed to buy something of such value. I'm sure Rickaby and I were only invited to Ambler's dinner to push up the price.'

Minke leaned towards Howells, elbows on his knees and his low voice starting to shake a little with restraint. 'But *you*?' he said. '*You* are Ambler's oldest and richest client. *You* were the one he should have sold the Metland Egg to. *You're* the only man who was snubbed, Howells, and everybody knows it.'

He jabbed a single sharp finger into Major Howells' chest.

'Everybody is laughing at *you*.'

Then Mr Minke stood up, straightened his dinner jacket, and left the Oological Society dinner – never to return.

*

Major Howells knew it was true.

He knew it the moment the Jew said it.

Everybody *was* laughing at him.

He knew it all through that first restless, sleepless night. And he still knew it the next morning, when he caught the early train back to London and then immediately a cab to Cavendish Square.

'Good evening, Major Howells. Is Mr Ambler expecting you?'

'He should have been expecting me these past four years!' said Howells curtly, and pushed past Edwards, who gave way in deference to the visitor's superior class, yet stood his ground just long enough to make a point about manners.

That point did not go unnoticed by Howells, and it only added to his sense of having been publicly snubbed. Even the butler was doing it now! To regain a little of the high ground, he slapped his gloves against the man's chest and demanded: 'Where is he?'

Edwards inclined his head minutely – *This way* – and led Howells to the door of the drawing room. There he put his hand on the brass knob and said, 'If you'd be so kind as to wait here, sir?'

Howells hesitated. He had rudely pushed past the butler into the house and so knew that he could not be denied an audience now without considerable embarrassment. But he also knew that Edwards was here reasserting the position for which he was paid.

Major Howells had no qualms about pushing a servant out of the way. He had done it before and would cheerfully do it again. But being *seen* to push another man's servant out of the way – as would no doubt happen if he circumvented Edwards and burst into the drawing room . . . ? Well, that was a different matter. In *that* case, Ambler might be justifiably aggrieved, which could undermine his own planned attack. Howells wanted this meeting to be all about the gross insult to his person, not derailed by some perceived breach of etiquette in regard to Ambler's household.

So Major Howells pawed the ground while the butler went in to announce him – although it irritated him further that Edwards closed the door to undertake that mission, thus denying Howells the look on Ambler's face when he realized that he was finally about to be challenged on his deception.

A long minute later, Edwards opened the door and ushered Howells in with another inclination of his head that might have been subservience or might have been insolence.

George Ambler rose from an easy chair that was flanked on three sides by glass-fronted cabinets filled with eggs.

'Major Howells,' he said. 'To what do I owe this pleasure?'

'Pleasure be damned!' Howells started strong, ignoring the man's proffered hand. 'This has gone on long enough, Ambler! *Where is the Metland Egg?*'

Ambler's brows rose. He opened his mouth, but Howells was too angry to let him speak.

'We have all been deceived and denied! Every last one of us! At least do us the courtesy of revealing the identity of this purchaser you hold in such esteem! Is it royalty? If it's royalty, then just bloody well *say* so! But this stupid mystery! This ridiculous silence! It's outrageous!'

'My dear fellow . . .' Ambler began.

'Don't you *dear fellow* me! I have not travelled the length of England to be called *dear fellow* by a man who has made me a laughing stock!'

'I assure you . . .' stuttered Ambler. 'I mean . . . ! *Who* is laughing at you?'

'*Everybody!*' shouted Howells. '*Everybody* is laughing at me!'

'Nobody *I* know, Major,' said Ambler. 'Everybody *I* know thinks you a very fine fellow.'

'A very fine fellow *who does not have the Metland Egg!*' cried Howells, and dug a meaty finger into Ambler's chest so hard that the smaller man stumbled into the nearest cabinet, which tee-tered – first backwards, then forwards, then settled again, but not before spilling dozens of eggs off their little plinths and sending them rolling and cracking against the glass.

There was a gasp and Howells turned to see a maid in the door-way, carrying a large silver tea tray. She was wide-eyed, and the china chattered like teeth.

How much had she heard? That everybody was laughing at him?

'Ah. Martha!' Ambler regained his footing and gave a short, embarrassed laugh. His voice cracked a little. 'Now do stop horsing about, Major, and have some tea.'

Howells shoved his big yellow moustache almost against George Ambler's sweaty top lip. 'Damn your tea!' he spat. 'I'll see you in court!'

And he stormed from the room, knocking the tray from the maid's hands with a mighty crash.

He saw himself out.

Fame

1933

For the first time, the bird seemed to know what was about to
happen.

It did not flap. Flapping had never worked. It did not squawk,
for squawking was pointless. It did not peck, for that had never
stopped the thief.

If birds can learn, it had learned.

This time the bird just watched Celie approach.

And, for the first time, Celie hesitated.

She was not frightened of the bird – she wore stout gauntlets
now, provided by Mr Ambler, who was forever imagining new
ways in which the Metland Egg might be lost to him, and had
been afraid that Celie would be pecked and drop it in fright.

But today there was no protest. And so Celie met the bird's
shiny black eye.

All around them a thousand guillemots shrieked warnings,
and here and there exploded from the cliff in whirring sparks of
chocolate wings.

While this bird just watched her, and waited.

Under its downy breast she could already see the prize. A
tiny shock of red on the shaded wall. The bird shifted and the
egg disappeared, and now there was nothing to distinguish this

guillemot from any one of the thousand others under the Metland overhang. As if it knew it could not fight her, but hoped it might still deceive her.

And yet Celie *knew* the bird. It was no longer about knowing the particular ledge, or the distance to the crack. As they stared at each other, Celie thought that she would know *this* bird anywhere.

And she . . . hesitated.

The rope creaked beside her ear and she could feel Robert shift his position at the other end of it.

Waiting for her.

Waiting for the Metland Egg.

Gently, Celie reached under the bird. It turned its head away a degree, and half opened its beak and made a low grunt that Celie felt more than heard.

Carefully she placed the egg in the satchel and tapped the rope.

The bird sat and watched her all the way up.

At the top a crowd had gathered.

Every year they came now, hoping to witness the annual appearance of the world's most famous egg.

Ambler had whipped them up – he'd *had* them whipped up – from the second year onwards. He'd considered it could only be good for business and, indeed, had sold several inferior eggs at superior prices, just because tourists wanted to boast that they had bought them from the man who bought the Metland Egg – and while on the very cliff where that red rarity might appear at any moment.

Metland was between Flamborough and Bempton, but despite the long walk and the poor access, as May drew near each year, excitement grew and word was passed to newcomers, so that the trickle along the clifftop became a thick flood that blocked the narrow track and made for some unseemly shouting and even a few scuffles.

Locals led tourists through crops – sometimes not *their* crops – to avoid the crush on the track, where a cart once dropped a wheel over the edge and was only saved by the quick thinking of the Hodgson crew, who left young Arthur dangling, and hauled its load of wives out over the slatted wooden side, until the pony could be beaten hard enough to recover the cart. Somebody had shouted that the Hodgsons had saved six lives, and there was a great hurrah, but then the wives and their grateful husbands had hurried on with barely a glance at the Hodgsons' eggs, so keen were they to secure a spot at Metland that might provide a view of history.

And a view of Celie Sheppard.

For Ambler's whipping-up relied heavily on the girl. He had made much to the local papers of her slender frame and her great beauty, even though the only beauty he ever saw in her himself was for that fleeting moment when she was in possession of the Metland Egg.

And Celie was not beautiful. While her family had grown big and strong on her spoils, Celie at thirteen was still not five feet tall, and as narrow as a stalk of wheat. Her skin was still pale, her hair still white, her limbs still like twigs.

No matter. By the time people had walked a mile along a narrow track and encountered an endless procession of dirty farm boys and grizzled labourers with cigarettes gripped in their yellowed teeth, Celie Sheppard appeared quite luminous, and each year there was an increasing number of boys clamouring for her mark in their books, or who brought her flowers and shells and trinkets.

It had all the qualities of a pilgrimage – although one where the object of worship was neither bones in a box nor a holy robe, but a slip of a girl and an egg.

Those lucky enough, or knowing enough, to time it just right would cluster at the edge of the overhang and watch Robert lower Celie over the cliff. Always there was a sharp intake of breath as she let go of the sides and dropped through the crack, causing Robert to brace and sometimes skid a little as he dug into his heelings. There was never any real danger, of course, for Robert was now a strapping lad, who could have dangled three Celies off the cliff without strain. But even he had come to recognize that this had become a show, in which he had his part to play.

And then came the wait – maybe two minutes – while the rope twitched and creaked and turned, and then suddenly vibrated as Celie slapped it to let Robert know that she was ready to return from the underworld with her prize.

Collective breath was held while Robert wound the unseen girl in, gathering the slack and looping it around himself, always keeping tension on the rope, as he and Celie each moved closer and closer to the fissure in the overhang, until finally a hand appeared in the split, and then a second, and then the white hair whipping upwards, so that as she emerged it seemed almost as if Celie were being blown up through the rock by the wind itself.

She always rested for a moment on her elbows, waist deep in cliff, while the crowd always broke into a ripple of spontaneous applause.

It was then – in a move he had perfected over the years – that George Ambler liked to step forward and hold up his hand for silence.

This was not what they had come for, his hand seemed to say.

The girl was safe, certainly.

But what about the egg?

Ambler would then walk towards the edge of the overhang,

while Celie twisted sideways, straightened her arms, and pulled the rest of herself up through the crack and on to the great slab. There Ambler always took her arm and helped her to her feet, as though she couldn't have done any of it without him.

Then, in a moment of pure theatre, he would plunge his hand into Celie's leather satchel, and raise the Metland Egg in triumph.

To cheers and wild applause, of course.

It was this scene that George Ambler always thought of whenever he thought of the precious eggs. This spotlight. This adoration. For in Ambler's mind he was the hero of the hour – of *every* hour – and deservedly so.

This very public event was the extent of the common man's involvement with the Metland Egg. Once it was over, none of those participating in its harvest or the witnessing thereof ever saw the egg again.

The beautiful jewel was immediately blown, wiped clean, and placed in a sheepskin-lined wooden box, which Ambler entrusted to a steady young fellow named William Slack. Then Ambler, followed by the obedient Slack, would stride back to Bempton with his prize, cutting a swathe through the ardent tourists, touching his hat to any pretty lady, and swishing his cane ahead of him now and then, to clear boys or dogs from his path.

In his wake he left hundreds of people speculating as to *who* might soon possess the famous egg, and at what possible price.

Robert unknotted the rope and helped Celie out of the apron.

She was more practised now, of course, but his hand always hovered close in case it was needed to steady her, for she was still an easy target for any gust of wind.

The rope was the same good one that had been left in the barn (by Mr Chandler, they always presumed) all those years ago. It was not subject to the same stresses and strains as were the ropes of the other gangs. Instead of four clims a day, it was only required for two clims a year, each just a short drop, and with a girl at the end of it who weighed less than a small sack of flour.

The apron was the same one too. They had tried other things, but Celie liked the way she sat deep in the old leather and it wrapped closely around her. It would be hard to fall out of the apron. And so Robert had spent many hours checking it and trimming it and softening it up with dubbin to make it more comfortable for her.

The satchel was new – provided by Ambler after he had woken sweating from a nightmare of the Metland Egg smashing against the rock as Celie clambered through the crack. The satchel was of stiff leather, and custom-lined with sheepskin to hold the treasure in suspension, so as to cushion it from any bump or knock.

Once Celie was relieved of the prize, the tourists crowded around to pat her back or her head – always thinking her much younger than she was – and the boys held out their books and pencils and gave her their tokens. She thanked them and carefully wrote her name, *Celie*, in their books and put their gifts in the satchel. Any overflow she handed to Robert to carry home in his pockets. Mostly the tokens were flowers or seashells, but sometimes they were sweets, and on this occasion – this seventh year – Celie and Robert walked back through the mallow and then across the hayfield to home with their mouths distorted by Bridlington rock and blackened by liquorice.

After Ambler was gone and Celie was gone and Robert was gone and the boys were gone and the tourists were gone, all that would be left to show for the miraculous event for another year was a lot of flattened grass.

And a tiny puddle of yolk.

Knickers

Patrick woke up with a twitch, and realized he'd been asleep.
He had no idea how far they'd gone, but his knees and back were protesting, and he wanted to pee.

It was dark now, and the car radio was playing something loud and metallic.

At least his breathing wouldn't give him away.

But what *would* give him away, if Garrett looked behind him, was the man-sized green tartan lump behind the driving seat.

Patrick almost laughed. He clamped a hand over his mouth to keep it in, but for some horrible reason, that made him want to laugh even more. It was agony. Terror and hilarity melded within him, making his throat ache and his eyes stream.

It was the rug's fault. The very idea that it might hide him. Why had he bothered? He tucked even more tightly into a ball and pressed his forehead to the dirty black carpet.

He thought of Finn Garrett swinging the sledgehammer and Matthew Barr's wailing . . . and so slowly willed himself away from hysteria and back to serious silence.

He wondered how far they had come and what Weird Nick was doing now.

He wondered where they were going and what would happen when they got there.

He tried to stretch little parts of himself without really moving.

He needed to pee. He tried to ignore it – to will his bladder into numbness – but it didn't work.

With great caution, Patrick poked his head out from under the blanket. If the worst came to the worst, maybe there was a bottle he could use.

Something.

Anything.

He raised his head a little and looked up towards Garrett. The headrest was broad with bolstered sides that blocked a good deal of the man's peripheral vision. In the dark, Patrick felt dangerously safe.

He turned to the back seat. There was a small first-aid kit and some RSPB leaflets.

Nothing useful.

There were elasticated pockets on the backs of the front seats. Weird Nick's mother used to keep little waxed bags in those pockets in her car, in case Nick got car sick on a long journey, which he often had. Patrick remembered a trip to Barry Island which had ended in a splatter of warm strawberry ice cream.

A waxed bag would be better than nothing.

Gently, Patrick reached into the pocket beside him.

Nothing.

He'd have to try the one on the passenger seat.

Patrick tried to gauge the angles between Finn Garrett's limited peripheral vision and the rear-view mirror, and the gap between the two front seats. Should he go fast or slow? Risk giving himself away by a sudden movement? Or increase his exposure time?

He realized he didn't have enough information to determine what Garrett might or might not see. But he still had to find something to pee in.

Very slowly, Patrick reached out and slid his hand into the pocket.

There was a can of de-icer.

There was a window hammer with a machined steel point.

And right at the bottom there was a pair of black knickers.

Patrick flicked them into the footwell in disgust, then held his breath again in case Garrett had caught the movement, but nothing changed.

Then Patrick thought of something. Soundlessly he slid the first-aid kit off the back seat and – under cover of the rug – unzipped it.

Inside were some blue latex gloves.

Like old friends.

One of those would have to do. He put it to his lips to blow into it.

Suddenly the car braked, stopped, then reversed in an arc, and stopped again.

Finn Garrett was parking.

Patrick tucked back into a ball and clutched the blanket around him like a scared child under the bedclothes. The car jiggled, then rose slightly as Garrett got out and slammed the door.

Patrick heard him walk away.

For good?

He wasn't sure, but he had to take the chance and get out *now*.

He twisted himself around and opened the door, then slid backwards out of the car and on to a pavement, staying low. It had been raining here, and Patrick's socks were immediately wet. He looked around. Garrett's car was one of many parked down either side of a street flanked on both sides by low, terraced houses and little shops.

Garrett himself was nowhere to be seen.

Patrick yanked the tartan rug off his shoulders and tossed it on the back seat. He started to shut the door, then hesitated. Quickly he leaned in and folded the rug and put it back where he'd found it. Likewise the first-aid kit. After a brief internal struggle he even leaned all the way across to the other footwell to pick up the knickers—

Then his world turned upside down.

One minute Patrick was leaning into the footwell, the next someone grabbed him by the back of his T-shirt and he banged his head on the door frame and saw stars, then sky and roofs and streetlights and finally the kerb against his cheek. He came to rest on his back in the gutter, where rainwater rushed around him as it hurried to a nearby drain.

Finn Garrett crouched over him, one hand on Patrick's heaving chest, the other brandishing a pint of semi-skimmed milk.

'What the fuck are you doing?'

Patrick's mind spiralled in shock.

What the *fuck* are you doing?

What the fuck are *you* doing?

What the fuck are you *doing*?

It was a good question, so Patrick felt compelled to answer, but right now he wasn't sure what the fuck he *was* doing. And which answer did Finn Garrett want to hear? Which answer would make him take his weight off Patrick's chest and put the milk bottle down? It was plastic, but it would still hurt.

Garrett shook the milk at him angrily. Still wanted his answer. 'What the fuck are you doing in my car?'

'Tidying up,' croaked Patrick.

'What the . . . ?' Finn Garrett dropped the milk and hauled Patrick out of the gutter and on to the pavement, then briefly, flailingly, to his feet. Then he shoved him backwards so that he was sitting on the back seat of the car with his socks in the gurgling gutter.

Finn Garrett wasn't a big man, but Patrick was astonished by how strong he was. Now he stood over him, blocking any escape.

'You're Matthew Barr's mate.'

'No, I'm not.'

'Don't lie to me. You were at his house. Earlier.'

'Yes, but I'm not his mate.'

'Why are you following me?'

'I'm not following you.'

'Then why are you here?'

'I was in your car,' said Patrick.

'*What?*'

'I was in the back. Under the rug.'

There was a long, confused silence, then Garrett folded his arms. 'Right. Start again. From the beginning.'

'The beginning?' Patrick squinted up at him. How far back did the man want him to go?

The tartan rug?

The Big Bang?

Patrick wished people would be more specific.

Luckily Garrett got more specific. 'What were you doing at Matthew Barr's?'

'We went there about an egg.'

'What egg?'

'My friend had an old egg in a fancy wooden box. Two men broke into his house and stole it, and we went there to see if Matthew Barr knew how to get it back.'

'So you're collectors.'

'No. Nick just found the egg in his attic.'

'Still, you know it's illegal to possess wild birds' eggs?'

'Well, we do *now*. But he wanted to know why anyone would want to steal it, so we went to the museum to see if Dr Connor could help, but he couldn't so we thought maybe Matthew Barr could.'

'And could he?'

'Not really. Mostly he talked about *his* eggs.'

Garrett barked a short, ugly laugh. 'You know why that is?'

Patrick shook his head.

'Because he's bloody mental,' said Garrett roughly, tapping a finger on his own head. 'Like the rest of those egg fetishists. Batshit crazy. You saw his house. Cardboard on the floor. All that money spent on fancy cabinets and he's living in a slum. Smashing his eggs won't stop him. Smashing his *legs* wouldn't stop him. Doesn't care about food or clothes or his own bloody family. All he cares about is eggs. It's an obsession. He can't help it. He's sick. They're all the same, these collectors. They're *sick*. And now that his eggs are gone, he'll just start again. Mark my words. I've been in this game a long time now and I know how these bastards think.'

Garrett leaned closer and closer to Patrick, who wished he could back away, but he had nowhere to go.

'And as for *Doctor* Connor? He's the worst of the lot! Sitting there on the biggest pile of eggs on the whole planet and he still goes crying to the courts to give him more!'

'But . . .' said Patrick warily, 'what about the science?'

'Science, my arse! You really think it's about the *science*? It's because he's a greedy little shit. He's got a million eggs in that building and still wants more – not because more is better, but because more is *more*. And they give him taxpayers' money to do it! That's why I fight him so hard. Because people like Connor make people like Barr think it's OK to keep killing birds and stealing eggs. They're as bad as each other. The only difference is Connor does his collecting in a suit and tie, and not his fucking underpants!'

Patrick laughed and Garrett looked surprised, then half smiled.

Patrick was taken aback.

Confused.

Smiling was good. Meg was always telling him to smile more so that people would understand he was a good, kind person. He made the effort when he was with her, but couldn't be bothered to think about it at other times. Still, Meg was always right about everything, so did this mean he was wrong about Finn Garrett? If *Garrett* was a good, kind person, then maybe *he* could help them.

Patrick took a deep, cautious breath . . .

'Have you heard about the Metland Egg?'

Garrett looked at him sharply. 'What about it?'

'Matthew Barr said the egg my friend found looked like the Metland Egg.'

Garrett snorted. 'How would *he* know? Nobody alive has ever seen it.'

'But you've heard of it?'

'Everybody's heard of it.'

'I hadn't heard of it.'

Garrett shrugged. 'Everybody who knows eggs.'

'Oh,' nodded Patrick. 'Matthew Barr said it was the greatest mystery in egg history.'

Garrett pursed his lips. 'It was the greatest *crime* in egg history, that's for bloody sure.'

'You mean George Ambler's murder?'

Garrett snorted. 'I'm talking about the crime of somebody stealing every egg that a bird ever laid. I'm talking about a bird dying without ever raising a chick. You tell me a worse crime than that.'

'*Every* egg?' Patrick was confused. 'How many eggs were there?'

'They say there were thirty.'

Patrick felt a shiver run up the back of his neck.

'*Thirty?*'

Out of nowhere, he wanted to cry. He thought of Meg, and wished she were here so he could share this feeling with her.

'Exactly,' said Garrett roughly. 'You steal thirty eggs from a bird? That's not about science, that's a war.'

'What kind of war?' asked Patrick.

Garrett shrugged. 'The kind *all* wars are about – greedy people wanting more than they need and taking it from the weak and the vulnerable. Selfish arseholes stealing the beauty from the world that belongs to all of us.'

Patrick nodded slowly. That did seem unfair.

'And Connor knows about your friend and his egg in the fancy wooden box?'

'Yes.'

Garrett pulled a face Patrick didn't understand. The man glanced up and down the road as if someone might be approaching, then fixed Patrick with a piercing stare.

'I'm warning you, don't get involved.'

'Why?'

'Because it might be an old, forgotten war,' said Garrett grimly, 'but people still get hurt. Some still get killed.'

Patrick nodded. 'OK.'

Garrett bent and picked up his milk. 'Where are your shoes?'

Patrick looked at his feet. They were so cold he'd forgotten they were there. 'Newmarket.'

'Fuck's sake,' Garrett sighed. 'Get in the car and I'll take you back.'

Patrick hesitated, but he was cold and wet and it was night and he didn't know where he was. He was in his socks. He really had no other option. And something in Garrett's manner had changed since he'd mentioned the Metland Egg. He was still angry, but Patrick didn't think it was with *him*.

'OK,' he said, and pulled his wet feet into the car.

Garrett closed the door on him surprisingly gently, then walked around and got behind the wheel and started the engine. 'Wrap your feet in the rug.'

'OK.'

Patrick reached for the rug. As Garrett manoeuvred into the road the streetlamps illuminated the interior of the car and Patrick noticed the knickers, still in the footwell where he'd dropped them. He reached over to put them back in the seat pocket.

But even as he did, his brain was rearranging them, re-evaluating their shape. Carefully he picked them up and – as they passed slowly under another streetlight he could see more clearly—

Panic rippled through him.

They were not knickers.

They were a balaclava.

Patrick threw himself against the door and fell out of the car. He hit the ground and rolled; grazed his knees and his palms; banged his head.

Brakes squealed and there was a long grinding sound as the tyres scraped the tarmac.

Patrick staggered upright and ran down the road in the rain, in his socks and with the balaclava clutched in his fist. Dodging cars, turning down side streets, across verges, through gates. So filled with adrenaline that he couldn't even feel his feet.

Until suddenly they were *all* he could feel.

He slowed then, and limped into a shop doorway and took out his phone and called Nick.

'Where the hell are you?' his friend answered.

'I don't know,' Patrick panted, 'but I think Finn Garrett stole your egg.'

The Visitor

Metland Farm had prospered as much as thirty acres occupied by a fatherless family possibly could.

John Sheppard had been a hard worker, but a harder man, and eventually Celie's siblings realized that it was not their father they had missed as much as the security a father had embodied. Once that security was restored by the Metland Egg their attitude to Celie thawed – although her relationship with them was never like the one she had with Robert.

He was a young man now, and his part in the Sheppard family's improved fortunes did not go unappreciated, or unrewarded. Enid put his money up so that he was earning what he should – although he still failed to spend it on very much other than soap and razor blades, and so asked her to keep it for him, which she did in an old flour tin on the top shelf of the pantry.

Robert continued to be a mainstay on the farm, but it was his twice-yearly labour on the overhang that had made the difference to his adopted kin.

Twenty pounds for each egg. There had been no further hampers after the first, but forty pounds a year before a lamb dropped or a bale of hay had been stacked in the barn was a comfortable cushion, and Enid spent it wisely. Year on year there was money for wheat as well as hay, for another pig and three more ewes, and for a dozen hens that laid enough eggs to sell and so that at least once a week they all ate omelette.

As each Sheppard boy had left school, his labour on the farm increased yields for no greater cost than his room and board.

After a few years Enid even saved enough money to pay an officer of the court to investigate the possible whereabouts of John Sheppard – who had never so much as written a letter. That officer traced him to a boarding house in London where the owner said he had gone to the Dog and Duck in Wandsworth one night and failed to return. The police had no record of his body being found but, given he had left behind his few possessions, his absence – from the room, from London, and from life – was deemed to be permanent. As soon as was legally possible, Enid had her husband declared dead, and by the time her youngest child was fourteen, Enid could call herself a widow, which elevated her a little in the eyes of the community.

Ever so little.

But every little helps, and that, combined with George Ambler's contract, made life at Metland Farm far happier.

Now Enid was never late with the rent.

Indeed, so prompt and fulsome were her payments that even Mr Bastard grew grudgingly polite.

And yet Mr Constable wrote with increasing regularity.

'Is the man never happy?' asked Will irritably. He had been stirred up by the lads at the Cock talking of the Communists fighting in Spain, and was disinclined to feel favourably towards any perceived oppressor.

'His wife is sick,' said his mother.

Will didn't see how that meant Mr Constable must write more often – and to his mother – but he was not an imaginative young man.

*

When Celie was sixteen, Mrs Constable died – as had long been expected. They all said prayers for the landlord and his wife in church on the Sunday, but Celie was the only one who cried.

Shortly thereafter, Mr Constable's letter suddenly announced that he would be coming for his rent in person.

This created a flurry. More than a flurry – it created such preparations that they became an event in themselves.

Enid absented herself from the pigsty and the fields for almost a week. Instead she walked to Bempton and caught the new bus to Bridlington and bought enough white cotton to make shirts for all the boys – even Robert – and new smocks and aprons for Molly and Celie. Once those were made and folded away, she set them all to cleaning the yard, then the barn and finally the house – and woe betide anyone who walked into it in shoes or with dirty hands.

Only the slurry pit behind the barn defeated Enid's attentions. Slurry was slurry, and there was nothing that could pretty it up, or keep it from stinking. She would have grown a hedge to hide it, if she'd only had the time.

On the day of the Great Visit, the Sheppards were washed and brushed to within an inch of their collective lives, and dressed in their new shirts and smocks, and ordered not to move or touch a thing, fully an hour before the landlord was due.

Will grumbled about the oppression of the working man and the iniquity of it all, but did not dare to refuse to get dressed.

Robert pulled on his new hand-stitched shirt with great care, and thereafter didn't like to move – or even sit down – for fear it might get a spot on it, or a wisp of hay. So much so that later he was discovered to have stood in the barn by himself for the entire duration of the landlord's visit, and missed the whole thing.

Enid herself spent that final hour in her room, and when she came downstairs she was nigh-on unrecognizable to her own children. She wore a dress they had never seen – for there had never been any use for its frills on the farm, and it was too fancy for church – and with her hair washed and curled and gathered into a pile on her head.

'So pretty, Ma!' cried Molly.

She was right. The family's change in fortunes had been kind to Enid. She was less tired, and the little plumpness that had crept back to her cheeks made her look younger than she had a decade before, while her figure had remained as willowy as a girl's.

They all sat at the table, which was laden with food they were not allowed to eat, until their stomachs squealed in protest and Stanley threatened a mutiny.

But just then there was the sound of an engine that was not a tractor, and in an orderly fashion they followed their mother into the yard to pay their respects to the great man who owned the very roof over their heads.

The car was grand – enormous and shiny, with maroon wheels and a chrome angel on its long black bonnet.

A young man in grey jodhpurs and a peaked cap got out as though about to deliver a telegram. But instead he strode around the angel and opened the back passenger door with a flourish, to allow his master to alight.

The Sheppards held their collective breath. So far, the much-trumpeted visit of the landlord was turning out to be worth every stitch on the shirts and smocks, and every minute they had all spent scrubbing. Molly thought the chauffeur alone was worth it, and even Will was on tenterhooks.

The oppressor of the working man got out of the car, and took off his hat.

The collective slump of disappointment was palpable.

Will actually snorted.

Mr Constable was very short and very thin. He wore a tight

collar and wire spectacles that made his ears fold down comically.

His hair and brows and moustache were all pure white, which made him look much older than his fifty years. His clothes were expensively tailored and yet looked like nothing on him – so ordinary were they made by his lack of either stature or presence.

Indeed, Mr Constable would have been unremarkable in every possible regard were it not for his eyes, which were bright and cheerful.

And the palest, palest blue.

The Drive Home

'**D**id you bring my shoes?'

Weird Nick rolled his eyes. 'Hello to you too, mate!'

'Hello. Did you bring my shoes?'

'They're in the back,' said Nick. 'Get in.'

Patrick got into the Fiesta and peeled off what was left of his socks.

'So what the hell happened to you?'

'My feet are cold,' Patrick said. 'Can you put the heater on?'

Nick obliged.

'Where are we?' said Patrick.

'Somewhere near Cambridge.' Nick swung back into the road.

'What time is it?' said Patrick. 'What about your mum's work?'

'Too late now. Don't panic. I called her and said we were in a little accident and having to get the car fixed, so play along.'

'Why?' Patrick hated lying. The truth was so much easier to remember. He could barely look Weird Nick's mother in the eye at the best of times. *Mrs Morgan.* He knew that now from the lanyard Dr Connor had given to Nick.

Nick Morgan and his mother. Mrs Morgan.

Jen Morgan.

Jennifer.

Patrick shuddered. It was all too *familiar.* He thought he would stick with nothing.

'Well,' Nick was saying, 'I don't want her thinking we were late because we're just off having a good time.'

'But we're *not* having a good time,' Patrick pointed out.

'Yeah, but she doesn't know that. Trust me, my way is better.'

Patrick thought that was unlikely.

'You might have to pay for the taxi,' Nick added.

'Why?'

'I told her you were driving.'

Patrick opened his mouth.

'Anyway,' said Nick, before he could say anything, 'what's this about Finn Garrett stealing my egg?'

Patrick dug in his jeans pocket. 'I found this in his car.'

Nick frowned. 'Knickers?'

Patrick pulled it over his head.

'A ski mask!' Nick swerved back into his lane. 'Oh my God! The RNLI stole my egg!'

'RSPB,' said Patrick, pulling off the balaclava.

'Sonofabitch!' Nick spluttered furiously. 'They're supposed to be these . . . these . . . charitable . . . old . . . naturists! But now we find out they're a bunch of paramilitary venge-warriors running round committing armed robbery! We have to call the RS . . .'

'PB,' Patrick helped out.

'PB,' nodded Nick, 'and get this nutcase fired! What the hell were you doing in his car?'

'He was going to give me a ride back to Newmarket. But then I found this, so I jumped out and ran away and hid and called you.'

'But! What! Why were you—'

Then Nick stopped himself, took a deep breath and said, 'Start from the beginning.'

Patrick rolled his eyes. '*Which* beginning?'

'From Newmarket.'

So Patrick did.

He wasn't used to speaking for long periods without a break, but Nick was an encouraging audience. He laughed about the tartan rug, then made a face at the idea of peeing in a glove, then widened his eyes and said *fuuuck* very slowly when Garrett grabbed Patrick and threw him in the rainy gutter and threatened him with a pint of semi-skimmed.

'Chris was right about him,' Nick said sombrely. 'He *said* he was crazy.'

'He said he was a philistine.'

'Same difference,' said Nick. 'The man's a maniac. I swear, when he and Eggman broke into my house I thought they were going to kill me. And you should have seen him at Matthew Barr's house. He made kindling out of those fancy cabinets and enjoyed doing it. Even I could hardly watch and I don't even give a shit about eggs. Or furniture! And Matthew Barr . . . Poor bloke was a-weeping and a-wailing so hard that afterwards he couldn't even speak. He went kind of *loony*. Seriously. All curled up with his head in his hands. I didn't know *what* the hell to do.'

'What *did* you do?' asked Patrick.

Nick shrugged. 'I just grabbed your shitty shoes and legged it.'

Patrick reached into the back of the car and retrieved the bag containing his shoes. He began to undo the knot in the handles.

'Don't!' shouted Nick. 'Put them in the freezer when you get home. It's easier to get the shit out.'

'Yeah,' said Patrick. 'My mother doesn't like it when I do that.'

'Fair enough,' said Nick.

They turned on to the A14 and headed west.

'Are you going to go to the police about Garrett?' Patrick asked.

'You bet I am! You finding that balaclava is *dynamite*. I mean he's supposed to be protecting birds, not wearing balaclavas and stealing eggs.'

'What if the police arrest you for having a wild bird's egg?'

Nick frowned. 'I'll work around that.'

'Garrett said it was a war,' said Patrick. 'He told me not to get involved because people get killed.'

'He threatened to *kill* you?'

Patrick was surprised. 'Did he?'

'Sounds like it to me!'

'OK.'

'And a war between *who*?'

'He didn't say.'

'Between . . . collectors and . . . *anti*-collectors probably,' said Nick. 'Or maybe even between collectors and *other* collectors!'

Patrick nodded. 'It is starting to feel like they're all the same. Garrett said Dr Connor's just as bad as Matthew Barr. Except he collects eggs in a suit and tie and not his fucking underpants.'

Nick laughed and then shook his head. 'Everybody wants something.'

'What do you mean?'

'Just that nobody does anything for no reason. They always want something in return.'

Patrick thought about that. 'You mean like the time I asked Meg to take photos of a cadaver, but in return she wanted me to read to a coma patient?'

Nick gave him a weird look. 'Well, that's not a typical example, but I suppose so, yes. I mean, Garrett can say what he wants about Dr Connor, but *he's* the one who stole my egg!'

'He knew all about it too.'

'All about what?'

'The Metland Egg.'

'Of course he did!' Nick frowned. 'That's why he took it! I swear, this is just bloody *typical*! I find a . . . an egg that's worth a fortune. And before I can make a bit of cash out of it, some eco-arsehole breaks in, steals it and smashes it to smithereens!'

'You don't *know* that's what happened.'

'Oh, come on! If you didn't think Garrett stole my egg when you found that balaclava, you wouldn't have jumped out of a moving car.'

Patrick nodded. 'True.'

'And you saw what Garrett did to Matthew Barr's collection,' said Nick mournfully. 'If he took my egg, it's gone for good.'

'Maybe not,' said Patrick. 'He smashed those eggs right in front of Barr. Why not do the same to yours?'

Nick frowned and then brightened. 'You're right. We could still find it in one piece!'

'Garrett said there were thirty Metland Eggs,' said Patrick.

'*What?*' Nick rolled his eyes. 'Great. Now we have to find *thirty* mythical eggs instead of one.'

'They were all taken from one bird,' Patrick went on. 'This was way back before the Second World War, but Garrett's still really angry about it.'

'Angry enough to steal my egg?'

Patrick thought about the sledgehammer arcing through the sky, and the view from the wet gutter of Finn Garrett's face, and that weird, primal fear he felt around the man that had forced him to run from him *twice* in one day.

'Definitely,' he nodded.

'Jeez,' said Nick, 'who knew the world of eggs was so cut-throat! Just as well you got out of that car, or you could be dead in a ditch by now.'

Patrick wondered if that were true. Stealing birds' eggs and murder were two very different things.

Weren't they?

'George Ambler was murdered,' he said.

'How do you know?'

'Dr Connor said.'

Nick shook his head in amazement. 'See what I mean? Bunch of nutters. We could *both* be dead in a ditch.'

Patrick frowned into the night. 'What did they say?'

'Who?'

'The men who stole your egg. What did they say to you?'

Nick shook his head ruefully. 'Mate, it all happened so fast . . .'

He was quiet for so long that Patrick nearly dozed off. His feet were so warm now . . .

'I was playing *Call of Duty* and they just came in and grabbed me. They threw me on the floor and my glasses fell off . . .

'And then they tied my hands . . .'

Nick stopped talking, and swallowed hard and looked at the black road ahead. When he finally continued, it was in a much smaller voice. 'I thought they were going to kill me, you know? And I just kept thinking . . . *Have they already killed Mum?*'

He stopped again and wiped his nose on his sleeve.

'But what did they *say*?' said Patrick impatiently.

'Shit, I don't know, mate! Gimme a minute here!'

'OK,' said Patrick. He watched the dashboard clock.

Waited a minute.

'What did they say?'

'Bloody hell,' sighed Nick. 'They just said *Where's the egg?* and *We know you've got it*, and it was right on my desk anyway, so it was all over pretty quickly.'

Patrick got a weird little electric feeling in his chest, like the hum of a rail when an important thought was coming down the line.

'They said *Where's the egg*. Not *Where are the eggs*?'

Nick thought about it and then nodded. 'Yes.'

'It sounds like they only expected to find one egg.'

Nick sniffed. 'Yeah. So what?'

'So,' said Patrick, warming to the idea, 'remember Dr Connor said collectors are completists? No egg left behind.'

'What about it?'

'Well, *if* your egg *was* one of thirty Metland Eggs . . .'

'Yeah?' Nick nodded encouragingly.

'And *if* the robbers knew you only had one . . .'

He stopped again to think and Nick waited with barely concealed impatience while Patrick struggled to connect the dots in his mind – the eternally murky dots of what people *said* versus what people *meant*. He knew he was on the right track; he could *feel* the amorphous excitement of it. There were bits of it that he knew were still out of reach, but there was something else that was close by – something within his grasp – if he just worked *hard* enough . . .

'Then,' he started again slowly, 'doesn't that mean that . . . whoever took your egg—'

'Already has the other twenty-nine!' Nick finished triumphantly. He clapped Patrick on the shoulder and grinned. 'Mate! You're a genius!'

Patrick shrugged. He didn't answer pointless statements.

Misery

Less than three months after Mr Constable came to collect his rent in person for the first time, he and Enid Sheppard were quietly married at the registry office in Scarborough.

The church would not have them, of course – thus depriving the parishioners of Bempton of the thrill of seeing Enid Sheppard marry the man who had so obviously fathered her bastard child. Naturally, nothing of the sort was ever *confirmed*, but that was no impediment to gossip.

Celie had often been confused by the disapproving looks and sly mutters she noticed in church and in school. It was only a month later, when she and Molly joined their mother at Mr Constable's home in Scarborough, that the big mirror in the hallway showed her what others had long seen.

Celie at nearly seventeen looked very much the way she had done the last time she'd stared into this mirror. She was a few inches taller and wore a better dress, but that was all that had really changed. Her shape, her white hair, her pearly skin and her ice-blue eyes were all as they had been.

But now that she knew Mr Constable, the resemblance was unmistakeable.

I look like him!

It was a cheerful idea to Celie, and it made her smile, but she was far too unworldly to think it anything other than just a happy coincidence. She understood that some people looked like other people. Molly looked like her mother, for instance, and Will and Martin and Stanley looked like each other. And now she looked like somebody too! The resulting kinship she felt with her new stepfather was quite divorced from any idea of *actual* kinship with an *actual* father. To her, it was just a lucky accident.

And while the connection between Celie and Mr Constable may not have been accidental, it certainly did turn out to be lucky. Mr Constable was kindness itself, and at pains to make them all feel at home. They ate food that Celie had never imagined existed – veal and scallops and blancmange, all served by the same kind maid who had brought her the doll cup a decade before. She had her own room – nearly as big as the barn! – with two tall windows and broad sills covered by golden silk cushions, where she could sit and look over the shady park where ladies walked their dogs while nannies walked the ladies' children.

She and Molly were given an outrageous allowance. A pound a week, for which they were expected to do nothing whatsoever.

Enid bought them all new clothes. Clothes that fitted and had never yet been mended. Molly was in raptures, and Mr Constable made much of how fine they looked, and even employed a photographer to take pictures of them all.

In Scarborough, every day was an excitement, and the months passed in a blur of shopping and society.

But after a short while, Celie began to be seized by inexplicable attacks of melancholy.

She was surprised by her tears and her sadness, and felt very ungrateful, but the longer she was in Scarborough, the more frequently she pined, and finally the bouts of melancholy spread like spilled milk, until they all joined up.

Then all pleasure leached from her life, and all she did was pine.

She pined for the big skies. For the chickens and their hot eggs.

For the pigs rolling in their own shit. She pined for the smell of the barn and the hay, and even of the pungent cliffs and the violent wind.

But really Celie pined for Robert.

Robert the idiot.

Robert who slept in the barn and ate with the dog.

Robert's silence.

There had never been a day in her life when Celie Sheppard had been without Robert, and now that she was never with him, she felt utterly alone.

She could not say so, of course. Could not tell her mother that this was why she drooped listlessly around the house, or always had a headache right before a party, or spent days in her beautiful bedroom, weeping on her golden cushions.

Her own misery left her confused and sometimes infuriated.

Why would she think of Robert now that they were apart, when she had never thought of him when they were always together?

Of course, she had not *had* to think of him then, because Robert was never more than a glance away – Celie had only had to look out of the window to see him repairing the fence, or cleaning out the chicken coop, or wheeling slurry behind the barn. Or just sitting on a bale, his face turned to the sun and with one hand on the head of the dog.

But now that Celie's gaze fell only on fine dresses and strangers, she found Robert in her thoughts, even when she didn't want him there, chipping away at her newfound pleasures.

She often dreamed of him.

It was always the same dream – that they were on the overhang and Mr Ambler had left with the egg, but there were no crowds, no clamouring boys. Just the two of them and the birds swirling below them and the purple mallow scenting the air.

Sometimes it was dusk and sometimes dawn and sometimes it was in bright midday sunshine. That changed – but one thing never did . . .

As she stepped out of the apron, Robert always took her arm.

Then Celie would wake up with a gasp and lie in the soft feather-bed darkness, so close to the dream that her arm could still feel his warmth.

It was so *real* – his rough brown hand on her bicep. The feeling of him steadying her. Of surrendering herself to his care. Of safety.

Only as her skin cooled did the sadness creep in.

Robert *used* to hold her arm, she was sure of that.

When had he stopped?

And why?

Did he no longer care for her?

And at that thought, tears would spill from the corners of Celie Sheppard's pale blue eyes and run into her ears and on to her embroidered linen pillowcase, until finally her misery would exhaust her, and she would sleep until morning and wake feeling even sadder than she had the day before.

When Enid asked her what was wrong, she admitted only that she felt tired, and then for penance had to endure a visit from a doctor with the coldest hands and the bitterest tonics.

When Mr Constable – prodded by his wife – tentatively asked whether Celie was happy in Scarborough, she told him how grateful she was for the big room and the golden cushions and the pound a week.

And when he said that he could provide anything she desired – if only it would make her happy – she said she couldn't think of a single thing more.

But she never mentioned Robert.

To anyone.

Of course she didn't. For who would understand it, when she did not understand it herself?

Celie took the first opportunity she could to return to Metland Farm when her mother and Mr Constable went there to inspect improvements that were being made.

There was a happy reunion with Will and Martin and Stanley, and no little teasing about her new dress. The sky was big and the hay just mown and there were warm eggs to be collected from the chicken coop.

All the time Celie kept looking around excitedly for Robert, but when he finally emerged from the field with a bag of oats, Celie found herself mute.

She was appalled to find that while she had been away, Robert had become a man – which made her feel that running through the hay or chasing piglets were no longer appropriate things to share. What might be appropriate in their stead, she had no idea, and her mind whirled with confusion.

Miserably, she trailed the little group as Mr and Mrs Constable were shown the new tractor and the new baler, and the repairs to the farmhouse windows. There was so much to see and to say, and yet Celie could find nothing to say to anyone, or about anything, that did not seem foolish or dull.

Robert still did not speak much, but when he did speak to Mr Constable or to her mother, Celie noticed that he said grown-up things. And, what was more, they spoke to him the same way – all respect and business, as though he were close to an equal and not *the idiot* or *the boy*. It seemed that their months apart had wrought in them all some mysterious change that meant they were now different people.

She hated it.

Robert did not talk to her the same way as he had when they last met. He seemed oddly formal, and did not use her name. He did not even *look* at her the same way. Their former childish ease with one another was gone, and Celie had no idea how – or even if – it could be recaptured.

All the time they looked around the farm, she kept noticing Robert's hands, and remembering the dry warmth of them in her dreams. It made her blush, but she wasn't sure *why*, which only made her inexplicably cross – with herself and with the whole world, including the dirty farm, the smelly chickens and the accursed big sky, none of which did a single thing to soothe her troubled mind.

The feeling of something beautiful having been lost was overwhelming.

And when Robert touched his cap to her as they climbed back into the car, Celie turned her face from him as if he were a beggar on the street.

All the way to Scarborough her throat burned with unshed tears.

Want

Private Patrick Fort kept getting killed. First by a sniper, then by a landmine, then by another sniper.

His body was destroyed, but his mind was elsewhere, circling a well-worn path.

What do people mean?

What do people want?

Too late he saw a soldier with a bazooka, and the screen dripped red. He didn't care, but he knew Weird Nick would, so he turned off the Xbox without saving the game.

Nick came in, tossed his phone on his bed and threw himself down on the beanbag. 'Bloody cops won't do a thing about it.'

'Why?'

'Because they don't believe us, that's why.'

'But why?'

'How should I know?'

'Did you tell them everything?'

'Of course not.'

'That's probably why,' said Patrick.

'I told them enough,' said Nick. 'They said there was no hard evidence linking Garrett to the robbery.'

'But what about the balaclava?'

Nick snorted. 'They said it's not a crime to own a balaclava.'

'But if you'd told them about the Metland Egg—'

'Forget it, all right?' said Nick irritably. 'Let's just— What happened to the game?'

'It went off,' said Patrick vaguely.

'Fuck's sake!' said Nick. 'I was about to level up!'

Nick turned the Xbox back on and they waited for it to reload.

'What do you think John du Pont wanted?' said Patrick.

'You what?'

'You said everybody wants something.'

'Did I?'

'Yes. So what did John du Pont *want*?'

'Guillemot eggs.'

'But Dr Connor said guillemot eggs were not rare, and have no great value.'

'So?'

'So why would one of the richest men in the world come all the way to England in person to buy something that had no great value?'

Nick frowned at him. 'What's brought *this* on?'

'I'm always thinking about what people *say* and what they *mean*. But then when you said everybody *wants* something, I started thinking about that too. And I thought, what did John du Pont want?'

'I don't know,' shrugged Nick. 'What do you think he wanted?'

Patrick spoke thoughtfully. 'The best. The best wrestlers, the best stamps . . . the best eggs.'

'So?'

'So what if du Pont believed that the Metland Eggs were still in Ambler's collection when he died? Maybe he had information that convinced him that it would be worth making the trip to England in person to make sure he got the right half of that collection.'

'But the Metland Eggs *weren't* there.'

'Right,' said Patrick. 'But that doesn't mean they were *never* there.'

'What do you mean?'

'The museum bought Ambler's collection after his death, but du Pont didn't come to England until years later.'

Nick's eyes widened as he caught up. 'Years in which *anyone* could have taken them!'

'Yes,' said Patrick. 'Dr Connor said the collection was a mess. Uncatalogued. Somebody could have stolen the eggs and—'

'And nobody would have even known they were missing!' Nick finished – flushed with excitement. 'You're right! Somebody could have nicked them right out of the museum!'

Patrick nodded slowly. 'Or hidden them there.'

'What do you mean?'

Patrick frowned and started to speak and then stopped and thought hard before starting again. 'Why didn't Dr Connor tell us about the Metland Egg?'

Nick was surprised by the question. 'I dunno. Maybe he just didn't know about it.'

Patrick shook his head firmly. 'Everybody who knows about eggs knows about the Metland Egg, Matthew Barr said so and so did Finn Garrett. And Dr Connor is the curator of eggs at the Natural History Museum, so I don't believe it's possible that he doesn't know about it.

'He invited us to the museum after seeing your photo. Matthew Barr saw the same photo and immediately thought of the Metland Egg, but Dr Connor didn't even mention it. He told us loads about *other* guillemot eggs. He showed us the guillemot room, and he told us about George Ambler and his obsession with guillemot eggs. And he told us all about John du Pont and his Rolls-Royce and his lackeys and how he bought fifty thousand guillemot eggs on the toss of a coin. We were only *there* because of a guillemot egg! And yet he never said a single thing about the most famous guillemot egg ever found.'

Nick stared into the middle distance, then nodded. 'You're right. It *is* weird. Instead he told us about the bloke sticking a pencil up a chicken's bum.'

'Although that *was* interesting,' said Patrick.

'Awesome,' agreed Nick.

'But Dr Connor not telling us about it feels . . . ummm . . .'

'Deliberate,' said Nick.

'Yes,' said Patrick. 'Deliberate. And he knew your egg had been stolen, so why invite us to the museum at all? I mean . . . what did he *want*?'

Nick frowned while he thought about it. 'Maybe he suspected Garrett was involved. I bet he'd love to see him behind bars. Hey! We should tell him about the balaclava!'

Patrick shook his head. 'But he didn't really ask much about the robbery. He just said the egg was probably stolen to order, and then he asked if the police had been any help. He didn't even ask how many men there were or how they were dressed or if you would recognize them again, or *anything* that could link it to Garrett.'

'True,' said Nick. 'He was more interested in what else I might find in the attic. He made that joke about the Holy Grail, remember?'

Patrick nodded.

'Oh,' said Nick with his eyes widening. 'You think he thinks *I've* got the other eggs? He did say to let him know what else I find there.'

Patrick got up and started to pace. That electric feeling in his chest was back, and humming, and suddenly he *knew*: 'I don't think he was talking about the other eggs. I think he *was* talking about the Holy Grail.'

Nick screwed up his face. 'Explain, please, Indy!'

'The data!'

Nick snorted. 'What? That little scrap of paper?'

'Yes!' Patrick felt right. His words tumbled out. 'He didn't ask about the robbery, but he *did* ask about the data. Remember? He asked you if you still had it. Then he asked where it was now . . .'

'He did look a bit cross when I said I'd thrown it away.'

'Of course,' said Patrick. 'Because *without the data you're screwed*!'

'OK . . .' said Nick. 'But why would he want the data if he hasn't got the egg?'

'Exactly!' shouted Patrick triumphantly.

Nick sat looking up at him blankly for a very long moment. And then he cried, 'Oh my God! Dr Connor's got my egg!'

'And if he's got one,' said Patrick, 'he's got them all.'

'Son of a *bitch*!' said Nick. 'But *where*? Nobody's seen a Metland Egg for a hundred years!'

Patrick shrugged. 'Where would *you* hide thirty priceless eggs?'

Nick frowned hard, and then started to laugh. 'With a million others!'

Patrick grinned and Nick punched the air, then suddenly got serious again. 'But how will we find them? We can't just wander into the museum and start opening drawers.'

Patrick shrugged. 'Dr Connor will invite you back.'

'And why would he do that?' said Nick.

'Because,' said Patrick, 'you're going to give him what he *wants*.'

The New Name

Mr Constable was a man who felt keenly that when he married Enid Sheppard, he had married not just the woman he had long loved, but her whole family.

Mr Constable proved himself a generous husband and stepfather. He spared no expense on comforts for his wife and stepdaughters in Scarborough, nor for whatever was needed at Metland, for he understood that for his wife the farm was more than just a tenancy, it was a family home.

Mr Constable was also aware that it would be wrong to favour one Sheppard child over any other. This he found most difficult, for Celie was so much his child – in appearance and in temperament as well as in blood – that it softened his already-tender heart just to look at her.

But he could see that she was unhappy, and did his very best to always consider her, and to bring her small pleasures, and to speak gently to her, so at the very least he might not add to whatever burden it was that she carried.

'You favour Celie,' Enid chided him gently one night as they prepared for bed.

'How could I not?' Mr Constable countered.

She nodded. Then added: 'As long as Molly doesn't feel left out.'

Then they both burst into laughter, because Molly was so giddy with clothes and money and with the young chauffeur in the grey britches (whose name was Stephen) that she would barely have noticed if Mr Constable had commissioned a marble statue of Celie and unveiled it on the prom.

Despite that, Mr Constable was at pains to prove to the Sheppard children that each of them was precious to him simply by dint of being precious to his wife.

Will, Martin and Stanley had continued to work Metland Farm for little more than a labourer's wage, and it was flourishing. And once Mr Constable saw that they were skilful and honest young men, he let them know that when they married, each would be settled on a small farm of his own in the vicinity.

This promise became widely known and naturally made them most eligible, so that within a year of Enid marrying and moving to Scarborough with the girls, only Robert and Stanley were left at Metland, and Stanley was all but engaged to the daughter of the landlord of the Cock.

However, there was no longer any problem finding or paying for labour, and Robert proved to be so capable a manager of those labourers that Mr Constable – with his wife's blessing – decided to transfer the lease of Metland Farm into his name.

And there lay a small legal rub, because Robert had never remembered his own surname, and the paperwork required that he have one.

After a little to-ing and fro-ing between his lawyers and the Land Registry, Mr Constable suggested it might be fitting to use the name Metland, to which Robert gratefully agreed, and a deed poll was drawn up, and Mr Constable and Enid made a special trip to the farm and arranged to meet a notary public there, so that Robert might make his mark upon both the deed and the lease.

Robert Metland

X

Mr Constable had brought a bottle of Dom Perignon to mark the occasion, but there were no takers and Enid made tea instead, just like old times. They all raised their chipped mugs to Robert Metland, who was so dizzy with gratitude that his mug might just as well have contained the champagne.

After the notary public left, Stanley hankered to go and look at the car, so he left with Mr Constable while Enid washed the cups. Robert lingered far longer than was necessary, so finally Enid asked him if he had something on his mind.

'Can I get some money?' he said. 'Mebbe?'

'Oh, Robert, you don't have to ask me for your own money any more!'

'Aye,' he said, but reddened, and Enid did too, as she remembered he had never been to school and could not read or count very high without great effort. He only knew if the flock was short because he recognized each sheep the same way he recognized people, and missed any that had strayed as though they were friends who were absent from a party.

So she retrieved the flour tin from the top shelf of the pantry, and together they counted Robert's money on to the old table where he now ate his meals, with his dog at his feet.

All that not-spending had really mounted up, and Enid was amazed to find that there was a shade over a thousand pounds.

Robert seemed no more impressed than if he'd saved fifty.

'But Robert,' she exclaimed, 'you could buy a house with that!'

'But I have a house,' he said.

'You do,' said Enid, 'and we're very happy about it. As long as you know that you have means now, as well as a home. Perhaps you should open a bank account. It would be safer than leaving it here in an old tin in the pantry.'

'Bin some time,' he said, 'and nobody's had it.'

'True,' said Enid, and realized that Robert trying to navigate the banking system would be hopelessly confusing for him. 'So how much would you like?'

'A hundred pound,' he said without hesitation.

'That's a lot of soap,' she laughed, and Robert smiled a rare, shy smile.

So Enid counted out the money slowly into piles of ten pounds while he watched attentively, as always.

Then he thanked her and gathered up the hundred pounds and Enid put the rest of his money back in the tin, and the tin back on the shelf.

Celie did not return to Bempton until late in the following May, when she had to in order to collect the Metland Egg.

She travelled alone on the train to Bridlington and then caught a cab the rest of the way.

Again, she felt the awkwardness grow as her destination approached, until, as she walked towards the house, she trembled – not sure whether she felt ready for a fight or a good cry.

She had put on the simplest clothes she now owned – a plain navy skirt and a white blouse – and had left Scarborough feeling quite dowdy, but here at Metland she felt as though she were off to church, not to the cliffs. She flushed as she saw Robert notice her ridiculous clothing, and longed for a smock and an apron.

Their hellos were clumsy and brief, and marked by not looking each other in the face. And when Robert seemed to be *just standing there*, Celie said, *Let's get on with it, then*, and headed for the horizon.

Robert shouldered the rope as usual, but for the first time he also insisted on carrying the apron, despite her protest.

'I'm eighteen years old, you know!' she said crossly.

'Nearly,' he said, but didn't give the apron back to her, and so Celie tossed her head and marched on ahead of him through the hayfield, oppressed by a silence that was broken only by the high songs of the larks that always nested here.

It was a typical May afternoon, sunny and blustery, hot behind the wall of mallow, then suddenly cooler as they emerged on to the exposed clifftop, where a great cheer assaulted them from the crowds who had gathered to watch.

Mr Ambler stepped on to the overhang and removed his old hat and bowed deeply in several directions.

Celie had dressed for modesty and had not thought about how she would get into the apron while wearing the skirt. She finally had to hitch it up – red-faced from the sudden shame of her bare legs showing, like a child's. In her hurry to get it all over with, her foot caught in the leather and she stumbled.

Robert caught her arm.

Immediately she shook him off and blushed furiously – suddenly feeling that more than just her legs were exposed.

He stepped back from her. Then – winding the rope around his waist and across his chest – slowly went to his place.

With her cheeks burning, Celie walked to hers, and sat down with her legs dangling through the crack. It was a squeeze to make it through nowadays, for although she was still a skinny little thing, she was not six. But despite her thinness, she was a strong girl and knew this crack in the rock so well – every twist she must make, and every ridge she could rely upon, and every one she could not. Even so, her heart pounded now in a way it had not since that very first time she had sat here, putting her life in Robert's hands.

Automatically she glanced at him to make sure he had her, and he met her eyes and nodded almost imperceptibly.

She hadn't needed to check.

He had her.

Always.

Afterwards Celie signed no books, and left before anybody could pat her head or give her liquorice. Instead she straightened her skirt and threw down the apron and set off fast through the hay-field, with Robert having to hurry to gather their equipment and to catch up with her. Once he had, he stayed a step or two behind her, just the way that *she* had followed *him* when they were both children.

The memory of that happier time, and its stark contrast to this moment, made Celie start to cry so hard and yet so silently that she nearly choked.

She dared not look around for fear that Robert would see her tears and say something, when she didn't know what to say back. Didn't know how to excuse her tears or shaking his hand off her arm. Could not explain the pain that seemed to squeeze her heart and her throat, as though she were drowning in sadness.

When they reached the farmyard, she went straight into the house and slammed the door behind her, even though this was *his* home now, not hers.

It was this thought – of all she had lost – that finally opened the floodgates. Standing well back from the kitchen window, Celie sobbed as she watched Robert walk blurrily back to the barn with the rope and the apron.

Truly, she hated him, and hated Metland, and couldn't wait to get away from this joyless place.

But she had arranged a taxi for six o'clock, and it was still only four, so Celie made tea. Two cups because she always made Robert one automatically, and then she could not bear to take it to him. Stanley came in with a bowl of eggs he had collected for the kitchen at Scarborough, and so she said the other cup was for him, and he sat and drank it and talked excitedly about the coming war and other things she didn't care about.

Mr Bonnington's taxi finally arrived in a cloud of white dust, and Celie rushed out and jumped into it and slammed the back door as though she had robbed a bank.

The car bumped slowly away across the yard.

'Celie!'

The voice was muffled by the window but she heard it and looked around, expecting Stanley with the bowl of eggs she already knew she had forgotten.

But a stranger was running after the car. In a suit.

It took Celie a long, frowning moment to realize it was Robert.

'Wait!' she said to Mr Bonnington, and the car stopped sharply.

Robert yanked open the back door, a little flushed and out of breath. And, despite the excellent suit and neatly parted hair, looking suddenly unsure – and more to Celie like the boy he had been than the man he had lately become.

Without saying a word, he dropped to one knee in the dust—

'*Oh, your suit!*' she cried, but he did not waver.

Instead he opened a small blue velvet box, and Celie Sheppard's heart near burst with joy.

Robert had spent months – years! – practising his proposal, but when the moment came, he did not need to say a thing.

He never had.

The Holy Grail

After half an hour spent watching Weird Nick falling over boxes and putting his foot into holes and stopping to try on funny hats, Patrick decided that he could not be party to such haphazard activities, and put himself in charge of the search for the data.

He went to the cupboard under the stairs in his own house and brought back a broom, as well as extension cables and work-shop lights, which he rigged along the beams that criss-crossed the attic.

When he'd finished and turned them on, Nick said, *'There, that's better, isn't it?'* as though he'd done it himself – and against Patrick's advice, to boot.

'Where did you find the egg?' said Patrick.

'In the trunk,' said Nick, pointing his now-defunct torch at a large trunk with a cracked black lid and brass corners.

'What happened when you found it?'

'Well, I was just looking in there, and I *found* it.'

'Did you open the box right away?'

'Hmmmm,' said Nick. 'No. I closed the lid and sat on the trunk, and then opened the box. Then I . . . mmmmm . . . sort of *half* took the egg out and had a quick look. Then I think I found the bit of paper—'

'The priceless data.'

Nick laughed sheepishly. 'Yes, that.'

Patrick tore a small strip of paper off a newspaper that was on the floor, then sat on the trunk and looked at his friend for instructions.

'Then I . . . uhhhhhh . . .'

'Screwed it up?' suggested Patrick.

Nick squinted – the better to view his own memory. 'A little bit, yes.'

Patrick crumpled the slip.

'Threw it?'

'Yes.'

'Underarm or overarm?'

'Ummmmm, sort of over my shoulder?'

'Left hand or right hand?'

'Right, most likely. Although could have been left.'

Patrick sighed. 'How far?'

'Not far.'

Patrick tossed the bit of paper over his right shoulder.

'Did you hear it land?'

'I don't think so.'

Patrick got up and looked around the trunk.

'Won't be there,' said Nick. 'I've shifted it about a bit looking for other stuff.'

'OK,' said Patrick. 'So the only thing we know for sure is that it's not *in* the trunk. So I'll take everything on *this* side and you take everything on *that* side.'

'Right ho,' said Nick.

Patrick had a system. He started by dragging the trunk and everything else on his side to one end of the attic, carefully side-stepping the hatch.

Nick continued to rummage through boxes, abandon them halfway, and throw them behind him – all the while keeping up a quiet running commentary about school reports (*Look at that, sixty-two for maths!*) and old copies of *Empire* magazine (*Five quid apiece, easy*) and Action Men (*Worth a fortune now. A tenner each, at least*).

Patrick ignored him. Now that he was working alone in his end of the attic, he felt better, and made good progress. He dragged boxes aside and swept the floor around them, then got on his knees and checked under the edges of the plywood with his torch and his mother's compact mirror in case the data had fallen down. He even ran the little silver penknife that Nick had given him along the joins in the plywood floor, in case something was lodged in there. After he had checked and double-checked the space, he brought each box into the clearing and unpacked and checked it, then repacked it and stacked it neatly in the opposite corner.

It was thorough and it didn't take as long as he had thought it might.

He started to enjoy himself.

He was going to get through his end of the room pretty fast at this rate.

An hour passed.

'Want a sandwich?'

'OK,' said Patrick.

While Nick was downstairs, Patrick finished his end of the attic and started on Nick's. No wonder he'd lost a tiny scrap of paper. In this chaos it was a miracle his friend had found a propellor and a stuffed badger.

By the time Nick came back with two sandwiches – both peanut butter – and two cups of tea, Patrick had made a clearing and was four boxes into an efficient search.

Nick sat down on the trunk to eat.

Patrick held up a stuffed badger. 'I found another of these.'

'Nah, it's the same one.'

'Why is it back up here?'

Nick looked uncomfortable. 'Well, there's a bit of a hitch on the old fundraising front.'

'Why?'

'Turns out this stuff isn't my dad's. It's my mother's. Or, at least, it was her father's stuff that was left here when my Granny Farrell died. Mum's not too keen on me flogging it on eBay, so . . .' He shrugged, then changed the subject. 'Say this data gets us back into the museum. What happens then? Where do we even start?'

Patrick was silent for a long while. Peanut butter was hard to talk through. 'I've been thinking.'

'Thought I smelled burning!'

Patrick frowned. 'What?'

'I'm joking.'

'OK.' Patrick had long since stopped trying to dissect Nick's jokes. 'I think we can narrow it down to just a hundred or so eggs.'

'Bollocks!' said Nick. Then: '*How?*'

'I think they'll be in the guillemot room.'

'You don't know that. They could be anywhere!'

'Yes,' agreed Patrick. 'But Dr Connor is a curator, and that's where guillemot eggs *belong* . . .'

Nick started to argue, then didn't bother. 'That's still fifty thousand eggs in that one room!'

Patrick nodded. 'And there are ten of those tall metal cabinets in each room.'

'How do you know?'

'I counted,' said Patrick.

'But why would you—' said Nick, then waved a hand at Patrick. 'Never mind. Carry on.'

'Each cabinet has two sides and each side has two hundred drawers – that's twenty vertical columns each of ten drawers, and all ten of those drawers are opened by a single key.'

'Are you sure?'

Patrick finished his sandwich. He got up and brushed his hands on his jeans. 'When Dr Connor showed us the guillemot eggs, he opened several drawers in that column, but only used one key to do it.

'So,' he went on, 'all we have to do is get the right key to the right column, and then we're only having to search ten drawers holding just a hundred eggs or so.'

'Oh, is *that* all we have to do?' said Nick.

'Yes.'

'Mate, did you *see* that keyring? It had *thousands* of keys on it!'

Patrick stacked yet another box on the 'done' side of the attic. 'But the big ring has five smaller rings – one for each room. Each room ring has ten smaller rings on it – one for each of the cabinets, and each of those has forty keys on it – twenty for each side. Once you know that, matching the right key to the right column of drawers is just a matter of counting.'

'Great!' said Nick. 'And how do we know which column of drawers the Metland Eggs are hidden in? Eeny-meeny-miny-mo?'

Patrick frowned at him. 'Eeny-meeny-miny-mo is not scientific. Depending on the numbers involved, it's easily manipulated to achieve a desired outcome.'

'I know,' said Nick a little wearily. 'We've talked about it before.'

'Then why suggest it again?' said Patrick.

'My mistake,' said Nick. 'Go on.'

'OK,' said Patrick, pushing another box into his well-swept clearing. 'This is where it gets a bit less obvious.'

'Oh, *this* is where that happens . . .'

Patrick was undeterred by sarcasm. 'You know the ladders?'

'Between the cabinets?'

'That's right. You know the marks they leave on the floor?'

'No.'

'Well, they're on wheels and they leave track marks on the wooden floor. More worn at the start of each row of cabinets and becoming gradually fainter towards the far end of the row, where they travel less often.'

'Logical,' said Nick.

'Yes, it is,' said Patrick, pulling junk slowly out of yet another box. 'Except that one ladder in the guillemot room has made much deeper track marks to the middle of the aisle. As if the ladder is pushed there often.'

'I'm lost,' frowned Nick.

Patrick piled the final box he had checked neatly on top of another. 'Matthew Barr said he liked to just *look* at his eggs, and *I* like having my teaspoons nearby, so I think whoever hid the Metland Eggs would want them somewhere nearby too, so he could look at them a *lot*.'

Patrick wiped the sweat off his forehead with the hem of his T-shirt. 'So that's where I would start,' he said. 'The sixth column on the second side of the fourth cabinet in the guillemot room.'

'You couldn't narrow it down some more?' grinned Nick.

'I don't think so,' said Patrick as he stared slowly around the now-tidy attic.

'So,' said Nick. 'Say I get the right key and distract Chris for long enough to get the eggs.'

'OK.'

'Well, what then? We just drive back here and wait for the police to arrest us?'

'I don't think he'll call the police. He stole the egg from *you*. I think he'll come after you himself.'

'And what happens then?'

'Nothing,' said Patrick. 'Because you won't have the eggs.'

'What do you mean?' said Nick.

But Patrick just frowned at him. 'Get up.'

Nick looked up at him nervously. 'What?'

'Get up,' he repeated, so Nick got up slowly, holding his plate, then stepped aside as Patrick tipped the trunk on to its back.

'Here it is.' He held up a slip of crumpled, flattened paper. 'I've been dragging it all over the room every time I moved the trunk.'

Carefully Patrick unfolded the scrap. It was dirty and a little torn, but by the strong workshop lights they could still read the faint pencilled words:

Guillemot, Metland, June 1926. GFA

'It's true,' whispered Nick. 'It's all bloody true.'

War

It was mid-morning on a warmish spring day when a car swept into the yard in a cloud of dust.

Celie got up from the table where she was chopping carrots and frowned at the old car as it made a half-turn, coughed, then ground to a halt. The back doors opened and two young men got out. Then two more.

'Stanley!'

The boy who shouted was Neil Pickering from over at New House Farm. She knew him from church, but only to nod to. She didn't recognize the others.

'Stan!' he shouted again, and headed to the back door.

She met him there. 'What's wrong?'

'Nowt!' He grinned up at her. 'Us is off to Bridlington to enlist!'

'Stanley can't go,' said Celie uneasily. 'Farmers can't go.'

'What 'em don' know won' hurt 'em!' Pickering winked and the other boys laughed, and suddenly Celie thought they might be drunk.

'He's not here,' she said firmly.

But then Stanley appeared from around the barn with an expectant look on his face, and the boys all turned immediately from Celie and surrounded him, and a great excitement arose.

Celie could see Stanley's dark head bobbing in the middle of it all, moving inexorably towards the dusty old jalopy. She hurried across the yard and grabbed his shirtsleeve.

'Stanley! Don't go!'

He turned to look at her, but one of the boys already in the car said, *Stanley, don't go!* in such a rude mockery that her brother reddened and then laughed and kissed her forehead. 'Don't worry so,' he said, and pulled his shirt from her grasp and squeezed into the back of the car.

It wasn't even out of the farmyard before Celie was running across the wheatfield, shouting for Robert.

He was on the tractor, spreading muck, and didn't hear her until he saw her. He leapt down and caught her in his arms.

Celie's skirt was filthy from the muck and she could barely speak for running and crying, but she told him what had happened . . .

'Please stop him, Robert!' she cried. 'Please don't let him go!'

Robert jumped back on to the tractor. He turned a slow loop around her and headed back to the farmyard, then through it, and down the road towards Bempton and then Bridlington as fast as he could go.

He didn't even stop to unhitch the muck spreader.

Thank God for liars.

This is what Sergeant Major Arthur Taylor thought every morning as he marched past the lines of keen young men and unlocked the door of the Bridlington recruiting office.

'Wink' Taylor had lost a leg and an eye to shrapnel at Loos in 1915, but every remaining bit of him was devoted to refilling the noble ranks he'd been forced to abandon. He took great pride in being the British Army's most effective recruiting officer in the north of England, with good numbers enlisted even during those difficult post-war years when the fathers and uncles and brothers who had come home without limbs or minds had rather taken the shine off death.

Luckily there would always be a mainstay of lads who knew no better, or who had known a lot worse, and were so grateful for three meals a day that they would march themselves silly and shoot on sight for the luxury of hot food, a bed and a uniform.

Taylor had been greatly helped in his work by his leather eye-patch and the tin leg that creaked romantically when he walked. Both were magnets to those boys who dreamed of killing things in far-off fields. Whenever he met boys like that in the pub or on the street or on a bus, the Sergeant Major drew them in with his many tales of derring-do.

And he was no liar. Before Loos, he really *had* done some derring.

No, the liars he was grateful for now were the boys themselves.

For war is a heady thing and once it had been declared Sergeant Major Taylor could not sign them up fast enough. At first it was just those aged twenty to twenty-two, but when it did not all blow over in a few weeks, that was widened to all single men aged between eighteen and fifty-one, and that started the real stampede. Recruits came mostly in gangs – on carts and buses and trains, loud and laughing and boasting. They jostled each other in the queue every morning, and in the afternoons they often came straight from the pub. Always in a great hurry, in case the war ended before they could get their chance at the Boche.

And many of them were prepared to lie if that's what it took to sign those papers and make their bid for glory.

Wink Taylor knew it, and thoroughly approved of it.

Because in places like Bridlington, he would bet good money that at least half of the lads who queued to sign up every day were farmers – and farmers were exempt from national service.

It had become clear to Taylor that farmers felt very hard done by in this regard. They were young, they were strong, they considered themselves the best possible candidates to be war heroes – and they were not going to be deterred by a mere Act of Parliament.

So, when some strapping young man smelling of manure sat before him and listed his occupation as *bookkeeper* or *clerk*, Wink Taylor asked no further questions. Or when some skinny child declared he was 'Nineteen, sir!' in a voice that had barely broken, he signed him up on the spot.

Put a gun in their hands: they would all be men soon enough.

Today – as was usual now – an encouragingly long line of youngsters snaked out of the Ministry of Labour door and along the seafront, smoking and shouting and flicking their still-glowing stubs in the air to tempt the gulls that hovered over their heads.

Taylor took a fresh registration card off the pile.

'Name?'

'Stanley Sheppard, sir!'

'Like the sheep?'

'No, sir,' he said, and spelled out his name while Sergeant Major Taylor wrote it in on the dotted line.

'Age?'

'Twenty-six, sir!'

Wink glanced at the lad – he was probably twenty-six.

'Occupation?'

'Shipping clerk, sir!'

The boy smelled faintly of pigs. Sergeant Major Taylor wrote it down anyway.

Shipping clerk.

'Employer's name and address?'

'Bridlington Shipping, Bridlington, sir!'

Taylor wrote that down too, as he already had twenty times today. He had never heard of Bridlington Shipping but he was fully prepared to believe it a behemoth of maritime industry. Yesterday it had been Bridlington Bricks they'd all worked for, tomorrow it would be something equally vague that someone would dream up and pass down the line to the other liars.

'Married or single?'

'Single, sir!'

Sergeant Major Taylor used to check their ring fingers but no longer bothered. If a married man preferred bombs and bayonets to his wife, who was he to deny him the relief?

'Can you sign your name?'

'Yes, sir!'

'Good. Sign here, keep your card safe and you'll be called for a medical.'

But before the lad could take the pen, somebody grabbed him in a bear-hug and lifted him off his chair and completely into the air. It was another young man – taller and broader and smelling even more strongly of pigs.

'He's a farmer, sir,' the bigger man said politely, then carried the writhing, kicking Sheppard from the office, and out past the line of hooting boys and shouts of 'Goodbye, Stanley!' and 'Back to the farm, Stanley!' and a mocking 'Don't go, Stanley!'

The two of them disappeared from Taylor's view, although he could hear the commotion rippling out on to the street.

'Can't blame a man for trying,' he shrugged cheerfully, and the shiny-eyed boys waiting their turn all laughed.

Then he tore up Stanley Sheppard's registration card and dropped the pieces into the wire wastepaper basket beside his real leg. 'Next!'

Another eager lad took the seat Sheppard had so unceremoniously vacated. His cheeks were as smooth as a baby's.

Wink Taylor smiled.

'Name?'

Robert put Stanley down outside. Immediately he was released, the younger man swung at him, but Robert ducked and he missed.

The lads in the line started to laugh and to clap and to shout 'Hit him!' and 'Hands up!' even though they didn't know Robert *or* Stanley, or what had just occurred or why. They were only excited about the war, and happy for the distraction a fight always provided while waiting for something else to happen.

Robert held up a placating hand and said, 'Celie—'

But Stanley was red in the face, with his shirt tail flapping, and was in no mood to be placated when he'd been so embarrassed in front of his friends.

He swung wildly again and Robert stepped backwards into the road.

The bang was loud, but it was the silence that followed it that made Sergeant Major Taylor throw down his pen, rise from his chair, and lurch across his office and through the throng of craning boys.

He knew that silence.

It was that same silence that had followed every bomb blast at Loos – that same deep, communal emptiness shared by men for whom life has suddenly halted, and who were now waiting for their shocked senses to recover so that they might learn whether their battle was all over for good, or just taking a moment to resume in some other form.

Out in the sunshine, nobody was moving. Not the shocked youngsters who had spilled from the car that had swerved and then skidded to a halt. Not the dozens who had queued all morning, keen for their chance to kill other young men just like the one who now lay at their feet. Not even that damned Sheppard boy, whose face was grey with horror and whose eyes swam with hope.

But there was no hope.

Sheppard must have seen it in Wink Taylor's face and he let out a terrible cry as he dropped to his knees beside his friend.

That's when the other boys slowly began to move. To back away from the tragic scene. The long, loud queue fragmented and dispersed in silence.

An ambulance bell rang in the distance.

There would be no more lads signing up today. No more boys desperate to die.

Sergeant Major Taylor waited for the ambulance to arrive, and then he locked the office door and went to the pub.

The Baby

A week after she had buried her husband at St Michael's church in Bempton, Celie found out that she was pregnant.

She wept anew – her grief compounded by the fresh thought of a fatherless child to add to that of a husbandless wife.

Her mother and her sister and Mr Constable took their turn in trying to console her but it was a thankless task. Even a tearful Stanley bravely tried to see her, but his mother told him it might be best to be somewhere else for just a little while, and Mr Constable bought him a train ticket to Scotland.

For two solid weeks Celie lay in her old bed in Scarborough, her curtains drawn against the view of the park, and could not eat or speak, so dreadful was her sorrow.

Until one morning she woke – tearless and calmed by a realization that had come to her in the night.

She had lost Robert. But she had not lost *all* of him. For part of her husband resided now in her own belly.

It changed everything for Celie.

Everything.

Suddenly her life was *still* about her and Robert. About something they would always share. Something that would endure long after they were *both* gone. Robert had left part of himself behind to comfort her always. Celie was not a young woman given to fanciful notions, but she had awoken feeling that this new thing inside her was . . . *magical*. And from that moment on, Celie knew that nothing would – or *should* – ever be the same again.

The doctor with the cold hands had told her that the baby was hardly the size of her smallest fingernail, but from then on she awoke every morning thinking of it, and barely stopped until her eyes closed every night. She did not know the child and yet she was obsessed by it, and her need to protect it was beyond logic, and all-consuming.

She could not even feel it, but she would die for it.

Would kill for it.

And – most strangely of all – Celie could not think of her sliver of a baby without seeing the blinking black eye of the guillemot.

Thinking of how, each year now, the little bird turned her head away just a fraction and opened her beak in silent, useless protest, as if she could no longer bear to watch while Celie slid a hand under her fluttering breast to steal her egg.

Her baby.

Her baby.

'I won't do it,' said Celie. 'I won't take the egg.'

'But Celie,' said Enid, 'what about Mr Ambler?'

'I don't care about him,' said Celie. 'Tell him I'm too fat to get through the crack. Tell him I'm sick. Tell him I'm dead, but I won't do it.'

Enid was gentle with her, but firm. 'Mr Ambler has been as good as his word, Celie. He has paid us forty pounds a year like clockwork. For two eggs! Without that money we'd not have been able to keep paying the rent. Without Mr Ambler's money, we could have lost our home!

'Honour dictates that we fulfil our side of the contract. *Until the bird lays no more.* It's what we agreed to, Celie. I gave my word.'

'Well, I didn't give *mine!*' said Celie, and she left her mother's company and sought out Mr Constable's instead, and appealed to him – thus placing him in the unenviable position of having to come down on his wife's side or that of their child.

Just like a real father.

He and Enid had had a happy and equitable marriage for nigh on six years, and Mr Constable was the unquestioned head of the house. But in family matters he knew that no man of wisdom contradicts his wife.

However, when Celie broke down in tears and told him all she felt about Robert's baby and of the bird, and of the *bird*'s baby (as she was now curiously wont to call the egg), Mr Constable could not help but be moved.

He recalled many similarly tearful scenes involving the first Mrs Constable, whose insipid health had deprived them both of the joy of children.

Now here *was* a child – *his* child. A child he'd sinned for, and a child he loved – suffering similar torments, not for herself, but for another of her sex, if not of her species.

Her defiance was so fierce and her tears so free that Mr Constable finally had to turn away and blow his nose. He told Celie he had a cold coming but that when he felt better he would think on it further.

Celie was disappointed. She returned to Metland Farm alone, determined in her refusal, whatever his answer might be.

But Mr Constable *did* think on it, long and hard, and finally came to the conclusion that because it involved a contractual obligation, this most delicate situation might actually have strayed out of family matters and into matters of business. And that, because they were now married, Enid's business was quite rightly *his* business and might, after all, come under his jurisdiction.

At a stretch.

Therefore within the week, and having discussed it at length with his wife and reached an amicable understanding, Mr Constable wrote a very decent letter to Mr Ambler, explaining that no Metland Egg would be collected this summer. He apologized for the interruption to service, which he said was due to 'tragic family circumstances', but said that he was confident that next summer the collections would resume.

He mentioned the contract to save Mr Ambler the embarrassment of doing so, and also said that – naturally – any payment should be suspended until further notice. Then, in a gesture of goodwill as much as compensation, he enclosed a twenty-pound note.

Mr Constable's letter made George Ambler very angry indeed.

That was not all Mr Constable's fault.

The broker was having a testing time of it.

Firstly, since the outbreak of war, George Ambler had noticed some funny looks and some strange remarks. Not from important people, but from shopkeepers and cab drivers and the like: people who really had no right to looks or remarks of *any* kind – let alone regarding a man of his standing.

He took a cab to the opera and the grizzled driver rather rudely refused his tip, saying, *If you can't be there yourself, sir, put it in a box for the boys.*

A girl at his tailor's boxed up his freshly steamed Ascot topper and said something unfunny about it not being made of tin.

A one-legged newspaper-seller handed him *The Times* and – as he touched his cap – asked him if he was *off 'ome to git yer boots on?*

It was a while before Ambler understood what was happening and, frankly, he would never have worked it out on his own.

It was only when his old school chum Roddy Bonnefort had complained to him of the self-same thing while they ate at the club that he'd gathered that he was being scorned and mocked – and all by commoners!

'Trouble is,' Roddy had said over a wonderful sea bass with samphire and potato dauphinoise, 'every other blighter seems to be in uniform! And you can't very well go around wearing a sandwich board saying *flat feet* or whatever the reason is you've been excused, can you?'

'Absolutely not,' Ambler had agreed.

'I mean, what's wrong with *you*?' Roddy had demanded, pointing his burgundy at Ambler.

'Flat feet.'

'Exactly! So hard to tell, you see? Sign of the times though, isn't it? The hoi polloi thinking they have a right to an opinion – even on matters that don't concern them! I blame the Communists.'

'Aren't they on our side?'

'For *now*,' Roddy had muttered darkly.

'I suppose so,' Ambler had said. 'Like protecting the miners and the farmers and the like. Who knows where *that* will end.'

'Ridiculous!' Roddy had picked a slender white bone from between his teeth and laid it on the side of his platter, carefully parallel to half a dozen others. 'I don't know who they think is going to keep making money while all this nonsense goes on. Believe me, if every man in the City were fit to serve, the country would be on its knees in a week!'

They had clinked glasses to that, and ordered another bottle of the '27.

Despite this affirmation that he was absolutely vital to the war effort exactly where he was, now that he knew what was happening, George Ambler had continued to feel the scorn of others. Right here in London, unworthy people felt it was their right to pass judgement on him. Openly. In public! To look at him and even *speak* to him as though he were not their superior. It had all the elements of a class war, and he had become defensive and prickly and sensitive to every possible insult.

There was another matter too.

For a while now, Ambler had been engaged in a careful correspondence with an American gentleman (if that was not an oxymoron!) regarding the possible purchase of . . . certain *items*.

The American was, of course, rich, and Ambler was, of course, greedy – and determined to relieve the man of as much of his wealth as was humanly possible. So, while the American's letters were always blunt and demanding, Ambler had been artful in his responses – hinting at magical things, and promising greatness in much the same way that he had whispered sweet somethings into the ear of Arthur Rickaby many moons ago, while reverting to the superior reserve of an Englishman whenever the Yank became too forward. Ambler had been a rank amateur in such matters in the Rickaby days, but his skills had been honed over time, with the result that he had managed to string the rich American along for almost two years – promising everything and delivering nothing – during which time the man's anticipation and desire had risen to very nearly fever pitch.

The spiral in the asking price was commensurate.

Ambler recognized that if he made the man wait much longer, his desire might burst and spill over into desperation – and from there it was only a short distance to anger, rejection and even revenge.

No, the apple must be plucked from the tree before the wasps arrived, and Ambler had decided once and for all that that moment would come as soon as he had collected this latest Metland Egg. For this one would make his own collection of thirty red eggs complete, and his fame and his fortune would both be assured.

All of which is why, when he received Mr Constable's polite letter and twenty-pound note, Ambler considered it the *final straw* (instead of no kind of straw at all) and was instantly furious. He shouted at Martha until she cried, and then strode about the house slamming doors while Edwards silently packed his valise, and within the hour George Ambler was on a train to Yorkshire to reassert his superiority.

Over northerners, at least.

The train took six hours to wend its way from the dirt and stress of wartime London and through the soft green hedges and ditches of England to the stone walls of Yorkshire, so Ambler had plenty of time to cool down, but instead he heated up. The simmering anger fostered by the past several months in the city welled up within him and became focused on Celie Sheppard and her dreadful stepfather.

After all he had done for these people!

Tragic family circumstances.

The scoundrel! There wouldn't *be* a family without *him*. They'd be out on the streets. *Forty pounds a year*. It would have bought the whole family thrice over, let alone a bloody egg. And *this* was the thanks he got? This contempt? This egregious letter? This *insulting* twenty-pound note? Presuming to pay him off like some underling? Some *navvy*?

It led him to ever more elaborate imaginary schemes for handling this outrage. Every manner of securing the Metland Egg while also punishing Celie Sheppard and her family for their lack of respect was toyed with and honed, while all the time his sense of having been cheated and humiliated burned so fiercely that by the time they passed Sheffield he was incandescent.

He had Constable's letter with him. When he had set out he

had had a vague notion of returning it *in person* with some cutting remark (yet to be confirmed) to let the man know that his unilateral declaration of breach of contract was *absolutely unacceptable* and that he (Ambler) expected the Metland Egg to be retrieved forthwith.

However, the angrier he got, the more spiteful he became, and between Sheffield and Bridlington, George Ambler started to form another – even more satisfying – plot where, having collected the egg himself in secret, he bombarded the Sheppard family with lawyers' letters so violently that they finally forced the brat through the crack, where she would spectacularly *fail* to find the Metland Egg in front of throngs of expectant tourists, while all along, he alone knew where it had gone.

What a moment *that* would be! To see her humiliation at failing to deliver. The discontent of the crowd. And the confusion on the face of that ignorant ox of an anchorman.

The train reached Bridlington before he could fine-tune this particular plan in his head. After the grand public shaming on the clifftop it all got a bit fuzzy and disjointed, with Celie weeping and the idiot shouting, and the tourists turning on them both, possibly with boys starting to throw eggs and maybe even stones . . .

No matter. These were finishing touches, but so far Ambler thought it all seemed to be going in a very satisfying direction. He would get his egg *and* teach these uppity farmers that he was not a man to be cheated out of what was rightfully his.

He would show them *tragic family circumstances*!

Eyrie

Alan Sweet had just opened a new packet of chocolate chip cookies when there was a terrible crashing sound and a dull thud.

'The tree!' shrieked Lynne.

They rose as one and rushed from the hide and ran the fifty yards to where the great Scots pine stood – their RSPB-issue torches flickering and bouncing through the forest.

The pine was still standing. They ran their beams up the trunk. The nest was there too – apparently intact.

'Oh, thank God for that!' said Lynne. 'I thought it had come down.'

'Me too!' said Alan, and for a moment they stood and caught their breath, smiling a little at their panic now that it was over.

'Then what the hell was—'

'Alan!' Lynne gripped his arm and pointed to the foot of the tree.

Almost hidden by the lower, sweeping branches, a man lay on the ground.

Motionless.

'Hello?' said Alan. 'Are you all right?'

There was no movement.

'Is he dead?' Lynne squeaked.

'Stay here,' said Alan firmly, and approached slowly.

The prone man was dressed in black and wore gauntlets and a balaclava. Strapped to his legs were vicious-looking tree spikes, with flecks of raw wood still clinging to them.

'Lynne! I think it's an egg thief!' Alan was nearly dizzy with the thought that the thing they had expected for eleven long years might actually have happened. He nudged the man's thigh with his foot. 'Hello?'

Nothing.

Through the holes of the black balaclava, Alan Sweet could see that the man's half-closed eyes were dull and lifeless.

He still clutched the branch that had snapped off in his hand.

Alan looked at Lynne and shook his head grimly.

'Oh, Alan!' She wrung her hands. 'Put him in the recovery position!'

'Love, he's dead,' said Alan gently. 'There's no recovering from that.'

He went over and hugged his wife as she cried a little bit from shock.

Then she gasped, 'Oh no!' and pointed at a black box that had fallen into the shadows a short way from the body. A camera lens case, with its silvered edges taped black so they would not catch the light.

They both knew what it was for.

With a sense of dread, Alan bent and opened it. Inside the hard casing, it was thickly lined with foam to protect its precious cargo.

'Empty,' he said.

'Oh, Alan . . .'

They hugged again then, and Lynne cried again – but this time from relief.

Finally they collected themselves.

'We need to call the police,' said Alan.

'Right,' nodded Lynne.

'I'll see if I can find some identification.' Alan turned to the body again and carefully peeled back the man's balaclava and shone his torch on his face. The dead man was unremarkable. Thin, pale, and with blood around his nose.

Alan went through the man's pockets, but there was no ID.

Only a motorway receipt for petrol and a cheese sandwich, and a faded photo of a small boy – with hair as ginger as a biscuit.

Doubts

'I'm not doing it.'

Patrick squinted at Weird Nick.

'It's off,' Nick continued. 'Over. *Finito!*'

Patrick didn't understand. They had planned meticulously. They had done their homework – poring over floorplans and going over layouts and anticipating obstacles and working out ways around them. They had even stayed last night in a Travelodge and spent the previous evening recce-ing the museum itself – scanning every inch of it from the cover of the trees.

It was very like a mission on *Call of Duty*, and they had both got more and more excited the closer it had got to zero-hour.

But now here they were, parked in a side road a quarter of a mile from the museum, and suddenly Weird Nick was full of doubts.

'Seriously, Patrick. The odds of us getting away with it are a million to one. A million to bloody *one*.'

Patrick shook his head. 'No, they're not. They're more like eighty to one.'

'Eighty to one?' said Nick, aghast. '*Eighty?* That's nearly a hundred to one!'

'Yes, but it's not a million to one.'

'But a million to one was just a . . . figure of speech! If you'd told me the odds of success were eighty to one, I'd have said *no* right from the start! I don't know why I said yes, to be honest. It's a bloody old *egg*. I've lived my whole life without it and I'm not risking prison now to get it back.'

'You won't go to prison. Dr Connor won't even call the police because *he* stole *your* egg.'

'What if he smells a rat?'

'*Where?*' Patrick twitched. He wasn't keen on rats.

'I mean, what if he gets suspicious?'

'Why would he get suspicious?'

'Look at me!' said Nick. 'I'm already sweating!'

'It's hot,' shrugged Patrick. It *was* hot. And the Fiesta didn't have aircon.

'Anyway,' Patrick went on, 'he'll be too excited about the data to suspect you of anything.'

Nick pursed his lips. 'No offence, but I'm your best mate and you don't understand how *I* think, let alone some bloke we've only met once.'

'Some *obsessive* bloke,' shrugged Patrick. 'I do understand *that*.'

'Fair comment,' said Nick, 'but now everything depends on *me*. *Everything!* If I screw it up, we'll both get caught!' Nick rubbed his nose nervously. 'Why can't *you* go in and steal the key and stall Chris?'

'I don't have your skills,' said Patrick.

'What skills?'

'Talking,' said Patrick. 'A lot.'

'All right, mate,' huffed Nick.

'And *you* can't get through the bathroom window.'

'OK, OK, don't rub it in. I'm just saying, however good I am at talking, Chris isn't stupid. He's a doctor!'

Patrick very nearly smiled. 'Doctors aren't invincible.'

He got out of the car and hitched his backpack on to his

shoulders. 'And this time you *will* have the element of surprise. Like that time on the oil rig.'

'Jeez, Patrick! That's a *game*. This is real life.'

'Same thing,' shrugged Patrick. Then he saluted his friend, and walked away from the car.

'I'm not doing it!' yelled Nick. '*Patrick!*'

But Patrick didn't look back.

Weird Nick pulled into the museum car park and turned off the engine.

He didn't get out. He just sat there with the windows down while birdsong filled the warm summer air, and let his memory unspool.

Trust Patrick to bring up the oil rig.

It had been his finest hour.

And he had not had many fine hours in his twenty-four years.

Nick's father had disappeared when he was still in nappies, leaving his name behind for his son to use, but no other support.

Times had been tough.

But when he was eight, Nick's mother had inherited the house from his Granny Farrell who'd always smelled of rubber. The house was small and remote, but it was paid for.

Nick still had vivid memories of the blustery blue-sky day they'd moved – everything they'd owned in the back of their battered old Beetle. Catching a glimpse of a boy standing, staring through the gap in the hedge, cradling something that Nick had thought was a hamster but would later prove to be a dead starling.

How lucky, his mother had said as they'd got out of the car. *You have a little friend right next door.*

Quickly though, Patrick Fort's silence and lack of eye contact had made Nick's mother nervous. The dead animals hadn't helped. She had told her son to stay away from Patrick, and bought him a PlayStation instead.

So for a while Nick had been friendless. At school he was too big and slow for games and, although he wore glasses, he was not bright enough for the nerds. The playground bully only had to call him *Weird Nick* once and it had stuck. And, having stuck, it had started to shape him.

But then, a few months after starting school, he had watched Patrick Fort knock that same boy off a swing with a rounders bat, and was so filled with awe that he'd determined to be his friend regardless of his mother's objections – or even Patrick's.

It had not always been the easiest relationship to navigate, for Patrick was pretty indifferent, but Nick had been dogged, and had managed to forge a friendship based almost entirely on video games, which did not require eye contact or conversation.

Together they'd graduated from *Mario Kart* to *Grand Theft Auto* to *Call of Duty*, and then gone through almost every incarnation of that title together.

Patrick was smarter than him, but Nick was always the superior player. While Nick rarely left his bedroom, his alter-ego, Sergeant Mick Savage, was absolutely fearless. He stormed in, guns blazing, and asked questions later, and had achieved an admirable Kill-Death ratio of 1.6.

Private First Class Patrick Fort's K/D ratio, on the other hand, was only 0.5 – the kind of score that might have been earned by a chimpanzee with a joystick.

Patrick gazed around gormlessly in clearings, distracted by architecture, crop identification, and pondering the exact model of every burnt-out car. He stood when he should be ducking, lingered on every skyline, and lacked the capacity to deceive the enemy during interrogation. Private Fort was shot, stabbed, bombed and executed on a regular basis.

Mick Savage bulged with muscles and bristled with weaponry, while Patrick's character looked very like Patrick, and remained a lowly Private. Patrick enjoyed the puzzle, the graphics and the location of the warzones, rather than the action, and stuck rigidly to military protocol – once even serving seven real-time days in lock-up for some minor infringement, instead of just restarting the game.

Now, sitting in the museum car park, Weird Nick Morgan laughed out loud at the memory. If *Call of Duty* had featured a gruelling bootcamp where recruits were required to clean toilets with toothbrushes, PFC Patrick Fort would still be on his knees.

But then there was the oil rig mission . . .

They had played that particular game nearly two years ago, but it still made Nick proud to think of how he'd handled himself. The rough sea crossing, the stealthy climb up the great steel stanchions, lashed by monster waves; the skill it had taken to reach the nukes without alerting the terrorist cell who threatened World Peace . . .

He'd reached the rig on six previous occasions, but had never got that far.

They'd set off together and it had been the first time Patrick had managed to get to the rig, but – predictably – he'd immediately been gunned down on the helipad. Nick had laughed so hard he'd had to pause the game. He'd saved the clip of the kill and later linked it to Patrick's incoming calls, so that he always answered his phone to the image of PFC Fort standing in the middle of a giant target like a human bullseye, and the ringtone was his character's final anguished cry of 'ARRRGH MY LEG!'

Once he was out of the game, Patrick had sat and watched Mick Savage advance to the bridge.

Now Weird Nick drummed his fingers on the steering wheel as he replayed every well-worn moment of the endgame . . .

Mick Savage had raged through the rig, kicking open doors, shooting everything in front of him. But it was Patrick who had maintained map-awareness, pointed out spawns, warned him of booby traps, and forced him to proceed with caution at the crucial moment, instead of his usual balls-out aggression. It was that restraint, that stealth – that *surprise* – which had led to the spectacular double kill that Nick had later screen-shotted and saved as his wallpaper.

Then Mick Savage had disarmed the nukes, won the war and saved the world.

But without Patrick, he would never have made it, and that was the honest truth.

Teamwork had made all the difference.

Weird Nick sighed deeply. If only this *were* a game, he'd be brimming with confidence. But this was real life – and there *was* a difference.

Or was it the same thing?

Nick got a little tingle, very like the one he got every time he sat down in his wholly inadequate office chair to play *COD*.

The plan Patrick had come up with to find the Metland Eggs didn't require guns or grenades, but it did require guts, guile, sleight of hand, courage, confidence and intelligence.

Nick wasn't sure they had all of that covered.

He pulled out his phone and watched the footage of his double kill on the rig.

Then he watched it again.

And again.

Slowly his chest swelled with courage.

What was he worrying about?

This *was* a mission.

And nothing was impossible.

Together, he and Patrick had defeated an entire platoon of heavily armed super-soldiers. Who was going to stop them now? Lance Corporal Jack Hammond with his crappy twenty-five ranking?

Never going to happen.

'Watch *this*!' he said to nobody in particular.

Then Sergeant Mick Savage – Kill/Death ratio 1.6 – pushed his spectacles up his scabby nose, and got out of his mum's Fiesta.

Stealing the Metland Egg

It was already past five when Ambler got to Bridlington, but immediately upon alighting, he had his bag sent to the Cock and ordered a cab to the cliffs.

On the train he had been so engrossed in his own scheme for wreaking vengeance on the Sheppard family that his plan for the actual retrieval of the Metland Egg was less than properly formed. So he thought about it all the way to Staple Newk, but by the time he set off along the windy cliff to walk the half-mile south to Metland, he had only come up with the most rudimentary scheme, which was largely composed of the absolute certainty that there *must* be somebody else he could drop through the overhang on a bit of rope.

He knew where each gang kept their rope, so that at least was not a problem. And he had watched Pricky Hodgson and Frank Artley and the like often enough, so he knew exactly how the rope should be tied around his own waist, then looped over his shoulder. It was not complicated. If farmers could do it, then he could do it.

All he needed now was a boy.

A very small boy.

Because of the hour (which was now nearly seven), tourists were leaving the cliffs in a steady trickle to go back to their guest houses and hotels in Scarborough and Bridlington.

Disappointingly, most of them were couples, or families whose small boys he could not detain.

The closer Ambler got to Metland Farm, the more annoyed he became, and the more perfunctory the tipping of his hat to the ladies. Did *nobody* let their children play on the cliffs alone any more? Why, when he had first started out, the place was awash with boys running hither and thither and making a damned nuisance of themselves! You could hardly stick a pin between the little sods. But here he was now, in need of a boy, and yet utterly boy-less.

The falling sun to his right had set the sky ablaze, and birds were coming in to roost in screeching waves to his left.

The trickle of people dried up entirely and for the first time Ambler faltered.

He was still a little way from Metland. Was there any point in going on?

He stood for a moment, undecided, and looking out beyond the birds to the ocean.

As he did, a great white gannet rose slowly on the wind from the cliffs below and stopped in the air a few feet before him, tilting only the fingery feathers of its wingtips to keep it steady.

It unsettled Ambler.

It was the size of a gun dog, and yet hung in the sky very near to his face, and seemed to be watching him with its angry blue eye. He tried to knock it away with his stick but it withdrew only inches, from where it continued to judge him as though *it* were the eminent egg-broker of Cavendish Square, and *he* were the dumb beast.

He swished his stick again, stepping more closely to the edge this time to try to connect.

Once more the gannet backed away from him, seeming to know just how far his stick could reach.

From that spot, at least.

It drew him further out.

Closer to the edge.

He swished at it again and frightened himself by teetering a little and then staggering sideways. 'Bugger off!' he shouted, but his words were immediately blown past his own ears.

The bird just sat in the sky on its cushion of air. Ambler felt bested and looked around to see if the contest had been observed.

And there – from the direction of Metland – came a boy.

A boy who seemed to be alone . . .

Ambler forgot about the gannet that had so nearly lured him off the cliff, and hurried south.

As he approached the boy, he smiled for the first time in years.

The boy *was* alone, and he was also a very small child. No more than eight, he should think, but one of those small eight-year-olds. It seemed to Ambler that nowadays boys of about eight came in two sizes – ridiculously tall, bulky and cheeky for their age, or painfully puny.

This boy was the latter.

If Ambler had been a religious man, he would have thanked God for this boy.

Even better, as he got even closer, he realized that he *knew* the boy! This was Little Tom Chandler, James's son and old Jim Chandler's grandson.

'Ah, Little Tom!' Ambler raised his stick in greeting and the boy slowed and then stopped and put down his bucket and touched his cap.

'Sir.'

'Hello, my lad.' Ambler had never called a child 'my lad' in his life, but he was just so inordinately happy and grateful to see this tiny boy – so well suited to his needs and just as his hopes had nearly gone – that his bonhomie could not be contained.

Little Tom had been carrying a bucket of egg. No doubt he was heading the mile or more to Bempton to earn himself a couple of pennies. It wasn't easy money. It was a long walk over rough, exposed ground, and Little Tom was small. A good amount of egg had already splashed on to his trousers – although it barely mattered, as they were already so crusty.

To Ambler it all pointed to the boy being in the market for a bob or two, and he could not have been more pleased.

'Where are they working today?'

'Cruddy, sir.' Little Tom waved an arm to the south.

Marvellous. Cruddy was two fields south of Metland. With any luck he could get the egg and nobody but he and the boy would be any the wiser.

'How would you like to earn five shillings, Tom?'

The boy squinted up at him sharply and, even though it was dusk, Ambler could see his grandfather already at work in his pinched little face.

'I would, thank ee, sir.'

'Right, then,' said Ambler. 'I have an exciting job for you. We've no time to lose! Follow me.' He strode past the boy, but Little Tom hung back.

'Come on, then!'

'What about my bucket, sir?'

'Just leave it here. We'll pick it up on the way back.'

But still the boy frowned and dithered.

Ambler ground his teeth. The boy didn't want to leave his bucket! For God's sake! An old tin bucket half full of raw egg on a clifftop at night, a mile from the nearest settlement. A jewel, indeed. The *stupid* child.

But a stupid child he needed to befriend, to persuade . . .

'Here,' he said, 'I'll carry it for you.'

Little Tom gave it up to him and followed Ambler back the way he'd come.

Ambler was surprised by how heavy the bucket was. The wooden grip was cracked and pinched his palm, and raw egg splashed on to his own trouser leg. He tried to ignore it all, and chatted to the boy.

'You want to be a climmer like your father?'

'Aye, sir.'

'Have you ever tried it?'

'No, sir.'

'Well, this is your lucky day, Tom. I need a climmer to fetch the Metland Egg!'

Instead of shrieking with joy and kissing his hem, Little Tom Chandler screwed up his face.

'Da says nobody works Metland. 'Cos of t'overhang.'

'Well, Da's wrong,' said Ambler sharply. 'You know Celie Sheppard, don't you?'

'Aye, sir.'

'Well, she gets the egg for me each year, doesn't she?'

'Aye, sir.'

'And that's at Metland, isn't it?'

The boy frowned as he worked it out slowly. 'Aye, sir.'

'There you are, then. And she's only a girl! If a *girl* can do it, *you* can do it, can't you!'

Little Tom nodded, but still did not look convinced.

Ambler sighed. There was only so much you could do with one so young and with such appalling breeding. The boy's father had told him a thing, and it would take more than logic and reason to make him let go of it.

They walked in silence until Danes Dyke where, in the fast-failing light, Ambler located the hole where the Hodgsons' rope and wheel lived, and yanked open the door.

Little Tom gasped audibly.

'What's ee about?!'

Not even a *sir*, so shocked was the boy by this transgression.

'Borrowing the rope,' said Ambler bluntly. 'The Hodgsons are my friends. They won't mind.' He gambled on the child not having the confidence to protest any further, and was correct.

Only another hundred yards.

The night was almost down now. The sky was white at the horizon, then green, deepening to navy overhead, with Venus already up, and a big yellow moon rising. They would have to be quick.

They reached the overhang, and Little Tom followed Ambler all the way to the crack.

The boy looked down at it doubtfully.

'Ee's reight small.'

But Ambler was already wrapping the rope around his own waist. 'Take your jacket off. Once that's off you'll fit through easily.'

It was cold and windy and Little Tom did not immediately comply.

'Come on! Do you want that five shillings or not?'

Little Tom looked up at him, plainly frightened. He shook his head. 'Mebbe I'll fall.'

'Don't be silly. You know the egg is only just under the overhang. I'll have you down and up again in two minutes. Five shillings for two minutes' work! Imagine telling the other boys *that*!'

Little Tom leaned slowly forward once again to re-examine the crack.

If he hadn't needed him so badly, George Ambler could cheerfully have kicked him off the cliff. 'Ten shillings!' he said in desperation.

Little Tom looked up at him with that same awful canny look as old Jim Chandler, and said, 'A pound.'

The child needed a bloody good flogging, but there was no

time to argue. In fifteen minutes – maybe less – it would be too dark for the boy to see the colour of the red egg under the shadow of the overhang.

It was now or never.

'A pound,' said Ambler crossly. 'Take off your jacket.'

Little Tom took off his jacket. His shirt underneath was thread-bare and flapped about his pipe-cleaner frame like washing in a storm. Ambler made a loop and tied a knot. He did not trust the boy to sit securely in the loop, so instead cinched it tightly under his arms and around his shivering chest.

'Now, you remember, when you're through the crack, the red egg is straight ahead of you. You make sure it's red and then you just put your hand under the bird and take it.'

'Will her bite me?'

'She might try,' admitted Ambler, 'so you be prepared for that and hold on to the egg, all right? Just you think of that pound and hold on to it. Then call out and I'll haul you in. She won't follow you, so just you keep hold of that egg, yes?'

He thought Little Tom nodded, although the boy was shaking so violently that it was hard to tell.

'I'm going over there by the heelings. You walk out to the edge, to where the crack is widest, and that's where you drop through.'

'A pound?' said Little Tom tremulously. 'Promise?'

'A pound,' said Ambler over his shoulder. 'I promise.'

Ambler had seen Robert use the heelings year after year. They were behind a big tussock on a lump of hardened soil over what he assumed was a rock. He settled himself behind it and made sure he had a good footing to hold himself in place. He sat and looped the rope over his shoulders to take up the slack.

Little Tom was prevaricating once more, silhouetted against the horizon.

'HURRY!' shouted Ambler. If he had to go over there again, he would give the boy a clip round the ear. With a pang he thought that if he'd done that from the start, they'd be walking back to Flamborough right now – the boy with his bucket and he with the Metland Egg.

He didn't need to clip him round the ear though. As good as his word, Little Tom sat on the edge of the crack, then lowered himself down as well as his skinny arms would take his weight.

And then he let go.

Little Tom *was* small, but even a small boy is a heavy thing to drop off a cliff on the end of a rope if one is not prepared.

And George Ambler was not prepared.

He should have been leaning all the way back, almost supine, with his heels dug into the tussock and his knees locked.

But instead he was sitting with his knees up like a fool at a picnic, and the weight of Little Tom hitting the end of the rope jerked him forward and over the top of the tussock, and dragged him several staggering, stumbling yards across the grass and the rough rock of the overhang, where he fell flat on his face.

The boy's muffled shriek floated up through the crack. It was only because his anchor was now lying down that his fall had been interrupted.

Ambler lay there and slowly regathered his wits. There was grass in his mouth, and his chin and hands and chest had been grazed bloody by the slide across the tussock and then the rock.

He'd lost his hat.

The rope he'd wrapped around his waist had not been tight enough (he now realized) and the entirety of the coils was now situated in a thick painful bulge under his armpits, along with his shirt and jacket. And not even as securely there as he would like. It almost felt as if the whole lot might be pulled over his head unless he kept his elbows down.

Little Tom was crying and begging for help. But it was under the overhang and against the wind, so only the faintest cries escaped into the night air.

Ambler recognized that from up here anything he might say by way of reassurance would be insincere *and* unheard, and so he said nothing at all. Instead, he slowly raised himself on to his sore hands and knees, and tried to crawl backwards.

But the rope tethered him there, a dozen feet from the crack. He could not reverse.

Ambler remembered watching the idiot reel Celie in. Once she tapped to come up, he always moved *towards* her and now he understood why – at this low angle the rope did not run through the crack, but merely became squeezed by the point and got stuck there. The harder one pulled, the tighter it held.

He needed to get closer to the crack – not further away. And he needed to pull the boy in as he did so.

He would have to stand up.

Leaning back all the while, he hauled himself to his feet and then started to work his way to the edge, turning slow circles as he went to keep the tension on the rope.

But the closer he got to Little Tom, the more he realized the danger – that in order to retrieve the child, at some point the rope must run freely through the crack. And that at *that* point he would need to haul the boy straight upwards using only brute strength. No angles, no levers, no wheel – and no mistakes. For any falter, any slip, and the boy would drop again, and risk pulling him clean off the cliff.

This was why nobody worked Metland.

George Ambler stood on the great rock, braced like a man playing tug-o-war with the sea, and knew he could not do it.

Not alone.

There was nothing for it. He would have to tie off the rope and go for help.

He inched backwards again, away from the weeping, pleading boy, and past the tussock and across the path in the grass and down the bank – all the time unwinding himself from the Hodgsons' taut rope – until finally he came to a hedge and a stile.

He climbed over the stile and squeezed back under it three times, each time hauling on the slack to try to keep the tension on the rope, and finally he was free of it, and it held, and he tied a mighty knot to keep it all firmly in place, and ran back to the crack and lay on his stomach and looked through it.

The boy was a shockingly long way down. Thirty feet at least. The rope was tight under his arms, but he was clinging on to it for dear life, and with his arms thus raised in front of his face, his shoulders looked dangerously narrow.

'Keep your arms down!' Ambler shouted, but Little Tom just cried more loudly.

From here Ambler could see the wall of guillemots, shifting and purring, and the narrowness of his failure was a bitter pill. Somewhere there was *his* egg. He could almost reach out and touch it.

The boy still might, if he could be calmed down.

'I'm going for help!' he shouted, and the boy's face turned up to his, pale and terrified. 'I won't be long!'

Little Tom bawled, 'Don't go! Don't leave me!'

But Ambler shuffled backwards and rose to his feet. He winced at his bloody palms.

He found his hat.

Then he turned and stood with his back to the sea and considered his options.

He looked up and down the empty path.

Cruddy was only a few hundred yards to the south. It was close to dark, and soon the Chandler gang would be heading back home to Buckton. They would pass this very spot.

If they saw what he had done, they would hurt him. Maybe more.

So instead George Ambler pushed his way through the mallow bank, and headed as fast as he could towards Metland Farm.

By the time he could see the farmyard by the light of a big yellow moon, Ambler's legs felt like rubber and his lungs burned like acid.

Celie was at the chicken run, and alone, thank God!

Ambler did not have the breath left in him even to shout Celie's name; he just ran out of the night and grabbed her by the wrist. The chicken she'd been holding burst into squawks and feathers between them, but he did not let go.

'Come!' he gasped. 'Come!'

'What for?' she cried. 'Why?!'

He could only shake his head, and keep a-hold of her. Then she saw the blood on his hands and shrieked and started to fight him. But he gripped her wrist and pulled her back with him into the long grass of the hayfield.

He was not much of a man, but a man he was, and Celie was only a very small young woman. Still, she fought him all the way – scratched at his arm and dragged her heels, but she was so light that, even in his panic and exhaustion, Ambler was able to keep a-hold of her.

At one point it seemed that she had given up. She stopped fighting and caught up and ran alongside him for a few strides.

'Good girl!' he panted.

Then she bit him!

Ambler cried out and let go of her to shake his hand in the air, then he slapped her face so hard that she fell backwards, deep into the hay, while he cupped his hand and called her furious names.

In that brief moment of freedom, Celie scrambled to her feet and ran back towards the farm.

Ambler went after her again. He was exhausted and injured, but he was desperate. The thought that at this very minute the Chandler gang might be discovering Little Tom dangling under the overhang lent speed to his weak London legs.

Celie was light and, although she was with child, she was young and fit from hard work. Almost anywhere else, she would have been faster than Ambler. But the hay was nearly up to her waist and she could not hope to outrun him, and relentlessly he gained on her. Once he even reached out and touched the back of her blouse with the tips of his fingers and she squealed in fear – but then he stumbled in his eagerness, and she drew away again and he chased her again, until suddenly a great black square loomed out of the night sky, and Celie angled towards it, then banged up against it and spun to face him.

Ten yards away, George Ambler stopped. If his lungs had allowed it, he would have laughed.

The stupid girl had run into the wall of the barn, and had nowhere to go.

She was trapped!

He bent for a moment with his hands on his knees, his breath burning and making him cough. Then he straightened up and looked at Celie.

She had given up. She stood, chest heaving – her ghostly blue eyes wide and frightened.

By the light of the moon Ambler looked at his bitten hand, then held it up to show her the blood coating his palm.

He would make her pay.

Celie scurried along the wall like a silly mouse. But she had nowhere to go. No escape.

Ambler ran at just the right angle to cut her off.

Now he had her.

It was dark when the Chandler gang crossed the Metland overhang on their way home, and they would have passed it without a glance, except that Pricky fell over. It was comical to see a big man fall over, and so of course they all laughed at him, before James noticed the rope stretched across the path.

For a moment they just frowned down at this familiar thing in an unfamiliar place and time.

Then old Jim Chandler moved so fast that the cigarette fell from his lips. He flung himself down on his stomach on the great rock, and looked through the crack.

An empty rope swung in the wind.

He pulled it in and held up the end where fresh kinks showed a knot had been recently tied.

Not well enough.

They all stood over the coils in horrible silence.

Jim Chandler was a tough old man, but the thought of poor little Celie Sheppard falling out of this loop and into the darkness brought murder to his heart.

'Whoever done this to her,' he said with quiet vehemence, '*I will kill him.*'

The others nodded their sanction, then James untied the rope from the stile and slung it over his shoulder.

In grim silence they set off again.

That's when they saw the bucket of egg.

*

Three days later, Little Tom's body washed up at North Landing.

On the same tide, just yards away, the fishermen who had pulled the child from the dirty surf found a battered top hat with a gash in the side, as if the wearer had been attacked with something very sharp.

That unfortunate wearer's name was printed inside the hatband in gold.

G. F. Ambler.

Leaving

When Mr Edwards received the news that his master was gone, he wasted no time.

'We're leaving,' he told the housemaid. 'Pack your things.'

Martha didn't ask why, but half an hour later, when he joined her in the hallway, she was standing next to a small bag and thirty extra-ordinary red eggs. One in a carved wooden box, and twenty-nine more in a glass-topped cherrywood case with silken rope handles.

'What's all this?' Mr Edwards said sternly.

'My things,' she said with an unusually defiant chin.

Martha was a thin, quiet young woman with chestnut hair, freckles and dark blue eyes. When she'd first arrived – aged just fourteen – she had reminded Mr Edwards of his own daughter, who had died along with her mother of the Spanish flu.

Martha's room on the third floor was next to his and furthest from the narrow staircase, so that the first time Ambler had visited her at night, Mr Edwards had known what was about to happen before she did.

It hadn't lasted long.

Not nearly as long as her sobbing . . .

They had never spoken of it, of course.

And they did not speak of it now.

Mr Edwards simply went into the attic and fetched the steamer trunk.

Then they took a cab to a house in Hammersmith where a dirty, frail boy with Martha's eyes and George Ambler's mercifully inoffensive nose took less than a minute to pack his whole world into his pockets.

They left, and nobody said goodbye.

They caught the milk train from Paddington and then a small, jerky train from Cardiff to Brecon. From there they got a small, jerky omnibus up the long, winding road that led to Pen y Fan. There was no stop but the driver let them off opposite an unmarked track, and they walked the rest of the way – Martha and the boy carrying the suitcases, while Mr Edwards dragged the trunk, mindful of bumps.

The stone cottage at the end of the track seemed tiny at first. The whole of it would have fitted into the dining room at Cavendish Square, and Mr Edwards's mother lived there too.

Martha and the boy took his old childhood bedroom – the one where Pen y Fan was framed by the window like a picture on the wall – while Mr Edwards cleared the box room for himself.

They walked two miles down the hill to chapel each Sunday, where their every move was observed by every eye. Mr Edwards knew that a man – even an old man – and a young woman living in a house together would never *not* be a subject for speculation. So they had agreed to tell people that Martha was his daughter and, because most had a hazy recollection that he had indeed had a wife and a child in London, the gossip slowly faded until it was confined to those few whose net of bad opinion was always cast so wide as to make any catch meaningless.

But still Mr Edwards worried about Martha's prospects, and felt she should have a place of her own if she were to be always respectable, so – a little awkwardly – he asked her if they might sell the eggs and use the proceeds to turn the old stables into a home for her and the boy.

Martha was already grateful enough to have *married* Mr Edwards if he had demanded it, so was delighted that all that was being asked of her was to give up the Metland Eggs.

The first egg in its carved wooden box had been gifted to her, as if it were not guilty payment for a hideous crime.

Inadequate payment, at that.

For what use had she for a shitty old egg in a box? And how could that – or anything – have compensated her for George Ambler's hideous assaults upon her person? And yet Ambler had made such a fuss of it, and was so terribly keen to tell her how lucky she was and how generous he was being.

Martha had been only fourteen, but was an intelligent girl, and so had not believed his distortion of history for a second. But she was also intelligent enough to suppress her urge to dash the red egg from Ambler's repulsive fingers. Instead she had accepted it and pretended to admire it, and had encouraged Ambler to tell her all about it again, and again, and again, and again and *again!* Until she had thought her ears would bleed from boredom.

Because every moment George Ambler had spent poring over the egg was a moment when he was not pawing her.

As each subsequent egg was collected, Ambler had placed it in a glass case under Martha's little iron bed. *These* eggs she was not allowed to touch, but he would visit them and gloat over them, and crow about paying *only twenty pounds for each* (all while he was paying her just ten pounds a year for every kind of service) and tell her how *if he could only hold his nerve* they would make him both rich *and* famous.

To Ambler, the value of the Metland Eggs was exponential.

To Martha it was immeasurable. Although it could never be sufficient for what she had suffered at his hands.

But *this*? This proposed exchange of the thirty red eggs she despised, for a new home and better life for her and her son?

This, finally, felt like it might be sufficient.

So Mr Edwards started to put out feelers for a buyer.

But almost immediately the plans ran into trouble from an unexpected source.

As a small boy, Philip's Sunday afternoons had been spent with his mother – the only few hours of every week when he had felt joy, and to which every other hour of the week had been an adjunct spent in sorrow at its passing, or anticipation at its next approach.

They had started off going to Hyde Park or to see the changing of the guard, but once they had been to the zoo, they never went anywhere else again. The penguins were always the highlight. He and his mother would stand at the futuristic new enclosure and watch the comical little birds waddle and flap, and slide down the curved concrete into the water, where they became slick black bullets – which his mother always pointed out and exclaimed: 'Look at how they change!' And then she would kneel down and squeeze him close and whisper at his ear: 'Everything will change for us too, Pip.'

'When?' he always asked.

'One day,' she always said.

And then she always told him about the wondrous red egg that had been presented to her in a fancy wooden box carved with penguins and puffins.

'And the box alone cost more than my year's wages,' she would tell him, hushed with amazement.

'And why did he give it you?' the child loved to ask.

'Because I'm the best housemaid in London!'

And little Philip would look at her with such pride that Martha sometimes thought her heart would fly clean out of her chest.

'And there's more!' he'd urge her on, 'in a big glass drawer—'

'—lined with cream silk, and every one—'

'—as red as blood and precious as rubies,' they always whispered together, with eyes wide and shining.

'And they're all under your bed!' he would whisper. 'And nobody knows . . .'

'Nobody but *me*,' she would say haughtily – but only so as to allow him the pleasure of pointing to his own chest and reminding her:

'And me!'

'Oh yes! And you!'

Then they would giggle and she would tickle him and he would run away from her and the penguins, laughing, and she would chase him to the tea rooms, where girls dressed in black with white aprons waited on his mother just as if she were a lady, and sometimes slipped Philip a stale bun to take away with him in a paper bag . . .

To Martha, the eggs had been buffers against much hideous abuse.

But to Philip, the thirty red eggs were symbols of hope and magical reminders of the small and fleeting joys his childhood had offered. Sometimes Mr Edwards or his mother would pass his room and glance in to see the boy sitting on his bed, with his back to the view, gazing instead at the red egg in its carved wooden box.

So when the grand plan for a new home was revealed to Philip, the thought of losing the eggs raised no little agitation in the boy. He was old enough to see what a home would mean to his mother, and never demanded an end to the scheme. Every time the matter was raised, he merely listened and nodded and listened and nodded until it all became too much for him, when big tears would spill out of his eyes and roll down his cheeks and off his nose, until his mother would hug him and rock him and tell him they didn't have to talk about it now.

Martha understood.

Mr Edwards understood.

The eggs were talismans to Philip, and he lived in dread of losing them, in case their own sudden good fortune might be found to be similarly fragile, and crack to reveal that it had all been a hollow dream – and that he might wake once again in London in a house that was not a home, under the care of a woman who did not care for him, nor he for her.

And so, while Martha was happy to sell the eggs, her son was not.

This situation persisted for several months, until the very first buyer Mr Edwards had approached started to pester him for a date.

Even after that point, Mr Edwards held back, for he felt only too sharply his own life of servitude, where decisions were very often things that were made for him and about him, rather than by him. For that reason he did not like to put pressure on Philip, or to come between the boy and his mother.

Finally – in the small hours of one rainy morning – he thought of a compromise. He interrupted breakfast next door to suggest that they sell twenty-nine of the eggs, but keep the very first of them in its beautiful box.

Philip took barely a moment to think about it, before smiling.

And so Mr Edwards proceeded to arrange the sale of the Metland Eggs, while Martha gifted her son the original egg in its box, to do with as he pleased.

And what pleased Philip was to keep it on his nightstand, where he could see it every day for the rest of his life.

Murder

A week after George Ambler's hat washed up at North Landing, Jim Chandler was arrested and charged with murder.

The police had heard of Jim's clifftop vow. How they heard of it was never properly established, but the Chandlers blamed Pricky Hodgson for blabbing, and so ended a long and profitable friendship.

Of course, it was not Celie who had died, so it might have been (and later was) argued that Jim Chandler's threat of vengeance was moot.

But once Little Tom's body was found, and Ambler's hat was recovered on the same tide, and he was found to have never checked in to the Cock (where his valise still languished), the police at Scarborough put two and two together and, inevitably, came up with four.

Their logic was sound: that if Jim Chandler had vowed to kill whoever had caused the death of a young woman he barely knew, how much more likely was it that he would be quite capable of murdering the man he believed to have dropped his own dear little grandson off a cliff?

It would have been more useful for the investigation had George Ambler's body washed up, yet it never did. But those things happen at sea and so, after a week of waiting in vain for that unhappy event, the police inspector decided that the damaged hat alone was enough to prove that the missing broker had met a violent end – and that that end was most likely to have come at the hands of the man who had, in effect, threatened to kill him.

Despite all of the contortions of motivation and method, the feeling in the neighbourhood, and well beyond the neighbourhood, was quite simple – and wholly in favour of Jim Chandler.

Of course, it helped that nobody had liked Ambler. But unanimous public opinion was that Mr Chandler had only done what any loving grandfather would have been right to do – avenge the ghastly death of an innocent child, and the law be damned.

So prevalent was this view that six months later at York, a jury of twelve good men and true took less than an hour to acquit Jim Chandler. It would have been five minutes, except that there were jam sandwiches on offer if the jury was required to sit through teatime, and there was a war on.

After the verdict, an editor from Scarborough postulated that George Ambler – filled with remorse at his part in Little Tom's death – may have flung himself off that same cliff and into the sea far below. This was not a popular scenario, as it attributed far too noble a sentiment to a man who had become a monster in the eyes of the general populace, and shortly afterwards the editor found that his services were no longer required in Scarborough, or anywhere else in the north of England, and the poor man had to move to Rhyl.

And so Jim Chandler was freed to continue his interrupted life and was accorded all the benefits of celebrity that Bempton could offer, which consisted of the awe of small boys, and free beer at the Cock.

In private, the Scarborough police always maintained that they had got their man – although even they were not sorry to see that man walk free. Subsequent to the verdict, however, they were naturally obliged to reopen their investigation. There was much talk of ill will between Ambler and some of his customers. Some old resentment about eggs, it was rumoured. But the more the officers delved into the matter, the more possible suspects they unearthed, to the point where even the inspector was heard to exclaim, *Did NOBODY like the man?*

After a few weeks it was decided that priority should really be given to the Second World War and no other person was ever charged with the murder of George Ambler.

Nobody complained.

Not even his brothers.

The Heist

'To what do I owe this pleasure?'

Nick shook Dr Connor's hand, and was surprised to find that his own hand was dry.

'Did I miss your call?'

That was a polite way of saying he should have called first.

'I wanted to surprise you.'

'And this *is* a nice surprise, of course.'

'I've got something to show you,' said Nick.

Connor leaned sideways to look behind Nick. 'I see no badger!'

They both laughed.

'Something much better than that,' said Nick, then glanced at the receptionist meaningfully.

'Sounds like fun,' said Connor. 'Follow me.'

The two of them went past the polar bear to the *Staff Only* door and then past the storeroom and the bathroom to the curator's poky little office.

In the middle of his desk the giant keyring sat like a spiky art installation.

'Take a seat.'

'Thanks.'

There were two chairs at the desk – one fancy one that was obviously the curator's, and the other a cheap plastic thing. Nick took that.

'Would you like a cuppa?'

'Yes, please, Chris. Two sugars, please.'

To Nick's delight, Connor left him alone in the room and went somewhere else to make tea.

He resisted the temptation to grab the keyring immediately. Once he had made his choice, he would have to stand or fall by it. So instead of seizing the ring and fumbling through the little silver keys, he studied it, trying to remain calm and to remember everything Patrick had told him about it.

Five halls of eggs. Five rings. The ring on the end is for the guillemot room.

Nick reached out his hand.

Then his gut lurched.

Which end?

There were five large rings, but there was no indication of which end to start from! The keys that opened the drawers of the guillemot room could be on either of the two outer rings. He could easily choose a key off the wrong ring and they wouldn't know until it didn't open the column of drawers.

Nick withdrew his hand with the sense of absolute deflation. Such a simple thing! It wasn't his fault. It wasn't anyone's fault. It was just over. Patrick would understand.

No, he quickly revised in his head, Patrick *wouldn't* understand. Nick frowned and tried to imagine what Patrick would do.

'Did you say two sugars?'

Startled, Nick blinked up at Connor's face peering through the door at him.

'Yes, please.'

'Right ho.' Connor disappeared again.

Shit! If he *had* been sure about which key to take, the curator would have caught him red-handed! Only his uncertainty had saved him. Relief washed through him, and he felt quite shaky at the closeness of his call.

Connor would be back any moment with his tea.

His tea.

Nick flushed with shame. Would Mick Savage sit here and drink *tea* with the man who'd stolen his egg?

No way!

This was the mission he'd signed up for. It was risky, but if it was easy, *everyone* would have a Kill/Death ratio of 1.6!

Confidence surged through him again and he chose the set of rings on the end closest to him and stuck with it. If it was wrong, it was wrong. He didn't touch the keys, just started counting. Fast. And with Patrick's voice guiding him: *The sixth column on the second side of the fourth cabinet . . .* Then – when he was absolutely sure of which key was his target – he quickly slid it off the ring and put it in his pocket.

There was no going back now. He was a thief.

Or a hero.

'Here you go.'

Connor put a mug down and sat at his desk, facing him expectantly.

'Thanks.' Nick sipped his tea to give himself a moment to calm his pounding heart.

'You had something to show me?'

'Oh yeah.' Nick nodded and took a matchbox from his pocket and handed it to Connor.

The curator opened it and stared at the slip of paper inside.

'Is that . . .' he stammered, 'the data?!'

'Yep,' said Nick. 'We searched the attic for hours. Finally found it *under* the trunk where I found the egg.'

'Always the last place you look,' Connor murmured. He opened his top drawer and took out a pair of long chrome tweezers. His hands shook as he removed the piece of paper, then twisted to read it.

'*Guillemot. Metland. June 1926. GFA.*'

He was silent for a long moment, and when he spoke again, his voice was husky. 'The first of them.'

'The first of what?' said Nick.

Connor looked at him blankly, then shook his head and half laughed. 'Look at me getting all emotional over a bit of paper!'

'That's OK,' shrugged Nick.

'I'm sure I can persuade the museum to make you a good offer for it.'

Nick paused. 'Nah . . .' he said. 'You can have it.'

Connor blinked at him. 'Really?'

'Really,' said Nick. 'It's no use to me. Without the egg.'

'Well, that's very generous,' said the curator. 'I appreciate it very much.'

'You're welcome,' said Nick with a smile, and they clinked mugs to seal the deal.

Nick felt calm. Confident. He had the key and Connor was in his debt. The first part of the mission – the first *level* – was over.

Level two was next. He had to go to the bathroom and give the key to Patrick. Then he must come back and take as long as was humanly possible over his tea to give Patrick all the time he needed to find the Metland Eggs.

Nick looked into his mug and took a deep breath.

Let the games commence!

'Can I use the loo, please?'

'Of course. Back down the corridor right before the door into the public halls.'

'Thanks.'

By the time Nick reached the office door, Connor was poring over the fragment of paper again – this time with a magnifying glass.

Nick glanced left towards the halls of eggs as he left Connor's office, but hurried right – down the corridor and past the bathroom to the *Staff Only* door.

He opened it slowly, and spotted Patrick looking into the glassy eyes of a kudu.

'Sssss!'

Patrick hurried over and slid through the door and then followed Nick into the bathroom.

'Did you get it?'

Nick held up the key with a triumphant grin.

'Nice one!' Patrick took it from him and put it in his jeans pocket.

'Easy-peasy,' said Nick. 'He's so distracted by the data he wouldn't blink if a bomb went off!'

There was a knock on the door.

They both froze.

'Nick?'

Dr Connor. Nick and Patrick looked at each other, wide-eyed with fear.

'Don't let him in!' whispered Patrick.

Nick flapped his arms in panic, but Patrick gave him a little shove, so he crossed the room and cracked open the door.

'Oh, hi Chris.' He squeezed sideways through the opening into the corridor. He jerked a thumb over his shoulder.

'I'd give it five if I were you.'

'I thought you'd left.'

'What? No. I just went to the loo.'

'Oh.' Connor frowned, then went over to the *Staff Only* door. 'The silent alarm went off.'

'Oh,' said Nick. 'Sorry about that. I got confused and then remembered the toilet's on *this* side of the door . . .'

'No problem,' said Connor. 'I really appreciate you bringing me the data, Nick, but I'm afraid something's come up which means I'm going to have to cut this visit short.'

Nick glanced down at the keyring in Connor's hand. Big as a basketball. He'd been spooked by the alarm and was going to check on the eggs.

His egg.

That thought made Nick cross enough to be rude. 'Umm . . . I haven't finished my tea.'

'Yes, I'm so sorry, Nick, but this is an emergency.'

'An *egg*mergency?' Nick laughed.

'Yes. Haha, good one,' said Connor with only the faintest of smiles. 'So anyway . . . sorry about this . . .' And he started to back away towards the swing-door into the first of the egg rooms.

Nick's mind raced. Any second now the curator would turn and leave, and then the whole mission would have failed.

'I hope you enjoy that data,' he said desperately.

'I will. Thanks again.' The impatience was rolling off Connor in waves.

Nick's mind scrambled for purchase on a slippery slope. In Connor's office, over a long hot cup of tea, he could have spouted meaningless drivel for an hour. Data and eggs and the RSPB and *Call of Duty* and *Resident Evil* and the propellor and the stuffed badger . . . But right here, right now, with Connor quite plainly wanting him gone . . . what more could he do?

'How do I get out again?'

'Just through that door,' Connor pointed, 'then turn right to reception . . .' He gave a half-wave and then turned his back on Nick.

'Past the polar bear, right?'

The curator barely glanced over his shoulder: '*That's right.*'

'*This* door?' said Nick.

The curator ignored him and walked away.

Game over.

*

Patrick didn't breathe. His ear was pressed hard against the bathroom door.

That's right. Connor's voice was faint. His footsteps receded. He was heading for the guillemot room.

This door?

Nothing.

Patrick's heart thumped. It would be only a matter of moments before the curator would realize that the critical key was missing—

'ARRRGH! MY LEG!'

Patrick frowned in confusion. That was *his* line! From the helipad!

'What?! *What happened?!*' Connor's voice and footsteps grew louder again.

'My leg!' howled Nick. 'My leg!'

Understanding broke out on Patrick's face. He grinned at the door as if he could see through it to the charade beyond.

'What *happened*?'

'I slipped! I think the floor was wet!'

'Shit! Can you get up?'

'I don't know. Can you help me? Ow!'

A squeak of strain from Connor.

'Owwww! OWWW! I think it's broken.'

Patrick was filled with admiration. Mick Savage: Weird Nick. Same thing.

'Here, lean on me. I'll take you to reception and we'll call an ambulance.'

'OK. Thanks, mate.'

Patrick listened to the sounds of them disappearing together, then very cautiously he opened the bathroom door and peered into the corridor.

It was empty. He had a free run at the guillemot room. But he'd better make it fast.

Game on!

Legacy

'You said there were thirty.'

The curator was a keen man, and fair too. It was he who had suggested meeting halfway to save Mr Edwards the inconvenience of a long trip to Hertfordshire, and here they were, sitting at a sticky table in a smoky pub across the road from Swindon Railway Station.

'I miscounted.'

The curator grimaced. 'I understood that thirty red eggs were collected.'

Mr Edwards could have asked him how he had understood such a thing, but years of discretion in service had taught him that the fewer the words, the fewer the complications. Many was the time he had stood by and watched his master talk himself into a proper pickle when silence would have won the day. So he said nothing.

'I have spoken to people,' the curator went on as if Mr Edwards *had* asked his question. 'People who know.'

Mr Edwards gave a small smile. 'I have noticed that what people know and what people have seen with their own two eyes are rarely the same thing.'

The curator said *hmm*, and Mr Edwards did not press the point. He himself had seen Ambler return from his trips north each summer. But apart from that first time – when Ambler had boasted of the Metland Egg as relentlessly as if he had laid it himself – even *he* had never seen another red egg until the very moment Martha had appeared in the hallway with them in a cherrywood case.

Only then had he realized that Ambler had hoarded each subsequent egg in the only place in the house where even the butler did not venture. That there he had kept his secrets – beautiful and bestial – where he could visit them both, and often.

Mr Edwards did not like to remember Ambler, but he did sometimes imagine his old master huddled in that tiny box room, seated on the rickety chair or on the rumpled battlefield of his latest cruel victory, salivating over the priceless eggs.

A good butler rarely spoke, but did a lot of listening. So it was on the many occasions when he had hovered over his master and his clients with a decanter or a soup ladle that Mr Edwards had learned that any collection's value increased exponentially with each new acquisition from the same bird; that two such eggs were worth more than twice the price of one, that five was a trove, that ten was a milestone of epic proportions. Knowing Ambler as he had, he felt it was safe to assume that, once ten had been achieved, twenty must automatically have presented itself as desirable to a man whose social ambition was matched only by his greed. And that thereafter, the thought of presenting thirty red eggs to the world would have been a *fait accompli* to cement both his fortune and his name in the annals of egg history.

'Thirty has a ring, you see?' said the curator, as if confirming his thoughts.

Mr Edwards did not speak.

'Twenty-nine does not.'

Mr Edwards knew that.

'Twenty-nine eggs cannot be displayed, you see? Not when

everybody knows that thirty were collected. It makes the Natural History Museum look . . . slapdash. Unscientific.'

'I see.'

'It means undertaking more time and even more expense to locate and secure the final egg before we can see any return on our investment!'

Mr Edwards raised an eyebrow.

'So,' said the curator with an air of finality, 'you have to understand that I cannot possibly pay the price we agreed upon for only *twenty-nine* eggs . . .'

Mr Edwards thought of young Philip in that filthy house in Hammersmith, and young Philip now – waking every morning to the twin miracles of Pen Y Fan in his window and the Metland Egg on his nightstand.

'I understand completely,' he told the curator with an apologetic nod. 'The error was mine.'

In the end it did not matter. The sum the curator *did* pay for George Ambler's collection was more than enough to convert the old stables into a dear little home.

They called it Ty Newydd – the New House – and Martha dug a garden and took in sewing, and Philip found work on a nearby farm and grew strong and brown.

Martha caught the bus once a week into Brecon and shopped for them all, and when Mr Edwards's mother died a year after their arrival she insisted on nursing her to the end, and did so with such tenderness that one would have thought it was her own mother on her deathbed.

Mr Edwards had put money aside all his life and now, with his own roof over his head and modest needs, he found that he no longer had to work. Instead he planted an apple tree and got a dog, a comedic little Jack Russell called Buttercup, and grew fitter and happier than he'd been for many years.

The gap in the hedge between the new house and the old was maintained by frequent passage of feet because Martha insisted on cooking him supper every night, while Philip tramped back and forth a dozen times a day, asking for or offering help of one kind or another.

Life became good to them.

Just before their first Easter, Martha came through the gap in the hedge to seek advice from Mr Edwards on a subject of no little delicacy.

Blushing, she confessed that she had never had Philip baptized.

'I did not know what name to call him, you see?' she said, red in the face and with tears in her eyes, and a damp hanky twisted in her raw little fingers.

'But why use any name but your own?' said Mr Edwards. 'It's a perfectly good one, Mrs Farrell.'

It was the first time Mr Edwards had ever called her anything but Martha, but when she caught his meaning, she laughed for the first time in his hearing.

And so, with Mr Edwards to attest to the fact that his daughter had once been married, Philip Farrell was thus baptized.

On that happy occasion, Mr Edwards gave the boy a small silver penknife engraved with his initials, and Martha became a respectable widow without ever having had to suffer the loss of a husband.

Or a husband at all.

At the end of their third year in Wales, as he walked the twenty unsteady paces home in the snow after a truly joyful Christmas dinner with Martha and young Philip, Mr Edwards stopped and looked up at the Milky Way, which ran like a river of stars over the Beacons – and permitted himself a rare moment of self-satisfaction.

George Ambler had been a terrible man, and had deserved whatever terrible end had befallen him.

But he *had* finally done right by that girl.

The Guillemot Room

The sixth column on the second side of the fourth cabinet . . .
The ladder glided gently to a stop, exactly where Patrick had predicted it would.

The little silver key slid into the lock and Patrick held his breath.

It turned easily and made a satisfying *click*.

Nice one, Nick!

Patrick opened the bottom drawer.

Guillemot eggs, of course. All shades of blue and each in a silken nest. Very beautiful.

But not red.

He slid out the next drawer. And the next. Patrick worked his way up the column. Blue eggs, brown eggs, green, pale, dark, scribbled, spotted, splashed. Some in silk, some on paper, some just rolling around the metal drawer, clicking against each other. Open, close, open, close. Faster. Faster. *Faster!*

He climbed further up the ladder, until he reached the top drawer. It didn't open.

Patrick tugged it, but it didn't budge. What was stopping it? He leaned back a little to get a proper look—

There was another lock.

He felt crushed. And then he felt stupid. *Of course* there was another lock. Connor was a collector. A hoarder. Obsessive. If this was the drawer, it probably opened with a key that was not even *on* the giant ring. It was probably on a chain around the curator's neck!

He looked down the row and felt his throat tighten with rare emotion.

This drawer was the only one with a second lock on it.

It told him everything he needed to know.

He and Nick had played well, but Dr Connor had won the game.

'Ow ow ow!!'

Weird Nick staggered sideways and left a big smear on the glass of the antelope display.

'Careful!'

He and Connor zigzagged to the big cats, where Nick slumped under the yellow-eyed gaze of a lioness. Connor bent over and put his hands on his knees to catch his breath.

A crocodile of schoolgirls in white socks walked slowly past – giggling and pointing at the panting, red-faced men as if they were just two more gibbons or wombats.

Up ahead Nick could see the reception desk silhouetted against the light flooding in through the main doors.

Annoyingly close.

Connor straightened and puffed out his cheeks. 'Come on, then!'

But Nick only shook his head. 'I think I might faint.'

'Seriously?' said Connor coldly.

Nick had to fake a coughing fit to hide his mirth. Thank God he had found the data. Thank God he had given it to Connor. Thank God the man owed him so huge that he couldn't just walk away from him – however much he wanted to.

'Seriously,' Nick nodded. Then he added feebly: 'D'you think I could have a glass of water?'

*

Patrick Fort stood atop the ladder, as still and as silent as the guillemot room itself.

Part of him demanded that he leave immediately. Nick couldn't keep Dr Connor at bay for ever . . .

But he didn't *need* for ever. And getting rid of Weird Nick was not as easy as it sounded. He himself had tried and failed . . .

Somewhere, somehow, his friend was doing his bit, and Patrick felt compelled to do the same – even if he was unsure how.

So he just stood where he was, apparently motionless. But all the while he ran a quick, careful eye over the drawers – looking for a way in. He tested the metal of the top of the cabinet with his fingers, hoping to find it pliable and breachable, but it did not even flex. He ran his thumbnail along the lip of metal at each corner, but could find no gap.

He could not break in. Not from outside anyway.

Stupid! he thought. The only way to break *into* something *is* from the outside!

But from nowhere he thought of his mother's potato masher. Always making the kitchen drawers stick, until finally it would fall down the back of the cabinet behind the bottom drawer. If he'd retrieved the masher from there once, he'd done it twenty times.

These were not kitchen drawers, but . . .

Hurriedly Patrick pulled out the drawer immediately below the locked one. He slid it off its runners and put it on top of the cabinet.

Then he stuck his arm into the dark interior, fingers probing all the way to the back . . .

There was a space.

Feverishly, Patrick started to yank the other drawers out and off their runners, piling them and their precious contents carefully on the top, and then – as he descended – on the platform of the ladder, opening up a gap in the middle of the column of drawers until it was big enough for him to crawl inside and stand in a lower drawer. He winced as eggshells crunched under his feet, then reached up and into the back of the locked drawer. There were eggs in there. On silk. Their delicate shells brushed his wrist and teased his fingertips.

Slowly, carefully, he drew one out and opened his hand.

The hairs on Patrick's forearms tingled upright.

The egg was red.

Not redd*ish*. But *red*.

A rich, royal colour undimmed by history, and which defied nature.

It seemed an impossible thing.

Enslaved by logic, Patrick had to turn the egg in his hand, frowning at it for flaws, for brush-marks, for some sign that would expose the trickery and tampering that must have created it – for it could not be real . . .

Until his brain finally agreed with his goosebumps.

It *was* real.

He was holding the Metland Egg.

Patrick worked as fast as he dared.

The first twenty eggs were easily taken and stowed in the sheep's wool lining his backpack. Then he started to stretch and to twist, the sharp metal of the drawer digging welts into his arm as he worked.

Twenty-five, twenty-six . . .

. . . twenty-seven . . .

He grimaced and stood on his toes.

Twenty-eight. Twenty-nine. Almost there!

And then his fingers found only air.

He worked his hand desperately from one side of the drawer to the other – as far as he could reach – but could feel nothing more.

There were supposed to be thirty red eggs.

What if they were wrong?

Disquiet stirred in him. He withdrew his bruised and tired arm and stood, deflated. Suddenly very unsure of everything. If there were only twenty-nine eggs in this drawer it would mean Dr Connor *hadn't* stolen Weird Nick's egg. And *that* would mean that they had no justification for *any* of this. That they weren't on a heroic mission. That they were just two idiots trying to steal stuff from a museum—

He's got a million eggs in that building and still wants more.

Finn Garrett's words rang in Patrick's ears. The last red egg *must* be here. It was the only thing that made sense!

His arm wasn't long enough, that was all.

Desperately he looked around him for something to use . . . Then, with a happy little skip in his heart, Patrick dug deep into his jeans pocket and pulled out his Highland cow teaspoon.

Perfect.

The last red egg had been lurking in the frontmost corner of the drawer and Patrick drew it out on his spoon like a child on sports day.

He placed it reverently into his backpack with the others.

The swing-doors to the first hall banged open.

Patrick froze.

Someone was coming – and cutting off his only way out!

For a single brief second it was the helipad all over again. Standing there thinking when he should have been running, shooting, kicking open doors . . .

And then Patrick *moved*. Feverishly picking up the wide drawers and slotting them back into place.

The second swing-door banged. And then the next.

And now Patrick could hear a man's footsteps echoing in the vast hall – and the rhythmic *chink* of the keyring.

It was Connor. Coming to see his eggs.

The last drawer got stuck. Patrick jiggled it, but it wouldn't close!

The fourth door swung shut.

Patrick calmed his breathing. Took the drawer out. Sized it up. Tried again.

As the door to the guillemot room swung open, Patrick closed the final drawer, scrambled up the ladder, kicked it away below him, and flattened himself on top of the high steel cabinet.

He heard the ladder clunk quietly to a halt at the end of the aisle.

He dared not raise his head to see Connor pass the first three rows of cabinets. He only heard the footsteps stop, and then the small squeak of the ladder starting to glide back towards him. As it did, Patrick slithered sideways off the cabinet, dropped lightly into the next aisle, and hurried out of the door.

Then he ran.

Before he even reached the next door, he heard Connor's bellow.

'*Bastard! BASTARD! I'll fucking kill him!*'

Patrick skidded to a halt at the *Staff Only* door.

The alarm!

Instead he turned into the bathroom and bounded on to the lid of the toilet and opened the high, narrow window. With the backpack hanging from his arm, he squeezed through and dropped into the shrubbery, staggering a little as he landed, then raced across the lawn, up the hill and into the trees.

It took Patrick ten minutes to make a wide loop through the copse. The sun was bright this morning, but that only made the shadows darker. He finally emerged where he could see the front of the museum. He dropped to his haunches, still flushed with adrenaline.

All was quiet.

Nick's car was gone from the car park and so was Connor's.

This was good. They had gambled on Connor not calling the police, although Patrick still half expected an alarm to go off at any minute. But he heard no sirens. No bells. Saw no flurry of activity . . .

A woman holding a file walked out of reception and crossed to another building. The gentle breeze blew her hair around her face and she stopped to clip it back. She was in no hurry.

Patrick allowed a little bud of optimism to unfurl in his chest: even at this moment of crisis, the curator wasn't sharing the secret of the Metland Eggs. For how could he report them missing when nobody knew he had them in the first place? He couldn't explain them to the police or the museum authorities without exposing himself.

Mission accomplished!

Patrick got up and skirted the museum grounds, cut through the allotments, and jogged across the road to the car park of the Castle Inn, where Meg was waiting to meet him in her battered old Polo. He put the backpack between his feet and fastened his seatbelt.

'OK?' asked Meg.

He nodded enthusiastically. 'Yep! It was crazy. Nick had to fake a broken ankle to keep Connor away! And the key he stole was the right one, but there was *another* lock on the actual drawer and I had to dismantle the whole cabinet – and then right at the end I had to climb out of a window. The whole thing was *nuts!*'

'Good to know my annual leave hasn't been wasted.'

'No,' said Patrick. 'Definitely not.'

Meg started the car and pulled out into the one-way system. The roadworks – *still*.

Patrick pointed out the sign to the ring road and Meg made the turn and they left Tring behind.

In two hours they would be in Cardiff.

With treasure!

'What do you think Dr Connor's going to do?'

'He's gone after Nick.'

Meg frowned and Patrick studied her face carefully. Usually he didn't like to look too long into a face, but Meg made it easy for him by not staring back.

'You're worried,' he said.

'Of course,' she said. 'Finn Garrett told you this is a war.'

'But it's over,' he said, a little impatiently. 'And we won!' Patrick was becoming used to sharing feelings with Meg; but she wasn't sharing this victory with him, and that made him nervous.

'If it's a war,' said Meg, 'Connor might call in reinforcements.'

'What reinforcements? He can't go to the police because he's a thief, and if he wanted the museum to know about the Metland Eggs, he wouldn't have hidden them away all this time.'

'What about the men who stole the egg from Nick?'

Patrick blinked.

'You said one of them lives in Cardiff. If Connor's called him, he could be on his way to Brecon right now.'

Patrick frowned.

'We already know he's a violent man,' Meg went on. 'And if Nick's not at home . . .'

Patrick understood. He pulled out his phone and called his friend on speaker.

Weird Nick answered, laughing. 'Mick Savage here! You got the eggs?'

'No. Listen—'

'*What?* What the hell happened?'

'Nothing . . . I got them. But you said not to talk about them on the phone.'

'Oh. Yeah. Too late now! Did Connor call the cops?'

'I don't think so. Listen, Nick—'

'Brilliant. I can't wait to see his face after following me all the way to Wales when he realizes I don't have the eggs!'

'It's *not* brilliant.'

'What's wrong?'

'Meg's worried.'

'What's she worried about?'

'This is war. People get hurt.'

'Fuck's sake, mate! What are you trying to say?'

'What if Connor's called in eggman456? He would get to Brecon before you . . .'

There was a pregnant pause.

'Oh shit,' said Nick. 'Oh shit. Mum! Oh shit!'

'Call her,' said Meg. 'Tell her to go and get Patrick's mum to drive them both somewhere safe until this is over.'

'OK,' said Nick. 'Shit. OK. Thanks.'

He hung up.

Meg and Patrick drove on in tense silence through winding roads to Aylesbury.

There was a road sign up ahead. Cheltenham and M5 straight on, M1 and the North to the right.

'The North,' said Patrick quietly. 'That's where the eggs came from.'

Meg didn't speak. Didn't look at him.

'I was thinking,' said Patrick slowly, 'maybe we should give them back to the birds.'

Meg bit her lip and nodded.

When they got to the lights, she turned right and they headed north.

'Are you sad?' asked Patrick.

Meg shook her head and smiled at him. 'Happy tears,' she said.

Patrick sighed. Another wrinkle in the vast lexicon of emotions for him to try to iron out.

'Do you know exactly where they came from?' Meg asked.

'Yes. Under an overhang on the cliffs at Metland Farm in Bempton, Yorkshire.'

Meg laughed. Of course he knew. He was Patrick. 'You think Nick will be OK with it?' she said.

Patrick shrugged, then smiled. 'I think he'll be OK with the gaming chair I'll have to buy him.'

Angles

Ambler had nearly caught her, and Celie made a desperate calculation of angles and distances. She might make it to the yard. But what would she do when she got there?

So she ran to the barn.

So fast that she almost bounced off it. Then she turned to face him.

Ambler stopped twenty yards away and doubled over with his hands on his knees. Wheezing.

Celie's heart thudded in her breast.

Then he straightened up, and came at her.

She shrieked and ran along the wall.

He cut the corner, closing fast.

Then—

Vanished.

Celie stopped.

She stood.

And the night – which had been filled with panting and terror – became very still and very beautiful.

The wind had dropped. The moon was up.

Celie pressed her back against the still-warm barn wall, and stared for a long, long time at the place where George Ambler had been.

But there was no movement.

Nothing to see.

Only an old stovepipe hat, floating on the slurry.

The End

The road surface changed from tarmac to dirt and gravel. It curved to the right and sloped down, and finally ran out in the dusty farmyard alongside Metland Farm.

Meg and Patrick got out and stood for a moment in a perfect dusk. The sky was the palest blue overhead, fading to white on the horizon, with a line of pink colouring the west. There was not a breath of air.

The old farmhouse stood facing them – whitewashed and squat and square and with a chimney at either end and four boarded-up windows. Behind the house was a ramshackle barn with a corrugated iron roof that hung down in places, rusting and buckled and showing the sky. Beyond the barn, through a lopsided wooden gate, was a hayfield – made blue by the fading light – which stretched all the way to the horizon.

'I can smell the sea,' said Meg, and Patrick drew in a long breath and nodded. The air was fresh and seasoned with salt.

He dipped his hand into the bag and handed her an egg.

Meg's laughter caught in her throat and her eyes widened. 'Oh my God! Is it *real*?'

Patrick nodded – then watched in fascination as her expression changed slowly from wonder to sadness.

He wanted to tell her that he recognized both feelings. Understood them both. Understood *her*, just a little bit, and meant to understand a lot more. It made a little bubble of happiness rise inside him.

'Look how big the hole is,' she whispered, and – like magic – he knew she was thinking of the acid. But he didn't tell her that. He understood that this was not a time for triumph. And not about him.

Instead he touched Meg's shoulder lightly, and pointed past the barn. 'The cliffs are that way.'

But Meg didn't follow his finger. She was still frowning at the underside of the egg.

'What's this?'

'What?'

'There's something inside it.'

He came close to her and she handed him the egg.

He tilted it and looked into the hole. Inside he caught a glimpse of something small and black.

'Looks like a bug that's crawled in there,' he said, and shook the egg a few times. When it didn't drop out, he poked his little silver pocket knife into the hole in the bottom of the egg and scraped it gently around the inside of the shell until the bug fell out on to his palm.

'What is it?' said Meg.

For a moment Patrick just stared at it. Then his heart dropped like a stone.

'Oh,' he said. 'It's not that kind of bug.'

'What do you mean?'

He held it up between his thumb and forefinger. 'I think it's a tracking device.'

Meg paled.

Patrick was furious with himself. *Of course* it was a tracking device! Connor was a collector, and obsessed. In the worst-case scenario, he needed to be able to find his precious eggs and this was the simplest way of doing just that. Patrick had an air tag on his *bicycle* – and yet he hadn't thought to check for anything like this in the eggs.

'You think he's followed us?' said Meg.

'Yes,' said Patrick grimly. He dropped the tiny bug on the gravel and ground it to dust with his heel, then put the egg back into the bag. 'We have to get going.'

'Right,' said Meg. Then: 'Shit. I hear a car!'

He heard it too. Coming fast down the hill towards the farm.

He hitched the bag on to his shoulders. 'Come on!'

But before they had gone twenty yards, a black Mercedes with its headlights on swept into the farmyard behind them and kept coming – fast.

'B1RDY'

It passed them at speed, cutting a swathe in the dust as it turned and skidded to a halt.

They stopped, shoulder to shoulder.

Dr Connor leapt out of the car, his face twisted and red.

In his hand was a gun.

Patrick felt sick. Not just because of the gun, but because Connor had tracked them all the way here, and that alone felt . . . *dangerous*. He could have caught them in Tring. He could have caught them at the services on the A1 where they'd stopped for food. But he'd waited to make his move here – in a deserted Yorkshire farmyard.

Where there were no witnesses.

'Put the eggs down,' said Connor breathlessly. 'Put them down, go back to your car, and drive away, and nobody has to get hurt.'

Slowly Patrick started to slide the backpack off his shoulders.

'What are you doing?' said Meg sharply.

'Putting the eggs down.'

'Don't you dare!'

Patrick stopped, as ordered. 'OK,' he said. 'I just didn't want to get shot.'

'He's not going to *shoot* us,' she said angrily. 'This is England! Nobody has a real gun!'

Connor fired into the air and Patrick jumped so hard that the eggs rattled.

'Just put them down,' said Connor. 'Carefully. And go back to your car.'

Patrick put the bag down at his feet. The eggs weren't his, and yet he felt a great sense of loss sweep over him. He wondered if this was the last time anyone but the curator would ever see the Metland Eggs. Stuck in a drawer to which only one greedy man had the key.

As they started to back away, Meg took his hand, as if she knew what he was thinking and felt the same way, and Patrick knew he'd remember this moment for ever – for all the wrong reasons *and* all the right ones.

Connor stepped forward to reclaim his property.

The air between them split with a high whine, and the windscreen of the Mercedes shattered white. Meg let out a tiny cry, but Connor and Patrick only froze. Their eyes met – each as confused as the other.

Connor turned two tight circles, the wobbling gun held out in front of him. There was nothing to see. He hesitated, then stepped forward again.

The second bullet spat dust up his leg, then punched a jagged hole in the Mercedes' radiator.

For a weird moment they all just stared in wonder at the steam jetting into the air. Then, with a squeak of understanding, Connor dropped to his knees, turned, and crawled around the back of his car, making a snuffling sound that made Patrick laugh, even as his brain worked overtime to understand what was going on.

Meg had dropped down beside the Polo. 'Patrick! Get down! Someone's shooting at us!'

But Patrick didn't get down. 'I don't think they *are* shooting at us,' he said. 'I think they're shooting at *him*.'

He stepped forward, and tentatively reached for the backpack.

Nobody blew his brains out, so he picked it up.

'It's OK, Meg.'

'Patrick—'

'Really,' he said. 'Look.' He held out his arms, the bag dangling from one hand, and turned slowly – making himself the easiest of targets. Just like on the helipad. But he came full circle and nobody shot him.

He breathed again, then shouldered the backpack and grinned at Meg. 'Come on!'

Meg rose to her feet and they walked briskly across the yard. Connor got to one knee and raised his gun as they passed him.

'Stop!' he shouted. 'Or I swear I'll shoot you!'

They both flinched at the crack, but the ping of metal reassured them that the bullet was not from his gun, and they did not stop.

Behind them, Connor yelled, '*Fuck!*'

'You think he's hit?' said Meg, sounding worried.

'I hope so!' said Patrick. 'Let's run!'

So they ran.

Past the old house, where Celie Sheppard had once reached for another sliver of ham.

Past the barn, where Robert had slept curled around a dog for warmth.

And across a patch of much greener grass, where once there had been a slurry pit.

Three more times they heard the crack and the whine of shots that kept Connor pinned down behind them.

'Why aren't they shooting at us?' panted Meg.

''Cos we're the goodies!' said Patrick, and she laughed.

By the time they were halfway across the big hayfield, all they could hear was their own jagged breathing as they ran towards what looked like the edge of the world.

There was a high bank between here and there – bright with purple mallow and humming with bees. It stopped them for a moment, until Meg found an indentation in the grass that spoke of an old path.

Then they pushed through the jungle of flowers and emerged on a grassy clifftop dominated by a huge flat slab of rock.

The view took their breath away. The green cliffs, the flat sea, the orange-pink sky – all through the whirl of seeds they'd disturbed.

And the thousands and *thousands* of birds.

'This must be it.'

Patrick met Meg's eyes and smiled.

Standing on the roof of his car, Finn Garrett focused his binoculars on the hayfield. Patrick and the girl had disappeared from view, but in the warm wash of sunset he could make out the shaggy silhouette of the mallow that he knew they must have gone through to reach the overhang. He had been through it himself a few times over the years, but most often he had hiked there from the RSPB centre to the north.

He too had stood on that great slab that had protected birds for centuries before someone very brave or very stupid had slid through the crack and stolen the very first Metland Egg.

The sorrow of it still had the power to pinch his heart.

A movement caught his peripheral vision and he trained the glasses on Connor.

The curator was running. Away from his car and through the darkening hay towards the cliffs.

Garrett ducked reflexively for the rifle at his feet – but then only sighed. He'd done all he could from here, bar murder. He'd bought them some time, and now he hoped for the best, but he couldn't stick around for the end of the story. He had to get out of here before somebody called the police about shots fired.

He jumped lightly off the roof and stowed the gun in its padded bag in the boot. Then he got behind the wheel.

He started the engine, but then sat for a long minute. And, instead of getting out of here, he drove the hundred yards from the field gate where he'd parked, down into the farmyard, and stopped beside the Mercedes.

He got out of his car with a crowbar.

But it was not necessary.

The doors were not locked. And right there – on the passenger seat, where the driver could look at it often – was the fancy wooden box that had once held the Metland Egg.

A lump rose in Garrett's throat. Patrick had only called it 'fancy', but no description could have done it justice. And it was all the more beautiful for being empty.

It was also evidence, of course, and shouldn't be touched.

But this was not a court case – or ever likely to be a court case. This was war.

And so he took it.

He put it on his own front seat, where he could look at it often.

As his car crunched out of the farmyard, it occurred to Garrett that sometimes things worked out the way you'd planned – and sometimes they worked out even better than that.

He was so grateful to have been spared the agony of deciding the fate of the Metland Eggs that it brought warmth to his eyes.

And then – because he knew the police would guess that any gunman at Metland would be heading west to Leeds or south to London – he swung his car around and drove north.

Maybe he'd go all the way to Scotland and see if those golden eagle chicks had hatched yet.

Finn Garrett looked at his watch and smiled ruefully.

He was already ten minutes too late for a chocolate chip cookie.

Patrick and Meg stood on the Metland overhang, close to a narrow V of a crack that split the great rock in two.

There was a proper breeze here, with the crack acting as a kind of chimney for the wind roaring up the cliff face, but it was still warm, and the view was incredible.

The sun had touched the earth behind them and now spread gold along the horizon, while the vast sky was turning violet over a sea so deep and blue that it was close to black.

But the real view was beneath their feet, where the edge of England plunged three hundred sheer feet into the indigo depths. To their left and their right. And beyond each little headland, more cliffs – as far as their eyes could see in either direction.

And every craggy inch of those cliffs was covered in birds.

Fulmars and gulls and kittiwakes and terns. Puffins whirring past their feet like rainbow bullets, and giant gannets that hung in the sky beside them like airships. But most of all, guillemots. Huddled shoulder to shoulder, they painted the chalky cliffs in glossy chocolate pixels.

'This is where they came from,' Meg whispered. 'This is where they belong.'

She looked up at Patrick and he saw tears sheening her eyes, even though she was smiling at him.

He didn't have to ask how she felt.

Happy tears.

Instead he put an awkward arm around her, and hugged her while she rested her head on his shoulder.

Then he carefully unzipped the backpack. Their heads touched as they gazed down at the dark red eggs nestling in the twilight.

A great rustling behind them made them jump apart, and Connor burst from the mallow in a swirl of seeds and with grass in his hair. He staggered sideways, looked around wildly, then regained his footing and rushed straight at them, gun at the ready.

'Give them to me!'

Patrick backed towards the crack.

'Patrick! Careful!'

He stopped. Connor stopped.

'Those eggs are the property of the Natural History Museum! Give them to me now and we'll say no more about it.'

Patrick laughed. There was so much more to say about it that he didn't know where to start! He glanced over his shoulder at the dizzying drop and the spinning birds, and felt his balance waver.

Then, in a single sweep, he turned and hurled the bag off the cliff. It arced high into the air, its precious contents tumbling free.

Connor let out an animal cry and skidded to his knees on the rock with his arms outstretched – as if he might yet be able to pluck the eggs out of the sky. Only Patrick grabbing his scruff kept him on the cliff. Connor tried to slap his hand away and they struggled—

'Stop!' cried Meg. 'Look!'

They stopped.

They looked.

The backpack had whirled out of sight, but the Metland Eggs weren't falling.

They were floating.

Emptied of everything but air, the thirty fragile jewels were cradled on first this eddy and then on that, so they didn't drop so much as *dance* between the wheeling, witnessing birds, trembling and tumbling in the arms of the wind.

Meg reached for Patrick's hand and together they watched thirty red eggs spin lazily down through the shadows like fiery red lanterns, until long after they lost sight of them against the black ocean.

Finally, as darkness fell, Patrick led Meg away from the overhang, past the weeping curator, through the wall of mallow, and back across the hayfield to Metland Farm.

The Beginning

Celie fetched the scythe from the barn and lifted George Ambler's hat out of the slime like a fish on a gaff. Then she carried it across the trampled hayfield and through the mallow and out on to the cliff.

The overhang was made silver by the light of the pearly moon. Celie crossed it as she had so many times before, all the way to the widest part of the crack, and with a single great sweep of her arm, she spun the hat into the air.

It curved smoothly away from her, before being caught by a little gust that flipped it over and sent it tumbling into the abyss.

Celie lost sight of it then, but she gazed down into the blackness anyway, until she knew it must have reached the water.

And even after that she remained, silhouetted against the indigo sky.

Lighter, somehow, despite a whole new person growing inside her.

She stood there for a long time, thinking of all that she had gained, and all that she owed.

And to whom.

Beneath her feet – in the shadow of the great Metland overhang, where neither Celie nor anyone else would ever go again – a thousand guillemots were knitted so tightly into a wall of chocolate feathers that nothing bird-shaped could even be discerned.

And yet.

Under one warm breast.

Nestled against one tiny heart . . .

A single, perfect, red egg.

Author's Note

What's real and what's not . . .

The Metland Egg is real. And somebody somewhere knows where it is . . .

In the past . . .

In the early part of the last century, thirty incredible red eggs were stolen from the same bird on the short stretch of cliff on Metland Farm at Bempton, East Yorkshire. It's unclear when the first Metland Egg was found, although it was definitely after World War One, and it's also unclear whether the eggs were stolen at a rate of one a year. A guillemot can live for up to thirty-five years, so it might have taken longer than thirty years to complete the collection. But it's also true that if an egg was stolen early enough in the season, another one might be laid that same year, so I condensed the timeline and focused on thirty eggs, rather than thirty years. This meant I could bookend the story between the wars and have my characters at around the right age for the story to play out the way I wanted it to.

The 'climming' gangs of Bempton are mostly correctly named, as they were family gangs who lived on the clifftop farms. Men really did risk their lives to collect the eggs, and there is at least one case where a climmer died after being struck by a falling rock. While their ropes were of the best quality and were cared for like babies, the rest of their equipment was ad hoc. Climmers would wear flat caps or Boer War helmets, tweed jackets and plus fours. They would fashion swings at the end of their ropes or sit in an old leather horse collar. They employed a variety of satchels, sacks and tackle baskets to carry their bounty. Their task was dangerous but lucrative – and also romantic. Thousands of tourists would walk miles along the blustery clifftops to watch them work, and business was always brisk.

Metland Farm still stands, at the very end of a long chalk track that takes a sharp right into a farmyard that faces only fields, then sky – then Norway. It was variously known as Metland or Metlands – one may be the natural extension of the other, and I found it in both forms in documents and on maps. But the eggs are known collectively in the singular. *The Metland Egg.*

The family who owned the farm at around the time when the red eggs were being collected was named Constable. I have given that name to the landlord, as a nod to them.

The stretch of cliff at Metland is very short, but alas there is no overhang. That I invented to explain the Sheppard family's poverty while everyone around them was getting rich.

George Ambler is based on a man named George Lupton, who apparently bought all thirty Metland Eggs. I changed his name because I needed my fictional character to be despicable and I have no evidence that George Lupton was anything other than a respectable family man, and a broker and collector in a business and hobby that was entirely legal at the time.

George Lupton lived in Holland Park, London, and is reputed to have paid the highest price then achieved for the first Metland Egg. I extrapolated that he must have had a contract of sorts with the finder, otherwise the book would have had to feature in-fighting between brokers, of whom three or four were always on the cliffs haggling over the best eggs.

I must give a special mention to George Ambler's unsuitable hat, which popped into my head – and on to his – the very first moment I began to describe him, and which played its part right to the end.

The character of Major Howells was inspired by the aviator Vivian Hewitt, who not only had his own vast egg collection but bought up the collections of many other rich men across Europe – including Lupton's. At the time of his death his collection was a shambles, as he had too many eggs for anyone to organize properly – or even to unpack.

After George Lupton's death, his collection found its way to the Natural History Museum at Tring, UK, via Hewitt, but it was in such a parlous state of curation that it remains largely uncatalogued to this day.

Celie Sheppard – along with her family – is an invention, sadly, as I do love her, and can see her in my mind's eye as clearly as any daguerreotype. Although why anyone would have photographed such an unappealing child would have been a mystery. Once I had thought of the crack in the overhang, Celie's appearance was a given – the skinniest, palest, most rickety child imaginable, whose diminutive size would be her greatest asset, along with her sheer doggedness.

Robert became involved because I needed someone strong enough to dangle Celie off a cliff, but without the authority or maturity to question the sanity of her scheme. So, when all the other hands left Metland Farm, Robert stayed behind. A big, silent boy – too undervalued to be paid his due and too young to know that he had other options.

In the present . . .

While historical egg collections with verifiable data can be legally held (with a very few exceptions), it has long been illegal to keep, collect, buy or sell wild birds' eggs in the UK. However, the crime continues to this day, with many 'eggers' undeterred by fines and even prison sentences.

So obsessive are these eggers that British museums no longer put egg collections on public display. However, scientific research using the shells of eggs already in their collections goes on behind the scenes, amid tight security, and researchers can be licensed to obtain small numbers of eggs for this purpose.

In the mid-1950s John Du Pont – 'the Foxcatcher guy' and infamous millionaire – bought half of Lupton's collection for his new museum in Delaware, which opened in 1957. Given his vast resources and the fact that he came to see the collection in person, it can be assumed that he hoped the Metland Eggs were to be found there, but they were never displayed in Delaware – or anywhere – and remain lost to history.

I must say that the current curator of eggs at Tring, Douglas Russell, is a very nice man whose character is unimpeachable. He was enormously helpful to me during my research and I hope he'll forgive me for EVERYTHING!

The Royal Society for the Protection of Birds is at the forefront of the fight against eggers. Their officers liaise with police to secure prosecutions and have been trained by British Army Gurkhas in surveillance and camouflage.

They are up against a determined foe . . . many of those prosecuted are found to have thousands of eggs in their possession and there is a thriving international black market for them.

My character Matthew Barr is based very loosely on Colin

Watson, a repeat offender at collecting, who fell to his death from a tree in 2006 while trying – yet again – to steal eggs.

Of course, Patrick Fort and his friend Weird Nick are inventions who appeared in my previous book, *Rubbernecker*. Due to his character and the situation in which we left him at the end of that adventure, it took me ten years to come up with another plot in which Patrick might conceivably be involved.

I hope you are as pleased to see him again as I was.

Belinda

Acknowledgements

I knew very little about birds, eggs or collectors before I started to write *The Impossible Thing*, so I was most fortunate to have been guided by the following:

Douglas Russell of the National History Museum at Tring, who offered invaluable expertise, insight, and a guided tour of the national egg collection.

Guy Shorrock of the RSPB, who shed sobering light on the continuing horrors of illegal egg collecting.

Jeff Wardlow of Bempton, who most generously donated his historical knowledge and resources to help with my research into the climmers of Yorkshire.

The whole team at Transworld for their patience and enthusiasm.

I would not have finished *The Impossible Thing* without the care of the oncology staff at University Hospital Wales and Velindre Hospital in Cardiff, and the immunotherapy nurses of Sciensus. Particular thanks to Dr Emma Hudson, Mr Robert Howells and Carole Mellish.

Belinda Bauer grew up in England and South Africa and now lives in Wales. She worked as a journalist and a screenwriter before finally writing a book to appease her nagging mother.

For her debut, *Blacklands*, Belinda was awarded the CWA Gold Dagger for Crime Novel of the Year. She went on to win the CWA Dagger in the Library for her body of work. Her fourth novel, *Rubbernecker*, was voted Theakston's Old Peculier Crime Novel of the Year. Her eighth novel, *Snap*, was a *Sunday Times* bestseller. It was longlisted for the Man Booker Prize and voted Crime & Thriller Book of the Year at the Specsavers National Book Awards.

Her books have been translated into twenty-five languages.